PENGUIN BOOKS

FREUD, A NOVEL

Carey Harrison was born in London in 1944. He has been a full-time writer since 1966 with the exception of a period spent as a lecturer in the Department of Comparative Literature at the University of Essex from 1972 to 1975. He has written ninety television plays and episodes, twelve stage plays and a number of plays for radio including the highly praised *A Suffolk Trilogy*, the first play of which, *I Never Killed my German*, won the 1979 Giles Cooper Award for the best play on Radio 3. Two of his short stage plays, *Lovers* and *26 Efforts at Pornography*, have been widely performed both in this country and abroad. *Freud, A Novel* came about as the result of his BBC 2 television drama series 'Freud'. Carey Harrison lives in Suffolk.

CAREY HARRISON

:FREUD:

A NOVEL

PENGUIN BOOKS

Penguin Books Ltd, Harmondsworth, Middlesex, England
Viking Penguin Inc., 40 West 23rd Street, New York, New York 10010, U.S.A.
Penguin Books Australia Ltd, Ringwood, Victoria, Australia
Penguin Books Canada Ltd, 2801 John Street, Markham, Ontario, Canada L3R 1B4
Penguin Books (N.Z.) Ltd, 182–190 Wairau Road, Auckland 10, New Zealand

First published by Weidenfeld & Nicolson Ltd 1984

Published in Penguin Books 1984
Reprinted 1985

Printed and bound in Great Britain by
Cox & Wyman Ltd, Reading
Set in Bembo

To P.J.S

DRAMATIS PERSONAE

Sigmund Freud
Martha Freud, née Bernays, his wife
Minna, her younger sister
Anna Freud, Freud's youngest daughter

Josef Breuer, doctor, scientist, Freud's mentor and collaborator
   in the birth of psycho-analysis
Ernst von Fleischl, scientist, inventor, scholar
Wilhelm Fliess, doctor, scientist, Freud's friend and collaborator
   in the birth of psycho-analysis
C.G. Jung, psychologist, Freudian disciple and sometime ally

Jacob and Amalie, Freud's parents
Alexander, his brother
Teresa, his childhood nurse
Max Schur, his doctor

Savants of Paris and Vienna
Jean-Martin Charcot, 'the Napoleon of the neuroses'
Theodor Meynert, professor of psychiatry
Rudolf Chrobak, professor of gynaecology
Hermann Nothnagel, head of Internal Medicine at the University
   of Vienna
Ernst Bruecke, head of the Institute of Physiology

Friends of Freud's youth, and colleagues
Ignaz Schoenberg, Minna Bernays' fiancé
Oscar Rie, Martha Freud's doctor
Carl Koller, re-discoverer of cocaine
Leopold Koenigstein, eye specialist
Ignaz Rosannes, fellow-student, later doctor
Lev von Darkschewitsch, sometime fellow-student
Alois Pick, partner at cards

Disciples, and allies, of Freud's maturity

Alfred Adler

Otto Rank

Victor Tausk

Sandor Ferenczi

Paul Federn

Wilhelm Stekel

Patients

Anna, the Baroness

Elizabeth von Rietberg

Herr Kaestner

Emma Eckstein

Anna Lichtheim

The 'Wolf-man'

Ladies

Mathilde, Josef Breuer's wife

Sophie, Emma Eckstein's sister

Ida, Wilhelm Fliess' wife

Paula, Freud's housekeeper

Mathilde, Freud's eldest daughter

ONE

Everything is here. Only I am not here.

I sit among my things, at my old desk from Vienna, among my statuettes from Vienna, my rugs and chairs from Vienna, my books, prints, and honorary degrees: among Freud's things, like a waxwork in a Freud museum. The other day a letter reached me, simply addressed 'Freud, London'.

Out in the garden the women sit in the sunshine, leaving me to you, doctor. You too, busy with my blood pressure, avoid my gaze.

You ask, am I still seeing patients, at eighty-two?

Yes, doctor. Hear my confession.

Between the women at the garden table sits a young man with the mark of death on his face. He rises as I come towards them, running.

'Am I late? Marty – Minna – forgive me . . .'

'We've been enjoying the sunshine.'

'Enjoying it? Look at poor Schoenberg!'

Minna's fiancé mops his brow, smiling, and sits once more. I pounce on Martha's hand and raise it for a kiss.

'We were just about to leave.'

Trouble, behind her teasing; both sisters study me as I take the empty chair, Minna shading her eyes against the sun.

'You look exhausted.'

'I ran all the way. First a patient refused to eat the hospital food and I had to feed him with a spoon –'

'Excuses.'

'Then I got waylaid by Breuer.'

'More excuses . . .'

'Schoenberg, come to my rescue!'

Schoenberg shrugs. The Bernays sisters have drained their glasses, waiting for me. Only Schoenberg's is full – but he doesn't offer me a drink. Consumption is catching. Do they kiss, he and Minna? Schoenberg meets my gaze.

'It's hot,' he answers, 'let's go inside.'

No-one moves. The girls are very still. 'What is it? What's the news?'

Schoenberg speaks, at last. 'I called Frau Bernays a selfish old woman. To her face.'

'Well done.'

'Sigmund!'

'Mother *is* selfish.' Minna looks past us. 'And she won't change her mind now. We're leaving for Hamburg in a week.'

So. It's happening, at last: and we sit there like blighted suitors in a romantic novel. Schoenberg, the tragic one, my twin. Anger wells up inside me as Martha and he fill the silence:

'It's only for a while – Mother said so –'

'I tell you it's for good!'

A week's time; one week. 'Cheer up, Schoenberg, we'll kidnap them and carry them back to Vienna. Deliver them from their Egyptian servitude!'

'This is hardly the promised land,' Martha rebukes me. 'The fact is, Mother doesn't want to live here –'

I can see Minna's colour rising.

'Vienna or Vladivostok, it wouldn't matter if we'd found two rich old husbands. Sometimes I think she doesn't even want us to be happy.'

'How can you say such things?'

'Oh Marty ... why pretend you don't know what she's like?'

'Pretend?'

'The way you spring to her defence, as if you were the only one who really cared about her.'

And Martha, scornfully: 'We know how much you love her ...'

'Of course Minna loves her.' It's out before I can prevent myself. 'That's why she doesn't feel the need to spare her.'

Too late now, as Martha wrestles with her humiliation.

'I hope when I complain of your behaviour that you'll take that as a token of my love.'

'I shall,' I smile. 'I do. Only you're usually much too good-natured to complain. Rather like Schoenberg here ... so when

2

you tell the truth it's with all the pent-up fury of the well-behaved. Whereas Minna and I ... ' Gleeful Minna. 'Are foul-tempered and frank. We can save our compliments for when we really mean them.'

Schoenberg coughs his faint dry cough.

'We seem to have chosen the wrong partners, in your opinion.'

'On the contrary. The right partners.'

In the harsh sunlight Minna looks raw-boned beside fragile Schoenberg with his wisp of beard. She has grown fat on frankness. While my slender Marty wastes away. I mean to feed her with kisses; instead I only draw her anger.

'Talking of rich husbands ... this morning I was quite convinced I'd made my fortune. With a new brain dye. I hit on the idea of using bichromate of potash, copper, and water, to make the cell structure stand out more clearly under the microscope –'

'Did it work?' Schoenberg looks hopeful.

'No. The wretched specimen was so slippery, just like a little piece of sausage ...' I can feel Marty shifting, restless. 'You'd never think it once transmitted thoughts and feelings –'

'I don't want to hear. Especially if it isn't going to make your fortune.'

Schoenberg's coughing gets the better of him. With a glance at the pair of us, Minna rises to comfort him.

'Come, Ignaz.'

'Forgive me ...' Schoenberg gets to his feet, still quivering. 'It's the heat.'

'We'll go indoors.'

As they make their slow departure I feel my hopes ebbing away, suddenly afraid. The twelve months of our secret engagement have shown Martha to be capable of deceit, of ruthlessness, tenacity. But now, removed to Hamburg with mourning Minna –

'He's looking better,' I murmur, 'don't you think? Perhaps he needs to lose his temper a little more often ...'

She stands and moves away. I follow. 'My sweet darling girl – my angel – ' I kiss her, a long kiss, a pause. 'You're very pale.'

'I'm quite well, thank you.' Studying me. 'You can be thoroughly unlovable sometimes.'

We walk.

'Marty ... you do understand: if you go back to Hamburg I must know that I come first in your life. That I count for more than anybody else. I shall work all the harder – I shall find the strength if I know I have your undivided love.' She knows it is a prepared speech. 'And if I don't, I must know now. "Let us consult, what reinforcement we may gain from hope ... if not, what resolution from despair ..."' I hold her gaze, smiling. '*Paradise Lost* ...'

Is she softening?

'I think ... if you could have heard how Breuer spoke to me today – spoke of his hopes for me. A post has come free in the neurology department. I could apply, he says. With Breuer's guidance –' Breuer, with his influence, his consulting room crowded with Archdukes, Breuer mentioning my name; still no response from Martha, and my impatience bursts. 'The man believes in me – as you should, without reservation.'

The time has come. 'Marty, one thing you have to face: your mother is the enemy of our love, and if you go on listening to her ...'

She halts, gazing down. 'I will *not* choose between you!'

'My God, you're obstinate –'

Turning back, I see her tears. She pulls away out of my grasp, and I catch her once more, kissing her cheeks, begging her forgiveness.

'Don't,' she struggles free, 'don't ... someone will see ...' She struggles free, and runs.

'Marty ...'

The two of us, away beneath me in a garden; Marty running, disappearing from view as I step back from the window. Inside the room a voice is speaking.

'With the unfortunate and premature demise of Nathan Weiss, there would appear to be a post free in Neuropathology – perhaps, dear colleague, you could put in a word for Freud ... in the appropriate ear ...'

Breuer is tugging gently on his ample beard. Now he draws himself up to impersonate Professor Billroth.

'"My dear Breuer," he said ... "we have enough of these

4

Jew-boys up from the country" –' he darts me an apologetic glance ... 'you know how Billroth is, he says it to my face!' and resumes the impersonation: '"... look at what happened to young Weiss, working his brain to shreds. Too much ambition – too much haste – *festina lente* ... what your Dr Freud needs is patience, and a few more published articles!"' He studies me, fatherly. 'Now that I look at you more closely – I think he is wrong. What you need is a bath.'

'Another day, Josef. Thank you.' Still that tender stare. 'I've been walking, that's all.'

'Then take off your coat, at least. Walking, in this weather! Come. Shirtsleeves are allowed. Mathilde is out shopping with the children.' As I remove my topcoat, Breuer comes to help. 'You shouldn't walk. Here ...'

With an awkward gesture he reaches for my hand. I find a banknote pressed against my palm, and pull away. He takes my coat, slipping the note into a pocket.

'At least take a *fiacre* from time to time. Of course, you could afford to – if it wasn't for such a cigar ...'

'It's your cigar, Josef.'

A fine cigar. I puff at it, dishevelled, luxuriating in Breuer's elegant apartment, and settle on a leather couch. Strike a Byronic pose: he loves me as his wastrel son.

'Anyway, I wanted to walk.'

If only I could tell him the truth. Breuer too has grown fat; but not on frankness. On a soothing bedside manner, stroking his rabbinical beard. He loves me, he has hopes for me.

'More published articles ...' I echo. 'I might have known!' The irony of it – when just eighteen months ago I was working at Bruecke's institute doing important neurological work ... no promotion prospects, twenty-five and barely earning, still living at home – but doing good work, interesting work! Then on the best advice – including yours, my dear patron – I give it up and move into the hospital to train for general practice. And now: my way forward is blocked because I haven't published neurological research! 'What do they expect of us? We're lucky to find time to eat let alone study. Surgery, Internal Medicine, Dermatology, Ophthalmology ... do you realize I've spent three months in the psychiatric wards, I can just about tell depression

5

from senile dementia – and I'm off to Nervous Diseases in a matter of weeks!' Breuer eyes me, weathering the storm. 'And when you do set up in practice, everybody knows you won't attract patients unless you've found your field and established a reputation in it. How? I'm not like Weiss – I don't pretend to be a genius. Poor man, he knew where he was going, or he thought he knew – but for myself, after three months struggling with dements, alcoholics, syphilitics ... I tell you I only know one thing for certain: I am not a doctor. I'm clumsy with patients ...' Clumsy with everyone. 'The psychiatric wards fill me with dread. Sometimes I think I'm going mad myself.'

No; not like Weiss. But I must tell Breuer the truth.

'For God's sake, Josef ... what am I to do?'

'Go home more often. At least you'll eat.' Mildly, smiling. 'And even take a bath.'

'Yes. If we had one, I would.' I hold his gaze, remorseful. 'I'm sorry. May I change my mind – and have one here?'

'My house is yours.'

Through rising steam I can see Breuer's dissecting table. Dead pigeons, instruments. Illustrations of the workings of the inner ear. Strange combination, in this opulent bathroom, of science and sybaritic pleasure. And pigeons with their necks wrung.

'I must apologize about the pigeons.' Breuer's voice comes from the corridor. 'It's the only room Mathilde lets me work in.' Breuer's hand appears around the door, holding a towel. 'Have you everything you need?'

I test the bathwater while the door swings back discreetly, not quite shut, and pour cold water from the magic of the tap. 'I usually frequent the baths in the Landstrasse.' The silence tells me Breuer knows: it's where Nathan Weiss hanged himself.

'You knew Weiss better than I did, Sigmund. Why did he kill himself?'

'He married the wrong sister.' The tapwater muffles my words; I turn it off. 'It was a mistake ... the girl he married. Shortly before the wedding she even suggested he marry her sister.' I climb into the bath and lie, perfectly still. 'Josef?' A grunt, from the doorway. Weiss' body hanging in the steam. 'You see, Nathan knew what he wanted. And what he wanted was catastrophe – to overreach himself once and for all. The honeymoon was ... unsuccessful, he told me so himself. In other words: it wasn't work that killed him, it was marriage.'

'You're lucky to be free of such entanglements, Sigi, believe me.' A change of tone now. 'Listen to me. Science is a battlefield, a bloody one, and its soldiers rarely emerge unscathed – you and I can think of many casualties ... suicides, drunkards, morphine addicts. But these aren't heroes,' – Josef, I know this speech; I know – 'they're failures, there's nothing romantic about their fate. I want to hear no more whining about your tribulations – or your loss of nerve: you *are* a doctor, and a fine one. So remember this – there is no urgency to find your field, you must hold on to that, because it isn't just a field you're looking for, it is your self, your soul. And think of Mephistopheles: "In vain you range from science to science ..."'

'"... each man only learns what he can learn."' But I have lost Breuer's attention. I can hear footsteps, voices in the corridor, Mathilde returning. Josef answering, 'Talking to Freud, my dear,' and then, low, 'he's in the bath.'

Don't laugh. Mathilde departing. Speak. 'Josef, I haven't been entirely truthful with you.' A moment. 'I'm engaged to be married. Hence the urgency ...' No answer comes. 'Josef?'

Faintly, 'God give me strength'.

I can sense someone in the doorway. Ignore him.

En cas de doute, abstiens-toi – St Augustine. When in doubt, don't: Marty herself set it in needlework, for my hospital lodgings.

'Meynert's just arrived.'

Bare lodgings: bookshelves, desk, washbasin, bed. Flowers, and a photograph of Martha, beneath St Augustine's words.

'Sigmund, did you hear me?'

Someone bending over my shoulder, eyeing the learned article in front of me. Flechsig advocates a gold chloride solution, as a brain dye. D'you suppose he's tried it out?

'Who sent the flowers? Fraulein Bernays?'

What is the man doing? It's Koller, nosy Koller. Picking up Martha's photograph.

7

'Nymph, in thy orisons . . .' He strikes a pose, retreating with Martha.

I rise and take the picture from him. For an instant I see my image, head and torso, in the dark of his eyes.

'Go on – you'll be late for the Professor,' warns Koller, slipping into my place at the desk, over the Flechsig article.

'The Devil! The Devil! The Devil!' The woman in the corner bed spits violently. 'There . . . my spit – he's licking up my spit. Look at his tongue . . .' I pretend I am not watching her, across the ward, as she lies back writhing. 'It burns . . . he gave me the disease . . . it's bleeding! Hurry, hurry!' We all pretend not to be watching her.

'Acromegaly. No doubt exaggerated by bulimia.' Red-haired, red-bearded, Professor Meynert strides past a gross, immobile woman, with us in tow. Obedient, black-coated crows. Meynert comes with greater interest to the next bed, where an elderly patient, head on chest and seeming to mumble to her breastbone, gets to her feet. 'Hurry,' cries the corner bed, 'she's going to jump, she's going to jump, jump, jump!'

'Some rigidity.' Meynert strokes her neck. 'Oculogyric problems. Catablepsia. Palilalic tendencies. Emprosthotonos, less severe today. Continue with the hydrotherapy.'

'Poor Klara,' sighs the corner bed, over and over.

'Admission report?' Meynert turns, beside the next patient.

'Confusion. Tics. Recurrent shivers, motor restlessness – akathisia. Intermittent torticollis. Some improvement after electro-massage.' Hesitating, Hollaender offers Meynert the report. Meynert reads out, unperturbed, 'Cure improbable. Father a syphilitic.' We eye the patient, the rhythmic drumming of her uncompleted gestures. 'Observe . . . how the greater the madness, the more mechanical the human being becomes, in its tics and tremors.' He means, if we could see better under the microscope, this ward would be empty; he means, if we had a suitable brain dye . . .

Tics and tremors. The corner bed is ticking like a clock now. 'Come quick, come quick, come quick, come quick!'

'Let her be,' Meynert calls, as the nurses restrain her. And now, beside a sleeping patient, he surveys us. 'Who admitted this one?' He can see who it is, in my eyes. 'Belongs with Schultz. Department Four.' As we move on, he holds my gaze. 'You'll see after the autopsy: brain tumour as big as your fist.' His smile adds: you'll soon learn.

At last we reach the corner bed, surrounding it, and can gaze freely at its occupant. 'Poor Klara,' says Meynert, addressing her directly. The woman starts to cry, soundlessly, her ranting done.

'Echolalia,' Meynert continues. 'Delusional insanity ... confusion ...'

'You mustn't think you have to choose between medicine and science, Sigi.' Breuer's drawing room is shuttered against the foetid summer wind. We sit in a darkened room, sweating. 'I know the laboratory seems pure and philosophical beside the rough and tumble, the quackery even, of general practice. What daunts every young doctor is his authority over that everyday thing, the body ... you in particular, I think, draw back before this seemingly godlike responsibility. Isn't that so? Why do you shrink from it?'

'Do I?' Breuer's beard is stippled with sweat.

'Diagnosis is a form of mutual reassurance, for patient and doctor. Witchcraft, if you like ...'

Witchcraft. We sit in silence, in Breuer's splendid drawing room. 'Once, years ago,' I begin, 'when I went home to Freiberg for a holiday, I witnessed a consultation by a country doctor. What he said was very simple, and the same in every case: you're bewitched, my good fellow ...' No matter what their symptoms were. Bewitched. 'And what impressed me most was that they all went out completely satisfied. At that moment doctoring seemed a fatuous profession.'

'But my boy, you can spend your whole life bent over a microscope, searching for some elusive chemical ... healing will always require more than drugs.' His plump cheeks shimmer with sweat. 'The body is as malleable as a dream ... and those who have the courage to explore that mystery will be called scientists, in time: if they're not afraid to be called quacks.' He hesitates. 'Until quite recently, I ran that risk myself.' Breuer? Respectable Breuer? He holds the pause.

'I've been treating a young girl, barely twenty when we began,

9

for two years now, week in week out. Daily sometimes. You understand: I tell you this in confidence. I knew the family well – the father, Pappenheim, was ill himself, and the girl nursed him like an angel, putting her own health at risk, going without sleep, without food. Until she herself was too weak to move. Her sight and speech were failing, she began to suffer from hallucinations – dreadful ones – intermittent paralyses, contractions in the limbs, severe headaches ...' I can picture her in the wards. Always the same hallucinations. Devils, death's heads; Breuer is describing them in morbid detail. 'Skeletons in her room, the ribbons in her hair turning into snakes. And if you could have seen her, before the illness set in ... she had a purity about her, a tenderness, chaste and kind –'

He is silent for a time, utterly absorbed. 'Other doctors were called, to no effect, sometimes she wouldn't even acknowledge their presence. For her the room was empty, except for the two of us. And I'd completely lost my touch. I couldn't penetrate her nightmare. Until at last her father died, and Bertha began to live again, miraculously ... *made* herself live again, as though by some auto-hypnosis. Her mind came and went now, at intervals, but the physical symptoms dragged on – and then I realized: if she could hypnotize herself, why couldn't I? Every evening I attempted to induce a trance – she was a willing subject – and for an hour she spoke freely about her illness. For an hour she was perfectly lucid.'

Breuer transported; we are at the girl's sick-bed, the shutters drawn, the *foehn* blowing. The hypnotized girl talking. 'Little by little, telling her she was well, her arms and legs no longer cramped in pain, her sight and hearing unimpaired – we freed the symptoms, one by one. Until there was no need for hypnosis. We only had to talk. Chimney sweeping, she called it.'

Breuer, rapt. As if ... is he in love? Witchcraft indeed. 'I didn't know you practised the black arts, Josef. Is this some free-masonry? Ernst von Fleischl claims to be a hypnotist –'

'Fleischl uses it as a party trick –' scathingly; I have his attention now, '... this was a patient in a state of living death, insensible to every kind of therapy. Hypnosis worked!' He breaks off, seeing my expression.

'And is she cured?'

He gives a nod, equivocal. 'She's travelling abroad. With a companion. I tell you this . . .' I watch him as he rises, heavily. 'I'd rather see her die than suffer as she did.'

Breuer at the window, his back turned, in silence. At last, 'While she was . . . briefly . . . at a sanatorium, recuperating, a young doctor fell in love with her. And she was forced to flee.'

I feel ashamed for him. A little angry, too; what young doctor?

'If there is a cure for madness, Josef, it will be found in the laboratory. And be sold by chemists.' But Breuer doesn't answer me.

'Yes, I hypnotized my parrot, once.' Sparks fly from the motor Fleischl is working on, some worn-out electro-therapy device that others have discarded.

'Successfully?' A few moments more; then I'll be ready.

Fleischl's head comes up, serene as a god. Dark curls, dark beard. He nods, grinning. 'Just don't mention it while Meynert's around, it's his *bête noire* – he thinks hypnosis is a kind of mumbo-jumbo with immoral side-effects.' Mimicking Meynert, ' "Erotic mumbo-jumbo . . ." '

'And is it?'

'Erotic? Not in my experience. I can't speak for the parrot.' He turns back to the motor. 'Or for Meynert.'

Minute adjustments as I steady the slide, under the microscope. We are alone in the hospital laboratory, Fleischl and I, in the lunch hour; he to tinker, I to be near him. And today, to prove myself –

'I think he gets his pleasure from dissection.' And Fleischl resumes the Meynert tone, as the coil showers him once more with sparks: ' "What we have here, my dear colleague, is a faulty machine . . ." ' He eyes it darkly. 'The question is, can the diligent brain anatomist find a cure for a simple short circuit?'

'Ernst, would you take a look at this?'

He comes, settles beside me, one eye to the eyepiece. Tightening the focus, between finger and bandaged thumb: infection, from a corpse on the dissecting table. He peers. 'What is it?' Casualties . . . I think of Breuer.

'*Medulla oblongata.*'

'But – what's it soaked in?' His fine strong face contorted, concentrating. 'It's a vast improvement on your previous attempt. The colours ... this is quite remarkable!'

A voice interrupts, cutting short my excitement. Professor Bruecke, in the doorway.

'What is remarkable, Herr von Fleischl?'

Hebrew grace, mumbo-jumbo. As Father draws to a close, I cannot disguise my brimming mood. Mamma can see.

'Well?'

My sisters follow her eyes, to me; Alexander too, darkly. The boy is learning. Only Father remains suspended, in the aftermath of grace. He breaks the bread. I can begin.

'I have some news for you all.' No place for modesty here. 'I think my search for a brain dye has borne fruit.' How can they understand? I tell them how for generations physiologists have tried to find a staining solution which would make the tissue in the central nervous system stand out more strongly ... and now: 'It seems that gold – dipped in chloride – may be the answer ...'

Amid the applause, 'And no-one thought of gold?' My father's eyes are on Mamma. 'That's always the solution ...' And the laughter, everyone laughing.

'A man named Flechsig thought of it. I'm the first to test it, that's all.'

His eyes are on me now. 'Is your hospital so rich, then? In gold?'

The mood is crumbling. 'Does it matter?' Mamma comes to my aid. 'The discovery belongs to *him*.'

He meets her eyes, smiling; how cosy it all seems ... and Alexander chooses his moment.

'I too have good news. From the first of next month my salary is being raised to six gulden – Herr Muenz is taking me on permanently, at the travel agency.'

I add my congratulations to the noise. Six gulden already, at seventeen; and how neatly he trumped my news. Our eyes meet, smiling. He knows I can trust his cunning.

'Pass Sigi his soup.'

'Yes Mamma.'

'How is Martha?' Now my sisters have gone silent. Mamma holds my gaze. 'Have you heard from her?'

'Not for a day or two. She's very busy at the moment. Did I mention that Bruecke himself –' Not that I've fooled anyone, I'll be interrogated later. I tell them instead how Bruecke straightened from the microscope to gaze at me and say I was a fine anatomist ... more, that my methods would make me famous yet ... 'Indeed, my friend von Fleischl says he's never seen so well into the nerve fibres.' I sip my soup. 'The implications for the study of all diseases originating in the brain –' Someone is interrupting.

'I understand the great von Fleischl has a few diseased fibres himself.'

'An infected thumb. From working on a corpse. One of the hazards of my profession, Alexander.'

'And that he's now a morphine addict.' The whole table is silent. 'Also one of the hazards?'

I dip my spoon into my soup –

'With what is Martha busy?' Mamma thinks she has me cornered. 'Is Hamburg so interesting?'

And sip my soup.

'Sigi?'

'Let the boy eat, Amalie.'

'Can't I ask him how his fiancée is keeping?'

'He doesn't want to talk about it.'

We eat, in silence.

'If he was happy,' murmurs Mamma, 'he would talk about it.'

Father, watching her. 'Who needs a brain dye,' he asks of his soup, 'when a mother can see everything?'

First, the meal. The boys' news; then the girls' news; then the gossip, as we clear the dishes. Then the excuses, each one finding a reason to withdraw and leave me to Mamma.

Long, sparring silences, by lamplight. I know there are questions she is struggling not to ask.

'Take a few days' holiday. Go to Hamburg.'

'When I can go in triumph – then I'll go.' Trying, by my tone, to forbid further discussion.

'And this discovery? Isn't that enough?'

'Papa doesn't seem to think so –'

'Of course he does!'

'Then why must he make a joke of it ... as if the hospital were to be congratulated for their facilities ... their hoard of gold ...'

Now she flares up; now it begins. 'You're as bad as he is – taking everything to heart!'

At least I've distracted her from Martha. She studies me, calming.

'Sigi, when a man's own ambitions have been thwarted –'

The son must make amends; a bitter compensation. Mamma sees my dull acquiescence, and her anger flares again.

'What is it? Can't you forgive him for being poor?'

Poor. A poor merchant; not even that – a man who was a poor merchant, who lives off schemes and dreams, who lives off his children, and his children's dreams. And loves them for their dreams, and hates them.

Fleischl's house, like Breuer's bathroom, a tableau: the Marriage of Art and Science. Graeco-Roman statuary jostles with hydraulic pumps, Classical landscapes with sectional drawings of electrical accumulators. Gilded pillars, Roman couches, champagne, drugs. Fleischl's fine torso beneath the billowing, expensive shirt; an athlete's frame. And poised above the elbow resting on the desk, the newly bandaged thumb, held high to keep the poisoned blood from draining into it.

With the other hand he re-adjusts the microscope, humming a tune, over and over. Lore, the parrot, watching him, shifts from foot to foot. I must speak first.

'These ones aren't as good, are they?' Fleischl makes no answer. 'I was up all night preparing them – they've been sitting in my room, congealing, while I patrol the wards. Unless ... the process is itself unstable –'

'I hear Weigert is trying something similar. You should publish at once.' At last he looks up, smiling. 'You've got there first, that's all that matters. The next step is to plant the flag, and then advance, exploring ... exposing the hidden trackways of disease – a Pizarro in the jungles of the cortex!' Rising, he moves swiftly to the bell-pull. 'A Cortez of the cortex! Come, we must celebrate this . . .'

He returns to the desk, hiding the thumb from me. 'You have the weapons . . . now you must hone them, and prepare for a seven years' war.' Both hands come to remove the slide, and he winces with pain.

'Would you like me to take a look? Shall I dress it for you?'

He nods, and I move to the cabinet. A seven years' war . . . does he doubt my discovery? 'Why say seven years? Why not say thirty . . .'

'What's seven years? Think what Galileo went through – or Darwin –'

'It's only a brain dye.' I bring the bandages and disinfectant; unwrap the thumb with care. 'I don't mean to remain a glorified technician all my life, no matter how accomplished. Do you realize Alexander brings in more than I do – gives my mother more?' And here I am, hoping to marry a girl without a scrap of dowry . . .

The last gauze comes away, exposing the festering thumb. Purple, ringed with yellow, bulging hideously. I can feel my hand begin to tremble. Fleischl watching my face.

'I understood the family Bernays was rich.' A sly grin.

'They've spent it all since Bernays died.' The disinfectant; then the fresh gauze, hiding the sickening thing from sight. 'That's why they've run off home to Hamburg.'

Fleischl begins to hum again, his shoulders waltzing, as I begin the bandaging. 'Hold still!' With his free arm he hugs me, accomplice in his fate, his secret decay. What is it? Why can't he hold still?

Lore squawks as the door opens, and Fleischl's strong fingers release me. 'Champagne.' The manservant darts me a glance before withdrawing. 'I intend to have a finer cellar than the Emperor – if my electrical work pays off. I may have found a new kind of accumulator –' his free hand waves disassembled metal into concerted life. Fleischl: neurologist, linguist, inventor, prodigy. I rest my shaking hand, put down the bandages. Those whom the gods love –

He smiles. 'A doctor must have hobbies. And if it brings

results, I could finance your thirty years' war, if you need that long . . .'

'I already owe Breuer almost a thousand gulden – never mind my debts to you, to Paneth . . .'

'And that distresses you? You should be proud we have such faith in you.' He eyes me. 'Are you going to bandage this thumb, or am I?'

'Forgive me. I'm a little tired.' I set to work again. 'To tell the truth I haven't been well since Martha left.'

'Symptoms?' Mock stern.

'Fatigues . . . migraines, depressions.' His smile declares: a normal Viennese in love. 'The nights are the worst. I mean – the dreams.'

'O . . . then I see Queen Mab hath been with you –'

'Sometimes I think the separation will cost me my sanity. I'm serious.' Yes; serious. And you're the only one I can tell.

'You mean the frustration. There's a simple remedy for lustful dreams.' A moment's silence. 'Girls aplenty in the Graben.'

'You're speaking from experience?'

He studies me. 'You've never been?'

'I swear –'

'On the Madonna,' he chuckles. A safe oath for a Jew. 'Go on fearing for your sanity, then.'

Dare I tell him about my nights, my dreams? The manservant enters with a tray, to further frenzied squawking from Lore's cage.

' "This great drivelling love . . ." ' Fleischl gestures, grandiloquent; his arm caresses me again. ' ". . . is like a great natural that runs lolling up and down to hide his bauble in a hole . . ." Have you ever noticed how madness and frustration go hand in hand? Now if there were a little antidote to lust, Sigmund, a convenient solution –' The door closes behind us. 'Pour me a glass, would you?'

'When I've finished.'

'Now.' Suddenly petulant, he holds my gaze till I obey. 'For the moment – take my tip: Alserstrasse 19 . . .'

'Get thee behind me, Satan.' Working the cork. 'I preferred you as Mercutio.'

'You prefer me dead, then.' He ignores my glance. 'If I hadn't lingered on like this, you could have stayed at Bruecke's Institute. Taken my post as his assistant . . .'

'Don't say that!'

'Sigi . . .' Pleading. I bring the glasses, set them down, and tie off the gauze at the dark, discoloured base of his thumb.

'*Prosit!*' He raises his glass. 'To the new conquistador – may he be forgiven his dreams.' A grin. 'Or fulfil them.'

We sip, we pause, I watch him drain his glass. And almost at once draw himself up, rigid, as a spasm racks his body. Fleischl, doubling up in pain. As I reach out to him –

'Wait . . .'

He tries to stand. Totters.

'Ernst!'

'In the desk –' Barely audible. Beginning to shake convulsively. I reach for the bandaged hand, he pushes me away. 'In the drawer of the desk! Quickly . . .'

The great metallic barrel of a syringe meets my gaze, as I open the drawer. Behind me, his unsteady voice.

'I've been without morphia for two days . . . without anything – spent them mostly in the bath . . .' Wrenching at his shirtsleeve, his voice rising to a shout: 'Come on . . .'

The syringe is ready loaded, the injection effortless, his good hand clenched in mine. Transferring the pain. Easing, as the fit passes, and he sits. I have pumped his body full of morphine. To ease a local agony? Or to feed an addiction? He sits, still shivering.

'Surely . . .' I try, 'Billroth can operate again, to drain the thumb –' The second time in six months.

His eyes mock my evasions. '"An embossed carbuncle"', he recites dully, ' "in my corrupted blood."' Death, his eyes say, is already inside the walls. Behind us the bird is screaming like a banshee. 'For God's sake shut her up . . .'

I cover the cage. Across the room, Fleischl grins at me, still speaking with difficulty. 'I've got the only Sanskrit-speaking parrot in Vienna. We've been learning together.'

A silence. 'You've been learning Sanskrit?' I stare, exhausted now. A brave task, for a dying man.

'Why not? It's a dead language.' Can he read my thoughts?

I'm so tired. 'Better now,' says Fleischl, after a pause. 'Thank you.'

I nod. His head on his chest, eyelids drooping. Time seems to pass, in silence; Fleischl like a broken reveller, slumped at his desk, shirt awry. Speaking again, softly.

'What a lot of Quixotes we are, Sigi. Will any of us see forty, do you suppose? Come ... sit down. Talk to me.' I sit, a little way away. 'How is your Esmeralda?'

'Surrounded by suitors. So she hints. She hasn't written for a fortnight.' Marty's last letter swims before me. 'Writers, sculptors – artistic riff-raff –'

'But she is chaste ...'

'As snow. A chaste Diana.' Silence. His eyes are closing once more. 'Did I tell you I'm thinking of emigrating?'

'Where to?'

'England.'

'Why not America?'

'All right. America.' I too am spent. 'Sleep. It'll do you good.' Some time later, I hear his voice. 'You will be here when I wake up, won't you.'

'Of course.'

The little square outside the university is empty, lit by gas-lamps. The church façade before me, pock-marked with vacant recesses. I can hear chanting, in the dead of night.

Coatless, I hunt the source of the sound, through empty cobbled streets. At the end of the street a procession along a street at right angles to mine, the Madonna seated high above the candles.

The street is narrower, the procession advancing towards me up the alley. They are Poor Clares. How do I know that? They fill the alleyway, I step aside, against a door, and their departing feet leave petals in the alley. Voices, in a doorway opposite. I remain invisible.

Three men emerge, opposite. It has begun to rain, louder than the receding hymn. The three men put on coats and hats, glancing down the street with a certain furtiveness. My heart thumps as I recognize one: my father.

'Gold ... that's always the solution.'

Above the door, the plaque reads '19'.

In the dark entrance hall, strangers jostle me, and then the room before me is bright with daylight from a single blaze of windows. The room is crammed with flowers, both bouquets and wreaths; among them busts, lightly festooned, and hung with Latin tags. There are beds. Fleischl lies on one, ignored, as I am drawn, tense with anticipation, so tense the dream grows dark till I can see only my feet, advancing, towards the far bed, thronged with people.

My face is in darkness; I cannot see, but I am filled with terror.

'Admission report?'

'Father a syphilitic.'

Breuer, before me, turning to me. 'You should publish at once!'

I turn away, shutting my eyes to end the dream, as in childhood, and open them once more to light: the window. Blank with light as I approach it, and stare out, hoping against hope.

In the garden beyond, at a table beneath an awning, sit Martha and Minna, two young women in summer dresses with Ignaz Schoenberg beside them. They turn, glancing up . . .

I hear my daughter's voice. 'Papa . . .'

I wake. I wake, no longer twenty-seven, I wake an invalid of eighty, shackled by age. Anxious faces peering down at me. I've slept off fifty years. Can you understand, doctor?

'Papa,' Anna takes my hand. 'Dr Schur is leaving now.'

I turn to the window. The garden beyond is sodden, rain-soaked, the table and chairs deserted. 'Where's Mama?' My jaw feels locked, bone without muscle.

'She went out shopping, when the rain stopped.'

The doctor's face. He can see the pain that speaking costs me, bends to his bag. 'I'll give you something now, before I go.' But my gaze stops him. Looks exchanged with Anna.

'Papa –'

'Aspirin.' I can still make the voice bark, from the throat. But in my jaw –

A nod between them, and Anna leaves, to fetch the blessed aspirin. In my jaw . . . I remember now, and I can feel it: no, not bone. Metal. A metal palate, metal gums. They've given me a mechanical mouth, sweet irony.

The doctor watches me still coming to myself. Watching the old man remember. Counting the operations. Our eyes light together on the faithful wooden clothes-peg, on the table beside me. I smile. 'Yes. One cigar.'

He fetches one, and watches, pained, as I prise my jaws wide with the clothes-peg. Sweet, chewed wood; it heralds a cigar. I clamp the wedge of leaf into the gap, and remove the wooden prop. Lean forward to the proffered flame, and take the first puff.

'In my dream too, it was raining.' Speaking has become a hell; this is no way to live. And I can see in your eyes, doctor, you too are impatient to leave. Enough. Enough of this humiliation. Silence falls.

'My dear Schur, you remember we had a little talk once, when we first met.' He remembers; he has gone very still. 'You remember? The disease was already inside the walls. And we agreed. When the time came, I should not be forced to suffer, more than is necessary.'

The speech has drained me. I can see panic in his eyes, he knows what I am asking of him. 'I remember,' he says.

'Don't fail me.' A moment's silence. 'I trusted your predecessor, and he failed me. For months he lied to me, while everyone else knew.' And it was *my* cancer, mine; my choice. My beloved, poisonous cigars. 'Don't you fail me too.'

Then Anna is in the doorway, holding a glass of water. Glancing from me to Schur.

I let the moment pass. Addressing the glass as it approaches, clouded by the dissolving aspirin, 'My best friend.'

Schur sees me work my mouth open with both hands, pushing at the machinery within. Quickly – too quickly – he tells me it's time to adjust the prosthesis again, '. . . if you'll let me administer some Evipan, we can remove it painlessly – '

Ignore him. No more operations. I raise the glass, watching the pill dance, rising to the surface in soft foam.

You know what Evipan is derived from, don't you, doctor? Don't you know? I watch the cloudy liquid in the glass.

Fleischl's voice. 'Is it expensive?'

I stir the liquid with a small, expensive spoon. 'Very, I was given to believe a gramme cost thirty kreuzer – instead it's three florins and thirty kreuzer. From Merck of Darmstadt.' I bring him the glass. 'My chemist has been supplying cocaine tea for years, to actors and singers. To soothe the larynx.'

Unshaven Fleischl, stretched out on a couch like Chatterton, the dying poet. Within arm's reach lie books, a basin, the remains of food.

'A man called Aschenbrandt, a regimental doctor, has been giving coca to his troops: he claims it revives their strength –' I have him now; he gazes at the glass with hungry hope. 'But the suggestion that it might serve as an antidote to morphinism comes from an American journal I've found.'

'A suggestion merely?' Yet he takes the glass. 'How much is in here?'

'One twentieth of a gramme.'

Holding my gaze, he drains the glass, grimaces.

'Trust me. It's a remarkable substance. It seems the Incas worshipped it for its medicinal and ... other properties ...'

'Other properties?'

'It's also a most powerful aphrodisiac.'

Fleischl begins to smile, the tenderness returning. 'How do you know all this? Have you tried it?'

I nod, teasing. Yes, but alone, in my room at night. In rapturous solitude. 'I've been spending hours in the library at the Gesellschaft – this morning I found a picture of an Inca goddess presenting coca leaves to the conquistadores ...'

He laughs, delighted. 'Do you have enough to take some with me?'

I return to the desk, to measure out a second dose. 'Ernst, it's a miracle drug, believe me – even in the smallest doses it alleviates all kinds of pain ... headaches, gastric disorders, skin infections – even the worst nausea disappears within minutes! Can you feel its effects?'

'Give me time. There is ... a certain numbness in my lips –'

I drain the glass, scarcely needing it in my own euphoria. 'You know Rosannes at the hospital? With his perpetual stomach cramps? I gave him a few drops – without letting him know what it was – and the pain vanished. Koller's tried some, and Koenigstein. I even took some home and gave it to Mama, to ease her lung constriction . . .' I come to Fleischl, place the box of powder in his hand. 'Can you imagine what mankind might owe this drug, in time? It gives you stamina to work without fatigue – with no loss of acuteness, no sense of being drugged, or over-stimulated . . . and without any craving once the first exhilaration passes! Imagine, if this could wean people off the worst addictions, without pain – without nausea –'

He takes my hand, hesitating. 'How on earth have you found time for all this . . . experimenting and research? Are you sure you haven't forgotten your hospital duties – in your exhilaration?'

'It fills my spare time. Every moment of it.'

'And the seven years' war? Gold chloride . . . already forgotten?' Hasn't he understood? Gazing at me with loving tenderness. 'What an absurd impulsive man you are.'

I take the box of powder from him, careful of his thumb. 'With this I can transform the *living* brain, and through it the living body. Ernst, this is the panacea that the ancients knew and revelled in. The elixir old Ponce de Leon spent his life searching for! Meynert is right – our salvation is chemical, it's real, not metaphysical! It's right here in this precious powder: health, and happiness.'

'Never mind its "other properties" . . .' Fleischl smiles. My hand still locked in his. 'I'm beginning to feel quite transported already.' A moment's silence, as his smile broadens. 'And . . . do you intend to slip some into Martha's tea?'

'We shall both partake. In the name of the gods.'

'How long will you be gone?'

'A week'. I shrug. Koenigstein leans forward to hear better, as triumphant cries ring out around us. 'A week, maybe two. It all depends.'

He grins. 'On how long your supplies last . . .'

Koller comes towards us, out of the milling crowd in the laboratory. My empire-builders, all brimming with cocaine, busily testing their reflexes on the dynamometer. Some in pairs, arm-wrestling with their newfound strength. I gaze round with a father's pride.

Koller shoots me a sour look. 'My tongue's quite numb –'

'Of course.' I turn to Koenigstein. 'While I'm away, you must try some on your patients. As an analgesic.'

'I'm an eye specialist, Sigmund – my patients aren't suffering from general debilitation.'

'Well, to alleviate iritis, say. But it will also find a wider application ... don't you think so, Koller?'

'No doubt.' A dry look; I glory in his envy. All round, elated faces, laughter. They look like men, not scientists. Discoverers, conquistadores. I am Manco Capac, king of the Incas: see, a gift from the gods, to satisfy the hungry, fortify the weary, and make the unfortunate forget their sorrows ...

A scene from the land of Cockaigne. The woods are still, the views as long and clear as any spring morning, the weather as light, warmth without the summer haze. Has there ever been such an autumn? The leaves have already turned, one breath of wind will bring them all down. Nature suspended, as if cocaine were all around us as we walk. Our first afternoon together, with the Inca potion in our veins.

'I may go abroad for a while.' I let it drop, offhand. Marty's glance comes quickly.

'When?'

I shrug. 'Next year.' I hold the silence. 'There's a travelling scholarship worth six hundred gulden, given by the Medical Faculty. I've been urged to apply.' I grin at her. 'It's true. For the first time in my life, people come to *me* – editors asking for articles, colleagues seeking advice ... even my professors deign to recognize me in the street: that's Freud, the father of cocaine.' We laugh. 'Don't you believe me?'

'Of course I believe you.'

'I'm going to put in for a lectureship next spring, resign from the hospital, and go to Paris. Then back to Vienna –'

'Wait ...' laughing, 'wait. Why to Paris?'

'To study, under Charcot. Breuer says he has the best collection of pickled brains in Europe. And he's promised me an introduction. Then: back in triumph to Vienna, a fully fledged neurologist ... lecturer in neuropathology ...' I see her smile brimming over, '... ready to set up in practice. You're not listening!'

She stops. 'I am. It's the cocaine ... making me laugh.'

Above us the yellow leaves, suspended, waiting.

'How would you like to spend your honeymoon in Lubeck ... when I return from Paris?' It sobers her. She gazes at me; wanting to believe. I take her arms. 'Perhaps, while I'm there – I should try my hand at hypnotism. It's Charcot's speciality. Who knows – the power of suggestion ...' I draw her close, and kiss her. Drawing back as I feel the laughter in her, through the kiss.

She struggles not to smile; a mock struggle. 'How much ... does a lecturer earn?'

I burst out laughing. 'Not enough!' We subside, slowly. 'Are you bringing me no dowry, then? A few kreuzer ...'

'Eli's invested them.'

'Sensible fellow.'

I take her hands, in sudden happiness.

'When I saw you at the station, coming towards me – it was like a dream –'

'That was the cocaine ...'

'A dream come true, I meant. Don't you feel it? Don't you notice the difference?'

She hesitates, smiling.

'I notice the difference in you.'

In the empty laboratory my cocaine lies return to mock me. How could I have said such nonsense? Freud the father of cocaine dreams ... the dreamer, surrounded by mocking opportunists –

Someone stirs, at the far end of the room. Koenigstein, looking up from his work.

'Sigmund ...'

'I've already heard.'

We stare each other out.

'You said a week or two ... you've been away a month.'

'A month.' Erupting now, in all my shame, 'Is it too long for a man like Koller to restrain his own ambitions – too long to respect a friend's priority? Do you dash in as soon as a colleague goes on holiday, steal his discovery, and proclaim it before the world?'

'You've already published –'

'An essay. An introduction. I gather Koller's already done operations – using cocaine as an anaesthetic. And there's been a lecture in Heidelberg . . . a paper here before the Medical Society . . . giving detailed accounts of Koller's triumph!' Control the black rage; sit. 'How could you let this happen . . .'

'Sigmund, it's not my job to protect your interests –'

'Your *job*? If you'd only done as I asked –'

'And offered cocaine as an analgesic?' The man's self-righteous calm – 'Koller's using it as an anaesthetic, Sigi, there's a world of difference – not just palliative treatment but to deaden the eye for operative purposes.' He studies me. 'You and I were concentrating more on the internal uses of the drug.'

He and I . . . I can hardly speak.

'Sigmund, listen to me. So far Koller's only tried it out on animals. He's due to read a paper to the Faculty on the seventeenth. You could give one too. It's happened before . . .'

To be the first, Leopold. The first. You know what it means.

As I feared: Nothnagel's waiting room is crowded. The Professor of Internal Medicine is a busy man, and I have no appointment. His patients eye me reproachfully, as if they can tell my intentions by my briefcase and embarrassed air.

The surgery door opens. Nothnagel's massive bulk appeared, white-coated.

'If I could see the Herr Professor on a most important personal matter –' I can feel the reproachful eyes on me.

'If it's brief, Dr Freud.'

I follow him into the consulting room, and shut the door. He stands beside me, gazing down, a head taller. Beneath the stiff blond hair, a face livid with warts. His pale Teutonic eyes survey me, seeing in me everything that he is not. Jew-boy up from the country.

Better, though, to know the worst, and know it now.

He is smiling. 'I approve.' I stare. 'The beard. Much better.'

'Ah –' It's newly trimmed. 'Yes.' Careful now. 'Herr Hofrat, I believe you are on the committee appointed to report on my application for a lectureship in Neuropathology. I should like to ask your opinion whether on the strength of my existing publications I stand any chance of being chosen ... or whether I should wait till I have more?'

He is moving to the desk, apparently untroubled by my audacity. Sits; reaches out a hand, wordlessly, for my briefcase. He brings out the little sheaf of articles, shuffles them.

'What are your papers on, Doctor? "Coca" I know.'

Impossible to gauge his tone. Impressed? Contemptuous? He lays the others out.

'You seem to have eight or nine here.' No: affable. Even indifferent. 'By all means send in your application. When I think of some of the people elevated to the rank of Lecturer ... really, there should be no objection.'

'I have several more things to be published,' I stumble, 'two of them in the immediate future –'

'You won't need them, these are more than enough.'

'But – there isn't much about neuropathology in them ...'

'Who knows anything about neuropathology until they've studied anatomy and physiology?' Under his gaze I feel myself transformed into a different person. Newly trimmed; clubbable. 'And I hear you are already a first-rate anatomist. Now: there are three people to report on this appointment – Meynert, Bamberger, and myself. There won't be any opposition, and if objections are raised by the Faculty ... well, surely we are men enough to push it through?'

I find my voice. 'Then – then may I take it you will support my candidature? I believe Professor Bruecke will.'

'You may indeed, my friend.' A moment. 'Is that all?'

'Thank you. Thank you so much –'

The door is only a few feet away.

'Dr Freud.'

I turn. Nothnagel is holding out my briefcase, with my articles.

'Thank you once more.' I fetch them, turn to leave.

'Herr Doctor ...'

His face, still affable. I wait.

'Some of my colleagues are disturbed by reports that this – "coca" ... taken internally, may have ... degenerative effects.' He measures the pause. 'No doubt you've come across some evidence of this. And yet – I understand that you still champion its use as a restorative. Even as an antidote, in the treatment of morphine addiction.' The tone is still the same; but the clubroom manner has vanished. 'Is that correct?'

'By no means. That is – I no longer advocate it with my first, unconsidered fervour. But I do think that with the proper supervision and – once the substance has been adequately tested ...'

The pale eyes wait me out.

I find a different voice. 'It's true. I don't believe we know enough about cocaine.'

Someone calling. Pounding on the door, distantly. I wake to cold sweat, in my clothes. Sunlight. I am sitting in Fleischl's bathroom, in bright light, Fleischl lying beside me in the wooden bath. Asleep, thank God. Arms dangling, hair matted, water up to his chest. I touch the water. Barely warm.

The knocking comes again. Breuer; I sent for Breuer. And the horrors of the previous night come back to me. Fleischl's face empty now.

I hurry through the bedroom, past the distraught parrot to the drawing-room door, and turn the key to open. Breuer and Hartmann, Fleischl's manservant, stand staring at me. My face tells the story.

'Where's Ernst?' In answer, I gesture. 'Is he all right?'

'He's sleeping.'

I let them into the room. Breuer puts down his bag, deposits hat and scarf.

'I can't stay long. I have a consultation at nine.' Breuer comes over to where I stand, dully, watching Hartmann discreetly tidying debris. Breuer follows my gaze; we pause. 'I gather Bruecke made a stirring speech to the Faculty, on your behalf.' Taking my hand, 'Congratulations.'

'It isn't ratified yet –'

'A formality.' He smiles. I meet Hartmann's gaze, and the man withdraws, shutting the door. Breuer turns swiftly back. 'Why did you lock the door?'

'I didn't lock it. Ernst did. To keep out the snakes.' Breuer stares. 'I thought you'd better see him. He's been sleeping for a while now, with the help of drugs.'

27

'Morphine?' I douse his alarm with a look. 'Thank God. I came as soon as I could. Forgive me –'

'I've refused him morphine for three days. This morning I felt I couldn't hold out much longer.'

I turn, alerted by the sound of water, splashing –

'You've been here three days? Alone with him?'

A shout. A shriek, from the bathroom. 'For God's sake – somebody! He's crushing me –' I run, towards the cries.

Water churning, splashing the floor as Fleischl beats at his legs, arms flailing. He hisses, 'Quickly . . . I can't move my legs!' Drawing his body up out of the bath. 'There! There! Can't you see him? There . . .'

I hurry to my bag. The syringe ready loaded.

'The great grey worm . . .' A sudden peal of laughter. 'Tickling my feet!'

Breuer in the doorway, gazing in horror, as I move to the bath.

'What are you giving him?'

Wrestling with Fleischl's arm. 'What do you think . . .' He breaks free, plunging forward.

'I'm – going to . . . throttle it!'

'Cocaine? By injection?' Breuer shouting now. 'Are you mad?'

'Works faster.' Shouting back. 'Help me!'

Together we pull Fleischl back. He screams, gazing at Breuer. I insert the needle, and we hold him fast. His eyes, fixed on Breuer, terrified. I withdraw the syringe, still gripping Fleischl.

'It's all right, just . . . leave me with him for a moment.' Breuer seems transfixed. 'Please . . .' He steps back, quietly. Fleischl is slipping into unconsciousness. 'The cocaine . . . at least . . . subdues him. I daren't give morphine.'

Breuer's voice comes from behind me, fierce. 'Don't you understand yet? He's a double addict!'

Kneeling, exhausted, I hold onto Fleischl as his eyes close, water soaking through my shirt. Silence, at last. I lay his head, limp now, against the wooden rim. Compose his arms. And let my own head droop.

'Josef?' No answer.

I find him, in the drawing room, hunched. Wearing hat and scarf. We stand in silence. 'Has this been going on all summer?'

Accusing eyes. 'How long have you been giving him cocaine like this?'

'I'm trying to keep him alive!' I watch Breuer slowly collect his bag. 'Josef ... in the Detroit *Gazette*, Bentley recommends a decoction of coca leaves as a specific against opium addiction –'

'Against opium, yes.'

'Of which morphine is a derivative.'

'It's *purified* opium! Don't you see the difference?'

'Just as cocaine is: the purified leaf. Fight fire with fire, Josef.' His face is livid. 'It's you who talk about having the courage to explore lost arts ... and new sciences –'

'Not to unleash a fresh scourge – replacing one addiction with another! If people believed your claims for cocaine we'd have a whole city full of degenerates!'

My courage fails, before his rage. He sees it, and turns away. I shudder, suddenly cold in my dripping shirt.

'Stay with him.' Breuer turns back to me. 'I'll come back after surgery.'

I watch him walk to the door and turn once more, to study me. I search for the dregs of my defiance.

'Could you ask Hartmann to bring up some more hot water?'

A moment, then he nods, sadly.

'Believe me – and I'm speaking from the heart ... I hope you win the travelling grant: the sooner you leave, the better.' Before I can retort, his anger breaks out again. 'Madness ...' My expression only provokes him. 'To think I recommended you as a sober-minded scientist – canvassed for your promotion ... and this is how you reward me.'

'Is that what you're concerned about? Your reputation? I can set your mind at ease on that! I've been assessed on my own merit – ' Ask Bruecke, ask Nothnagel!

'Oh yes ... no doubt you told them what they wanted to hear – that everything the human soul requires will one day be sold in a chemist's shop! If the Faculty had known what you were doing here ... they'd have dismissed you as a reckless fool!'

I feel tears in my eyes; out of control. We glare at each other like lovers in the torment of separation. Beyond words.

'You'd rather let him die?' I ask. 'Is that it?'

He turns away as my tears come.

Then, in a different tone, 'Let your emotions get the better of you ... and you are no longer a doctor.'

Nel mezzo del cammin di nostra vita, mi ritrovai per una selva oscura –

'Sigmund.'

A sudden movement, as if in cramp. Fleischl is awake.

'Are you in pain?'

'No.' He smiles, gazing at me. 'Just a little drowsy. Otherwise ... remarkably good.' He stirs in the bath, lying back. 'What are you reading?'

I show him. Dante; Fleischl's own copy, painstakingly annotated. He smiles, pleased.

'Is there anything you need?' I make to rise. 'There's food next door –'

'It's for you.' I resume my seat. A pause. 'You know, it's strange ... my brain's racing again. No wonder the ancient philosophers did all their thinking in the bath.' His face clouds. 'Was I ... did I hallucinate, just now ... or was I dreaming?' A shudder racks him. 'Breuer – like a great mangy crow ...'

Fleischl turns away, and I reach out one hand to his shoulder. Calming, he brings a hand to rest on mine. And meets my gaze.

'Remember,' he murmurs, 'in the *Purgatorio*, the man who reaches out for Virgil's hand? *Or puoi la quantitate comprender, del amor ch'a te mi scalda ...*'

Such is my love, that I, poor ghost, forget – and treat as solid flesh the stuff of shadows. I leave my hand in his.

'How much cocaine have you been taking in the last few weeks – without telling me?' He gazes back, expressionless. 'I came across your supplies, in the cabinet. Where did you get it all?'

'From Merck of Darmstadt.' Innocently. 'Same as you, Herr Doctor.' Then firmly, serious. 'No need to confiscate it. You've not become an addict – and neither will I.'

He smiles at me, guileless. And I say nothing.

My hand held tight in his. Is there not a level of the Inferno reserved for those who send others to hell?

Hartmann leads me once more up the marble stairs to Fleischl's apartments. I have become a stranger here. So much to do: making travel arrangements, attending farewells. So busy. We are at the drawing-room door.

'Herr Doctor Freud ...' Hartmann announces me, with unwonted formality. In it I hear a reproach for my absence; worse still, amusement at my new clothes. Imagined slights. The true cause greets me as I enter: Fleischl erect, rising from behind his desk, shaven and dressed as if to receive the Emperor.

For a moment I can find no words. Only relief and shame at once, and from some guilty place, anger. Fleischl smiles at my bewildered face.

'Yes – I've decided to rejoin the living.' A nod to the withdrawing Hartmann. 'I was beginning to feel like Marat in that bath. Waiting for Mademoiselle Corday.' He eyes me with a new expression. No dagger today? 'Is this better?' He draws himself up, as I approach.

Letting me see: it is all show. The face is ravaged, a death mask. Suddenly he cocks his head, like Lore.

'You've got the grant?'

'Yes.' Emotions jostle in his eyes. Quickly – 'My rivals were both Christians ... they split the vote and let me in. I've resigned my post at the hospital. Everything's in the balance now.' He nods, contained. 'I need you more than ever. When I return from Paris –'

Your guidance ... the words stick in my throat. And already Fleischl has turned away, striking a strange, stiff pose, one hand in his jacket.

'I understand Maître Charcot models himself on Napoleon!'

A rakish grin; our awkwardness dissolves. He comes to hug me.

'It will be a magnificent opportunity for you –'

'More pickled brains ...'

'Never mind pickled brains, think of the Louvre, think of Notre Dame, the Comédie Française ...' Slyly now, 'Sarah Bernhardt ...' He draws back. 'And they say Charcot's demonstrations rival anything to be seen in the theatre. More long lost magic, Sigi – and in return for the secrets of mesmerism, you can open Charcot's eyes ... to our Inca potion!'

I nod: indeed. But he sees me falter.

'What is it? Don't you want to make your mark, in Paris?'

'By all means. But I shall waste my visit if I neglect laboratory work –'

'By all means,' he mimics, still smiling. Waiting me out. 'Don't neglect laboratory work. There speaks the lecturer ...'

'Ernst, I'm going there to study neurology, not to announce a cure-all of my own. We've made great strides with the drug – you in particular have shown what can be achieved ...' It is so patent a lie that I plunge on, heedless now, '... but in the wrong hands, magic potions can prove to be scourges in disguise –'

He nods, as though to say: you Breuer. A moment, then quietly, 'No need to tell me where you've been, these last weeks. Whispering with the great black crow.' I turn away, looking for words; Fleischl's rage catches me off balance. 'Look at me!' Holding up his bandaged hand. 'This is my scourge! A blood disease contracted from a corpse – not morphine, not cocaine. D'you think I regret the risks you've taken? Spare me your homilies – I thank God for your drugs!' He studies me, calming. 'And beware of the Breuers of this world, Sigi – they don't mind taking risks when it suits *them* ... then justifying it with some high-minded, puritanical cant ...'

Bewildered, I rise to his angry tone. 'What risks ... what cant? If you mean his dabbling in hypnosis – it seems you admire Charcot for it, but when it comes to Breuer ...'

'Breuer's fished in deeper waters, believe me.' Fleischl's gaze is malign. I feel the whirlpool gathering about us. 'Alas for a certain young lady of his acquaintance. One Fraulein Pappenheim. Perhaps he's mentioned her?'

Coldly, 'I'm acquainted with the case.'

'Poor ghost – she's in the same boat as I am now: wrestling with the dark angel of morphine.' A moment, as he sees me wordless. 'You didn't know? Sigmund, the man's a hypocrite ... or have you guessed his secret?'

'That he fell in love with her? Why not ... with a beautiful, innocent girl? It's of no consequence –'

'Shall I tell you how innocent she is?' Brutal now, exulting. 'Chrobak used to attend her, and I have his word for it: Breuer was called out to her bedside late one night, to find the girl in

labour. Yes – and screaming with the pain of the contractions.
Screaming ... Dr Breuer's baby's coming!'

'It's not true –'

'Ask him whether it's true or not!'

'His child?' I stare.

'Oh, not in fact. In fantasy. There was no baby, as Breuer
quickly discovered. Whereupon ...' he glares at me. Glares;
lovers, in the throes of separation. 'He left the house, and never
went back. Rushed Mathilde off to Venice on a second honeymoon and left the girl to drugs and not-so-innocent dreams.'
Fiercely, 'It's Breuer who's the innocent! That's what I find
inexcusable – that virginal self-righteousness –' Pain, as the
black mood bursts, shaking him now. '*You* suffer from it too! So
go on, go to Paris, go and learn the black arts on the boulevards:
isn't that why you became a doctor? "Learn to handle women,
that make sure ... the doctor knows one little place to cure – "'
Silky, Mephistophelean; a spasm racks him but he will not let
me go. '"A bedside manner sets their heart at ease – and then!
They're yours, for treatment as you please ..."'

The barriers are down, all his despairing love visible in his
face. I hesitate, and he staggers against the desk, the array of
medicines clattering. Fleischl stares at them.

'Did you know – Johannes Merck, the founder of this ...
treasure house ... was Goethe's model for Mephisto?' The smile
fading under my gaze. 'I shan't be here when you return.'

'In God's name –'

'Enough of this charade. There have been days when I thought
you would understand and ...' slowly, '... not force me to suffer
longer than was necessary –'

Not force; not longer than was necessary, doctor. Do you
hear?

Fleischl is still speaking.

'I would have taken steps long ago, but for my parents with
all their high hopes ...' Then, 'Perhaps –' I can see his face; can
see it now. Pleading. 'As well today as any other day –'

No.

I said no. In shame. There was a long silence, and then he made
his way to a cabinet and brought out a figurine. A farewell gift,

33

he said, in the name of the gods. And embraced me for the last time.

An Etruscan figurine, you can see it there on the desk, beside the little Hermes.

Go now, doctor. I have my aspirin. We'll talk tomorrow.

'No argument. A farewell gift.'

'Ernst, I can't –'

'In the name of the gods.'

He offers me the statuette, presses it into my hands, and I take it, too moved to speak, letting his arms embrace me.

Now he draws back, holding me at arms' length, and speaks. Speaks with the voice of others. Measuring each syllable.

'Don't fail me . . .'

TWO

'Good morning, gentlemen. Today we shall address the problem of seeing.'

The stocky figure muses, head bowed. His assistants take up their positions, bringing a small table, a pincushion, a gong, three feathered hats. The dandies murmur in the back row; a glance quells them. Silence.

'Suppose ... you have before you this morning not Charcot, a man evidently in the prime of life – I hear no dissenting voices –' The smile is short-lived. 'But instead ... a little old man, pale, stooped, convulsive ... shaking ... who with a trembling hand extracts a little piece of paper from his pocket ...'

He seems to age and shrivel, fumbling, drawing laughter and now, from his trouser pocket, a scrap of paper –

'From which he reads a list – a long list! Of symptoms and complaints.' In the old man's voice, 'Convulsions, vomiting, diarrhoea, urinary ... difficulties ... sometime headaches, sometimes backache, toothache, earache – but always this shaking of the limbs, doctor, this trembling ...'

He straightens, Charcot once more.

'A figure from Molière, gentlemen?' Grave now. 'You will find him on many a street corner. And in every hospital in France. But what is he suffering from? What did you see, just now? Epilepsy? A parkinsonism, a palsy, a chorea? Or mere unbridled senility?'

A wave towards the wings: three female patients are admitted, each in the grip of compulsive tremors. They are led to the side of the stage, and left to stand, living exhibits.

'In these ladies, all of them inmates here at the Salpetrière, you may observe a variety of tics and tremors. One of them suffers indeed from a species of parkinsonism ... but which is the patient in question? And to what do we attribute the uncontrollable conditions of the other two? Gentlemen ... there are certain combinations of the anatomical substrata which do not present themselves to the physician's eye with that appearance of solidity, of objectivity . . .'

We are elsewhere, enthralled by the shuddering patients.

'. . . some indeed would banish these phenomena to the category of the unknown: it is hysteria which especially comes under this type of proscription. But before we venture into that mysterious territory . . .' he is moving back, towards a blackboard, unravelling a chart, '. . . let us first examine the devil we know. Organic damage – here in the cortex . . . is responsible for Mademoiselle Laforet's condition.' The assistant propels one of his charges towards us. A pale, proud face. 'The case of parkinsonism I mentioned.'

Muffled voices at the back; have they been laying bets? Charcot is fetching one of the feathered hats, bringing it to the Laforet girl. She gazes ahead, indifferent. Indifferent even to her humiliation.

. . . Marty my love, my princess: I hardly know where to begin. I miss you so . . .

'The manifestations will now be made clearer,' the hat descends onto the twitching head, the plume begins to shake, 'with the aid of the milliner's art . . .'

Friezes of painted stone, towering above me. Sphinxes.

. . . My sweet princess – Paris overwhelms me. I never knew what it was to feel so provincial, until now. To my relief, the great man has welcomed me most cordially, and arranged a cubicle in the laboratory, with all the pickled brain tissue a devout neurologist could wish for. But alas –

No, not sphinxes. Calendar beasts: the mythical animals, part man, part bird, part beast, of the ancient Assyrians. Faint laughter, from the next room. Two men and a girl, giggling at Grecian statuary.

. . . But alas – brain tissue! When I look through the microscope I might as well be in Vienna. So I flee into the streets, to the Cité, to Notre Dame, to the Louvre . . . where I feel a cultural being once more . . .

On the Faubourg St Denis I stroll at ease, inconspicuous among the passers-by. Eyeing the ladies of the night.

... Yesterday, my love, I walked in a daze down the allées at Versailles, with its stone guardians overlooking a nature trimmed and tamed ...

Nature untamed calls cheerfully to me, from a doorway.

... What splendours, Marty – and what a barbarous people! The streets are filled with shouting newsvendors and partisans of every revolutionary creed under the sun. The parks are crowded with lovers, wet-nurses feed their charges openly, *en plein air* ... even in the Louvre Frenchwomen can scarcely stand before Grecian manhood without sniggering ...

... I am avidly reading Hugo – *The Hunchback* –

I force a passage to a table at the cabaret. Dancers in purple boas, feathered hats. I sit.

... Believe me, the French people haven't changed. This is the place to read it. And how it makes me ache for you! When Dom Claude, the priest bound by eternal vows, conjures up pictures of Esmeralda his beloved ... one night in particular, so Hugo writes, 'they so cruelly inflamed his priestly virgin blood that he tore his pillows with his teeth, leaped from his bed, threw a surplice over his night-gown, and thus half-naked, wild, with fire in his eyes, he left his cell ...'

The feathered dancers strike a pose.

Applause. All three depart, their plumed hats bobbing. Charcot raises a hand, waiting.

'Strange, don't you think, gentlemen ... that our playwrights should be so negligent, so unobservant – Shakespeare is an honourable exception – as to make shaking limbs an attribute of old age? These young people are not old before their time. They are sick. And yet for two of them – two out of every three in the wards where they live, some violent, some catatonic, some merely unpredictable – we can offer no diagnosis beyond a name: hysteria.'

The audience restless, between acts. Charcot bides his time.

'With its manifold symptoms, its mysterious origins ... what is hysteria, this Proteus? Its sufferers come before us like so many sphinxes. But gentlemen, if we cannot tell what it is, we can at least – with the help of an unusual therapeutic tool – ascertain what it is *not*. I am referring to the art evolved by Mesmer and Puysegur, the much maligned art of hypnosis ...'

Through the door in the back of the lecture hall, a portable bed appears, and carried on it a young woman, not in a hospital smock but in a skirt and tightly corseted blouse. There is something different, too, about her expression. She has no need of pride: she does not see us.

'Mademoiselle ...' Charcot beckons, from a distance, extending a hand. The doctors, and the *beau monde* at the back, are hushed now. The girl slides her legs off the bed. Slowly, mechanically, she stands up, and the assistants move forward, arms at the ready. She sways, but remains standing, as Charcot comes to her, raises one of her arms and lets it fall, slack. He turns.

'No – this young lady is not, as you might think, already hypnotized. And yet, gentlemen, do you not see at once in her physical bearing that waxen flexibility, and in her face that dullness ... *la belle indifférence* ... which links the hypnoid and the neurotic states?' He pauses. 'Gentlemen, the lady is in love.'

He takes her hand, without mockery.

'Four years ago, on November the twenty-first, the object of her love parted harshly from her – with words of shocking finality – on the Rue St Antoine. For a time ... she stood rooted to the spot. Then she walked home. Ten days later – mark the interval! – she found that while she could rise from her bed at home, without difficulty, a strange impediment had descended on her during the night.'

Charcot releases her hand, steps back, beckons once more. After an instant's hesitation, the girl takes a step towards him: the assistants have closed in to catch her as she sprawls, helpless. They restore her to her feet, redress her balance. Their hands withdraw cautiously, as if from a precarious figurine.

'Our tests show undiminished muscular strength, and when examined in bed she is capable of normal movement, with normal vigour. She can stand – and strange to say can perform quite complicated actions: jump, dance, hop, even run. But walk she cannot. We can guess why ... yet how, gentlemen – *how* has she unlearned to walk?'

Without pausing, Charcot turns his back on us. Facing him in the doorway is another patient, accompanied but unsupported.

A man of thirty, muscular, one hand clenching the other, and kneading it involuntarily as though it were a cap. But his eyes are nervous and alert, avoiding Charcot's gaze.

'Our second patient derives his illness from a less romantic event: a minor railway accident leading, several days later, to a localized hysterical paralysis. I say hysterical because, once more, no organic damage can be found in the lifeless right hand upon which, as a master mason, the patient's livelihood depends.' The man glances at Charcot now. 'And I say it with added emphasis, because – as you will have noted – the patient is male. Without benefit of a "hysteron": a uterus. In short – hysteria, my friends, despite what the ancients held – and some of our contemporaries lost in the fogs of time – has no more connection with the uterus than it does with the liver!' In a gentler tone, nodding at the mason, 'Step forward, please ...'

Uneasy compliance. Charcot moves briskly to the table with the pincushion on it.

'You will recall the tragic railway collision at Clermont-Ferrand earlier this year, resulting in several fatalities. This gentleman was among the fortunate: he appeared to have escaped the crash without injury, having thrown out his right hand to save himself as he was flung across the carriage. With the onset of paralysis, however, he has joined the long queue of those suing the railway company for damages arising from loss of health and employment. Your right hand, please.' Urbane, as he approaches the mason; turning once more to us. 'Railway accidents are a prolific source of legal claims from members of the general public, and it will scarcely surprise you to hear that billions of francs – billions – hang in the balance, around the world, on these disputes. The question arises – are all these claims justified? Are there no malingerers among the claimants? Here is a man with a paralysed hand ... and yet, gentlemen –'

Charcot pauses, hatpin glinting in his hand, surveying us.

'There are half a dozen witnesses, including those who broke his fall at the moment of the crash, who will testify that this man's hand never encountered the floor, the wall, or any part of the railway carriage in question! All it struck –' he raises the pin '– was thin air ...'

The reaction, as Charcot plunges the pin into the man's right hand, is entirely from the audience. Not a gasp, not a trace of emotion in the mason's face, as Charcot repeats the stabbing procedure.

'Gentlemen,' smiling now, 'I have a patient in my wards who dreamt that he was run over by the coach of Monsieur le Duc de Varennes ... dreamt it! And he has two useless, lifeless legs to prove it! To whose agency, then, do we attribute these self-inflicted wounds? To the sudden onset of cerebral tumours ... as our esteemed colleagues in Vienna maintain?'

For an instant – I recall it only later – his gaze meets mine. Only later, when I have come to myself ...

'Professor Meynert believes himself able, I understand, to trace even melancholia and mania to the cortical circulation of the blood. Indeed,' mocking, 'if not ... where else are we to find the source of this many-watered Nile? In what name are we to save these patients from the surgeon's knife?'

Under our gaze, Charcot bows his head, gathering his forces. Then moves slowly across the stage to the corseted girl, still standing there, mirroring our own trance. An assistant relieves him of the pin, and Charcot takes the girl's hands, clasping them in his right hand; his left, as if in benediction, rises to close her eyelids. He begins to murmur to her.

'Mademoiselle ... you are on the Rue St Antoine ... listen carefully: the Rue St Antoine. It is midday, hot and dusty –' He repeats it, over and over. No-one stirs. 'Your lover is walking away ... you can see him, you are staring after him, standing staring, longing with all your might for him to turn. Willing him to turn. Can you see him ... walking ... walking away?'

The faintest of nods; Charcot has removed his hand from her brow. He is retreating softly from her, towards us. Tears forming in the girl's eyes.

'His step, his pace, is growing slower, more reluctant. He feels your eyes upon him, he is slowing. Slowing. He has stopped. Will he turn around? He's turning to you, you can see his face, his eyes. He takes the first step towards you, coming towards you, quicker now ... he wants you to join him, he can see the tears in your eyes. Will you go towards him ... go to him? Come ... come to him ... walk ...'

A first tentative step, then a moment of uncertainty.

'Come. Come!'

Charcot opens his arms. The girl walks to him firmly, eyes only for the face in front of her. Reaching Charcot, she falls sobbing into his arms. He holds her for a moment, as applause breaks out at the back of the hall; an applause dismissed, dispersed by one gesture from Charcot, as his assistants gently prise the girl from his arms. Hand still raised for silence, he watches her being escorted back to stand beside her bed.

'She is still in the arms of her beloved. But only for a short time. Unless we release her, unconsciousness will intervene. This is no cure, gentlemen! It is a passage from one abnormal state into another even more removed from reality. And yet ... reality's counterfeit, forged in the mind. Observe once more ...' Turning to the master mason, 'Now, monsieur. Kindly close your eyes. Listen attentively. Raise your right arm, palm upwards, and extend the fingers. Slowly, I say, extend the fingers ...'

The body is as malleable as a dream, Sigi ...

Like children before a conjuror, we gape at the paralysed hand: no hand, an idea merely. Once more the pin; Charcot probes down the arm, the patient winces, now the wrist, he still flinches, and then the hand. Dead. So dead not even Charcot's hypnotic insistence can move the fingers. Charcot transfers his attention to the left hand, murmuring words until it too is paralysed, indifferent to the pin. He turns back to the stiff right hand, murmurs once more. Motes play in the shafts of light above them, dust.

'Whereas in the afflicted hand ...' Charcot lightly stabs it, and the man pulls it away in pain, clenching it into a fist. 'Sensation has returned.' The motes dance, as we roar our applause, and Charcot acknowledges it with a bow.

'Where are these tumours now, gentlemen? And the cortical blood – has it begun to run backwards, at my command? One last experiment ...'

An assistant advances with the little gong. Charcot raises his arms for silence; if he were to soar out of the room, above our heads, we should find nothing strange in it. He glances at either patient, in turn.

'Mademoiselle, when you hear the gong, you will walk to-

41

wards me, your right hand extended. It is paralysed. Utterly paralysed. And you, Monsieur, when you hear the gong, you too will walk to me – or try to. Only now it is *you* who have unlearnt to walk . . .'

The assistants are in position. At the gong, the pair advance, from either side, towards Charcot: the man falling, caught by ready hands, the girl approaching, hand outstretched for Charcot to plunge into it the final pin –

Hand raised, 'Monsieur, Mademoiselle . . . when you hear the gong once more – you will be as you were when you entered this lecture hall . . .'

And as the gong sounds once more, reviving the one and causing the other to slump once more into her waxen dream, our tumult shakes the rafters. Charcot turns away, patting a private applause to his entourage as they lead the patients out; and discreetly mops his brow before turning back.

'Enough for one day.' His tone has changed. He scans the dandies at leisure, then fixes us with a long mocking look. 'Yes . . . these are tricks.' We sit very still. 'What you saw . . . it is for you to decide. The power of the mind over the body? It is a short-lived power, gentlemen. You saw me suspend one illusion and replace it with another . . . but the first illusion returns, intact. Why? Why, of the many victims at Clermont-Ferrand, was it this man's fate to bear a timeless witness to the event? Why *this* girl . . . of all the rejected lovers of the world? We can only suppose that a single, traumatic moment stirred from sleep some hereditary disposition in the psyche, which in the ensuing days – that fateful interval – mulled over the material like a busy dramatist, to make of it a passion play.' Stern now, the sternness of exhaustion. 'And here at the Salpetrière, what can we do for these poor actors tyrannized by their predestined role? Will hydrotherapy or tonics interrupt its flow? The best we can offer them is a fresh setting, gentlemen, a change in their moral environment – away from families too weak or too complacent to challenge their diseased will. With care and vigilance, with the constant promotion of hygiene, we can set the stage for a recovery sometimes as sudden as the onset of illusion. When once more . . . we are obliged to watch – and wonder.' One quick incline of the head. 'Thank you.' And he sweeps from the hall, leaving us to a final round of applause, chastened but still dumbfounded.

Blood returning slowly to my limbs; the physical world has lost all compulsion.

The stage is empty, my notes still on my lap. Weeks of reading about hypnosis have not prepared me for its impact – or for Charcot's abrupt dismissal of its therapeutic uses. Why such caution, when others in the same field –

A figure, hovering beside me; I look up blindly: 'Monsieur?'

He smiles. 'Don't you recognize me? Lev Osipovitch von Darkschewitsch ...' The hall is empty too, around him. The smile, importunate. 'I spent some months at the General Hospital, under your guidance.'

Vienna; now I place him. 'Of course – forgive me ...' Idle Russian. Dilettante.

'I too am a stranger here,' striking a Charcot pose, 'tyrannized by my role.' The mimicry is gross. 'I know nobody, and the Parisians are ... Parisian ... '

And the Russians, Russian. By his clothes I might have taken him for a visiting dandy. And yet – to talk to someone, to someone outside my head –

'Did you notice that what was paralysed was not his real, physiological hand ...' I ignore his patient smile '... but the mason's *idea* of his hand?' We emerge from the winding stairs, into the cold air on the parapet. Paris spread beneath us. 'The anaesthesia stopped at the wrist – despite the fact that the muscles which animate the hand and fingers are here in the forearm ... D'you suppose there might be an article to be written – on the hysterical paralysis of a given part of the body, as defined by the popular idea of its limits rather than the anatomical facts? There's a paper in it somewhere –' Seeing his smile, I add lightly, 'I'm full of schemes.'

And full of talk; lacking Gentile discretion, I can see it in his face. Clubbable men wear their ambition lightly.

Darkschewitsch leads the way, around the tower. 'I understand Charcot's lost touch with his German translator ...'

'Indeed?' Is the man mocking me? Notre Dame's gargoyles gaze down on us; I know each one by his sneer. 'I must confess,

I am tempted to follow in his footsteps: I hope to practise a little hypnosis in the wards myself.'

'Professor Meynert would be shocked.' No, his eyes are indulgent, amused.

'But there's one thing I don't understand – why Charcot denies its curative properties. Why impose limits on the powers of suggestion?'

Darkschewitsch hesitates, windblown, studying me. 'You think it's true that under hypnosis the subject will do anything you command?'

'Within reason.' Sensing his slyness, 'That's to say . . . unless you try to violate their moral will.'

'But isn't that just what attracts *le tout-Paris* to Charcot's demonstrations? I've attended one where he persuaded a girl to stab and kill a number of imaginary assailants – in self-defence, I grant you. But when he left the hall some medical students suggested to her that she was in the bath, and should undress.'

'And did she?'

'No. She went straight into a hysterical crisis.'

'You see?'

Guarded, he returns my smile. 'All the same, don't you find it odd that she was so quick to perceive the difference between their intentions and Charcot's?'

'Odd?' In what respect? '*I* have no base designs, believe me.' He laughs; a pleasant laugh. 'Come . . . tell me about yourself: are you married yet? I recall a devoted Russian fiancée . . .'

'Still devoted.' He moves along the parapet.

'And waiting . . .'

Nodding, 'Waiting for me to obtain a post in Moscow, at the University.' We are above the square now; milling heads beneath us. It was just here . . . 'And you?'

'A similar story. Transposed to Vienna.' I feel him warming to me. He follows my gaze downwards, in silence. 'It was just here, you know, that the Hunchback pushed Dom Claude over the parapet, as they watched the gypsy girl hanging from a gibbet in the square down there –' I glance at him '– left to the executioners by the treacherous priest, because she would not submit to his lust . . .'

'Ah, if only he'd known about hypnosis!'

Laughing, 'I think Paris has infected your brain, my friend – as it has your clothes.'

'What's the matter with my clothes?' He stares. 'Look at yourself, you look like a German peasant at a funeral. You really can't go round Paris like that ... in fact, I think I'd better introduce you to my tailor.' A critical eye. 'And my barber. A good French haircut. What do you say?'

... My love, I hypnotized my first patient today. Twenty minutes of murmuring 'you feel drowsy ...', and finally she slept. It was a close-run thing; another minute and I should have been asleep myself ... the closed world of two individuals, Kluge calls it – I think he means *'folie à deux'* ...

Green wallpaper. Hotel furniture. Martha's picture.

... It is our closed world, yours and mine, that has sustained me here. If you could only see this miserable room ... the wallpaper a bilious green. I've even tested it for arsenic. It's New Year's Eve, my treasure, and I raise a glass of water to you ...

Cloudy with cocaine; I drain it.

... I shall have to come home soon. I've spent my grant on the theatre and clothes and books, books full of esoteric wisdom. You are no longer engaged to a budding neurologist but to ... to a ... to what?

My eyes, closing.

... Write soon. You are my lifeline ...

Moonlit gargoyles. A crowd below, invisible, baying. I must not look, I must not look to right or left, I must not look up. Up: to the hunch-backed gargoyle.

Slowly, he draws my fascinated gaze. His stone face turns to me, beneath the hunched back. I see his eyes.

It is Charcot.

Above the voices of the crowd, a voice:

'*Monsieur le docteur Freud!*'

The major-domo's voice rings out beside me. No faces turn, among the throng of guests. A flunky takes my overcoat.

I stand, in a cocaine dream. Grand dukes and cardinals mingle with scholars, busy with one another; my new dress coat, bought for this soirée, seems wasted. And Charcot is nowhere in sight.

Amid the splendours of his drawing room, the crystal and the porcelain, I glimpse a cigar box.

Open the box. 'Monsieur Freud?' An owlish face with pince-nez smiles at my schoolboy embarrassment. 'The Freud ... of cocaine?' Can he see it in my eyes? He bows. 'Delboeuf. You see ... your reputation precedes you.'

He too takes a cigar, and lights them both in turn.

Studying me, 'Oh don't worry – I am strongly in favour of cocaine. In certain circumstances. Are you here to bring some new pharmaceutical discovery?'

'Merely ... neurological research.' Across the room, I see Charcot, scanning the new arrivals. 'While attending the Master's lectures.'

'Ah, the lectures ...' While Delboeuf prattles on, I try in vain to catch our host's eye. '... an admirable showman, is he not? And his willing ingénues: they rival Sarah Bernhardt.'

Puzzled by his tone, 'In a sense ...'

'In every sense.'

Charcot moving towards the door. 'I'm not sure I understand you.'

'Oh, I think you do.' Delboeuf puffs at his cigar. 'Surely. They've all been rehearsed, these ... obedient hysterics.' The pince-nez glitters. 'Didn't you know? Don't tell me you've been taken in ... it's a delightful game –'

'Rehearsed, Monsieur? By whom?'

He shrugs. 'Not by Charcot. I dare say not. But certainly by his assistants. Down to the last –' malign, he mimics a palsy – 'tremor ...'

Behind us, 'His Excellency, Prince Karl-Heinrich of Saxony!'

'You have been listening to gossip, Monsieur ...' I watch Charcot greeting the Prince. 'And I hardly think this is the time or the place to impugn Maître Charcot's honour as a scientist and a servant of truth –'

Delboeuf exhales softly.

Charcot turning his guest towards us – approaching – 'If I might introduce you ...'

'Good luck with your researches.' Smiling, Delboeuf slips away in a cloud of cigar smoke.

'... My new German translator: Doctor Freud. Prince Karl of Saxony ...'

I bow hastily; Saxony bows. '*Enchanté*.'

'Please –' Charcot's smile includes us both '– feel at liberty to use your native tongue ...'

'When in Paris ...' the Prince demurs. 'Though of course, we are aware of your linguistic accomplishments, Maître.'

I follow the pleasantries, in a daze, trying to put Delboeuf out of my mind. I have the pages in my pocket – quickly now – but the Prince is turning to me ...

'Have you been a member of this international community for long, Herr Freud?'

'Indeed not, your Excellency –'

'But he is a quick learner!' The German anchored now, Charcot's eyes seek the next port of call. 'And he will soon – I hope – be our Ambassador in Vienna. In a manner of speaking.'

I leap in, 'A *slow* learner, I assure you, Maître ... but a quick translator. I have a draft of the first chapter –'

'Yes, yes. Bring it to me in the morning.'

Saxony takes the initiative, with good grace.

'And will you also spread the gospel of hypnotism in Vienna, Herr Doctor?'

'The seeds are already sown – my esteemed colleague Josef Breuer has already used the technique on a young patient, with astonishing success. The girl was afflicted with multiple paralysis and a variety of delusions – the family had despaired of her until Breuer took her in hand –'

'I should be most interested to hear about the case.' Charcot turns back, glancing at the Prince. 'But if you will excuse me for a moment ... your Excellency – *cher collègue* –'

We watch him descend on an isolated lady.

'He found that ... first by hypnosis, then simply by talking,' I stumble on, 'he could free the patient from her morbid compulsions ...'

Saxony nods, polite. 'How very fascinating.'

... Free her. Release her from her guilty dreams ...

47

'To me it seems a miracle: somehow, Bertha was able to learn the secret of auto-suggestion and defy the commands of her disease –'

Charcot is all mine now; the guests departed. My chapter in his hands. He scans the pages, at the window.

'Lancing the painful memories one by one ... until she re-possessed her past, entire. Her soul. I understand ... it was as tortured as a mediaeval exorcism.'

'Remarkable.' He does not turn. 'And did it last?'

'She is greatly improved, and leads an active life –'

'There are such cases. But we, the doctors ...' he comes towards me, holds out the pages '... must learn to walk before we can run. And some of us ... must sleep.' Curtly, 'This is a promising start. Very promising. Send me the rest from Vienna.'

I hesitate. Dismissal in his eyes.

'Maître ... are you sceptical about Breuer's treatment?'

'I am sceptical about miracles, yes.' Waving a hand at crowded bookshelves. 'And – I know a great deal about mediaeval torture.'

'There are hazards, certainly ...' I hear my old presumptuousness; ashamed now, at his smile. 'That's to say, in this case, Maître – the patient fell in love with her torturer.'

The smile broadens. 'Of course! Of *course*. So did the witches. The seat of hysteria, my friend, is not in the mind but in the genitals!' He laughs at my startled face. 'I tell you: in the genitals. Without sexuality there would be no such illness.' Pitying, now. 'Don't you believe me?'

I stare. A joke surely, and in poor taste: Parisian taste.

'You find this ... in many cases?'

My mockery is wasted, his smile remains intent. 'In every case.' Thrusting his head forward, hands on his desk. 'You are a man of some intelligence, with ... I hope ... a capacity for self-examination.'

I watch him, wary.

'No doubt – you suffer intermittently from migraines? Neurasthenia? Fatigues, depressions ...'

A moment's pause.

'You appear unmarried.'

I nod.

By the time I reached Hamburg, I had conducted every possible
conversation with Martha, in my head. I was exhausted, over-
wrought, determined that I would return to Vienna with a date
for our marriage, or no marriage at all. No no, defeat was
unthinkable. Marty's resistance had become neurotic: should I
not use the weapons at my command, the appropriate weapons?
Under hypnosis, the moral will remains intact ... and is it not
her true, her moral consent I seek? Why not breach her equivo-
cations, then, with strong suggestions?

But such decisions melt like dreams in the other person's
presence. Marty's eyes meet mine, in the little Wandsbek garden
– a confined arena – with suppressed amusement, with some
undisclosed secret. Foreknowledge of my tricks? She agrees to
the experiment, humouring my vanity: Sigi, can you really hypnotize anyone? Even here, at this peeling wooden table, in this
suburban garden? Promise me you won't leave me sitting here
like a statue ...

But she bites her lip to hide the laughter as I soothe her into
trance, into sleep, long long sleep. Your eyelids are growing
heavy, you want to sleep ... you're feeling drowsy ...

'No ...' She softly mimics my tone. Charcot's tone.

'You're not supposed to answer, you must listen to what I'm
saying!' She gazes at me now. 'Once more –'

But it's too late. Her eyes dart anxiously towards the house,
as though anticipating mockery. Rightly: we are being watched.
At a ground-floor window, Minna gazes out at us, her face pale
above the black dress. Then she withdraws from sight.

At last Marty turns back to me. I smile, conceding: not even
Mesmer could work under these conditions. Marty's face is
drawn, expressionless now.

'Since Ignaz's death she won't even leave the house. She sits
... reading ...'

'She must burn his letters.' I receive a sharp glance. 'Burn
them. Tell her. It's important – to clear her mind of it.'

The certainty of my tone, the finality, holds her attention.
This is the moment, now before mourning covers her retreat.

'I heard you call my name one night, in Paris, in the street.' I take her hands. 'It was as if I'd caught a fever ... sometimes I imagined I was Danton, rescuing you in a runaway carriage –' Paris: with its centuries of ferment. And my own toxins, my violence. I try to describe it all – the boulevards and the laboratory, Charcot, my hotel room, my dreams, the dictates of the psyche. The word elopement, unspoken – 'Marty, it's been four years! I know your mother was engaged for nine ... but I can't go on waiting. I've come to ask you – to forgo the ceremony – rings, presents ...'

'To ask me?' The smile has returned. 'Or to hypnotize me?'

'I'm serious.'

Now the tender gaze; her tenderness, presaging bad news. She pauses.

'I must talk to you about our plans. Our financial situation has altered –'

'I know: Eli's lost your dowry.' It's spoken too quickly. But I must know the worst, and I'd seen it already in her brother's guarded eyes.

'Lost it?'

'Playing the market. Speculating!'

'He hasn't lost any of it – I told you, he's invested it. It's safe –'

Invested! A fine word. Anger surges between us, frightening and predictable at once. Coming home. 'Then why does he avoid the subject every time I bring it up?'

'It's not for you to ask him where the money is!'

'No wonder your mother's so quiet ...' I can feel peace descending, in the midst of fear. This anger *is* her moral will, her self.

'My dowry is secure, believe me – what there is of it! As for Mama ... we discussed everything at Christmas. Her objections are now purely practical, and –'

'Doesn't she understand?' I can let myself go now. 'Paris has changed my whole standing in the profession – I'm his chosen translator, his ambassador, he said so himself. People will listen to me ... even Meynert!'

'Will you let me speak!' She seems near tears; no – 'Last week ... Aunt Lea offered me a wedding gift –'

A gift? No tears; instead, a shamefaced smile.

'Of twelve hundred and fifty gulden. Now ...' she sees my bewildered expression, 'add that to Uncle Josef's legacy, subtract a thousand gulden, say, for –'

Her voice, teasing, pedantic. I find my voice: 'You mean we can get married?'

As before, 'A thousand for my trousseau and our house linen –'

'House linen?' I rush to her. 'Marty –' Not caring if we have a sheet to our name.

She submits to my kisses; but now, as I draw back, the smile is serious. 'Wait – wait.' Slowly, 'Sigi, you must understand: my mother will not countenance this marriage ... unless you learn the ceremony. And the proper wedding responses.' Before I can speak – 'In Hebrew.' A pause. 'Eli will teach you.'

'I'll say them in Sanskrit if that's what you wish –'

'In Hebrew,' she interrupts. 'And with a straight face.'

Marty: I am someone else, someone quite else, with your love. If I could only show you: four years waiting for this marriage; this moment. I know the words, every one.

And speak them now. The bridegroom's responses: '*Haray ut mekudeshet* ...' Behold, thou art consecrated unto me ...

Her gaze is answer enough. We stand in silence. What ceremonies, what words can match this?

Lightheaded, 'I've already learnt them ...'

A young man in a green cloak extends a hand to me. An open, innocent, compellingly attractive face.

'Sigmund ... Doctor Wilhelm Fliess, a colleague from Berlin.' Breuer gestures, a solemn pandar, and turns back to me. 'Doctor Freud, our principal speaker today.'

Fliess' smile radiates more than politeness. Warmth, encouragement; I seize his hand like a lifeline. All around us, silent colleagues remove their coats, shaking the rain from their clothes. Are they always so silent? Am I the only one choking with tension?

'You haven't come specially from Berlin, Herr Fliess?'

'Why not? I am also a former student of Maître Charcot's – his work is of the greatest interest to us in Germany.'

And we are in Vienna. He understands, I can see it in his eyes. Small talk fails me, and we stand, mute.

'Excuse me, gentlemen ...' A figure squeezes past towards a vacant coathook.

Breuer intervenes once more. 'Professor Chrobak you know, of course.'

'We've passed in the corridors.'

Chrobak nods in answer, distant. Smiles. Fliess has withdrawn discreetly to remove his cloak. I watch Chrobak, who makes no further sign, returning to the crowded lobby outside, the cries of greeting. A flushed, familiar face looks in on us, briefly: Meynert, the red beard stippled with rain.

Gruffly, 'Good luck.' He vanishes, only to put his head back in once more, as though in belated recognition. 'And congratulations. On your marriage.' His departure is unsteady.

'My God.' I glance at Breuer, who is studying his shoes. 'Is he drunk?'

The small doorway of the antechamber darkens with Hermann Nothnagel's bulk. No coathooks free, he flings his coat onto a bench.

'Good luck, my boy!'

The voices in the lobby recede, towards the lecture hall. Fliess follows Nothnagel out with a nod, a glance. Breuer and I are left to ourselves, among the dripping coats.

'You know ... rumour has it that you walked to Hamburg for the wedding.'

I find a smile. 'An exaggeration.' I borrowed the train fare; from Minna ...

'You could have come to me ... '

'And be further in your debt?' A clean slate. 'This way ... you're free to approve or condemn my lecture, as you please.'

Ignore his aggrieved eyes. The lobby is silent now, waiting.

'Hippocrates affirmed that epilepsy belonged to the natural order, and in Charcot's view – in the view of the Salpetrière – hysteria too obeys certain rules which, he maintains, "attentive and sufficiently numerous observations permit us to establish" ... '

Barely any need to consult my notes; as if my voice, not my

mind, were finding the words. Another's voice, more certain. Is this how an actor feels? Each phrase finding its mark, deferential or contentious. 'Hippocrates ... natural order ...' I have not looked at Meynert yet.

'The four stages of *"grande hystérie"* – the epileptoid state, the phase of muscular relaxation, the hallucinatory passage termed by Charcot *"attitudes passionnelles"*, and the post-hysterical derangement – represent a standard, or maximum, to which hysterical seizures aspire in widely differing degrees.' No murmurs; silence. 'In response to those who have pointed out that some hysterical patients are aware of this "standard" and are thereby empowered to imitate it on demand, Maître Charcot has made use of a pneumograph to distinguish genuine from artificial contractures of the limbs, which bring about a marked variation in the subject's breathing patterns. Thus ...' Now I hear them. Now they know me. '... while investigating numerous cases of so-called "railway spine", following railway train accidents, Charcot has come to share the American opinion that cases of malingering are relatively rare ...'

I can see them: vested interests bulging angrily, those with lawyer friends in the generous pay of the railway directors, of comfortable employers in every dangerous industry. I wait for silence.

'As regards the treatment of hysteria, the staff at the Salpetrière employ balneotherapy and other hydrotherapies, gymnastics, and the direct application of static electricity as well as the familiar tonics and restorants.' Pause now. Never mind Breuer's warning gaze. 'I also had occasion to witness the remarkable effects of suggestion therapy, by means of hypnosis. In my opinion, Charcot's success with this technique – the spontaneous generation of hysterical symptoms and their equally peremptory removal, on command – would appear to justify his description of hysteria as "less a disease ... than a peculiarly constituted mode of feeling and reaction".'

The snort comes from Meynert. Spittle on his beard, cheeks mottled. I focus all my attention on him.

'In Charcot's view, the hypnoid state is "an experimental neurosis" ... a kind of temporary, artificial insanity ...'

I can hear footsteps in the corridor. Marty's voice: 'I'll take it.' The maid retreating. Silence. Marty entering on tip-toe. Don't disturb the bear.

Sets down the tea-tray, noiselessly. Goes to fiddle at the curtains, to glance at me. Walks back, out of sight. And now I sense her behind my chair, soft soothing arms descend round my neck. I kiss her hands, in turn.

' "He went to Paris a neurologist ... and he has returned a crank." ' I make no attempt at mimicry. 'Meynert's words, apparently.'

Marty's silence says: But you expected it. You knew.

'What did Breuer say?'

'Smiled. Like a fond parent at a delinquent child. Then he took me aside and asked me what I was charging for consultations.'

Martha comes round in front of me, to see my face.

'What did he mean by that?'

'Oh, nothing ... insulting. Merely to remind me that a doctor in his first year of general practice – a doctor of controversial reputation – would do well to set modest fees.'

My dry tone fuels her anxiety. Must I explain everything? Reassure her, when I need reassurance?

'Josef means well,' I coax. 'He's invited me to an external consultation ... with one of the richest women in the city.'

Still her troubled eyes.

'To hypnotize her?'

'I doubt it. She's deranged enough already, by the sound of it.' Sly now. 'A baroness. It could be lucrative.'

Now she looks happier, now I need somewhere to put my anger. The sheaf of papers in my lap: Meynert stamping past me without a word, slapping something against my chest. 'As Meynert left the hall, he stuffed *this* ... into my hands.' Cutting off poor embarrassed Fliess in mid-sentence.

'So he had his answer ready.'

'Hardly an answer.' I finger the miserable offprint. 'An old article ... on the "fraudulence and immorality" of hypnosis! He actually claims it liberates the sexual impulses in the subcortex ... I dare say he imagines he can *see* the things, springing to lewd attention under the microscope.' Finding the place: ' "In the hypnotic state a human being is reduced to a creature without will or reason, and the nervous and mental degeneration of the depraved is only hastened by it ...." The depraved ... "Most hypnotic 'cures'" – in inverted commas – "are the result either of lies or self-delusion on the part of doctors and patients, whose activities ..."' I glance at Marty '"... are achieving the proportions of a psychical epidemic among the gullible and the corrupt"!' Marty silent before my rage; the papers scatter as I fling the pamphlet down. 'Narrow-minded, drunken ... bigot!'

After a moment, she bends to gather the pages.

'Leave them.'

She continues, till I come to her, gripping her arm, lifting her. Put my other arm around her still, stiff shoulders. Kiss her neck.

'Let the girl do it.'

Barely resisting as I turn her round. 'It's mid-afternoon ...'

'Didn't you know?' I speak into her ear, 'that's the hour of depravity, in Vienna.'

'"Pentheus", a poem ...' declaims the Baroness. She looks up from the slip of paper. 'Dedicated to my dear friend Professor Rudolf Chrobak, gynaecologist and magus.'

Chrobak nods solemnly, head on one side. Flattered, by his expression: the handsome, drawn, unsmiling face of an old campaigner. Breuer, by his side, smiles in polite anticipation. Neither meets my eyes.

> 'Out of the gates of timid Thebes
> Strides the Daring One, at dead
> Of night, drawn to the moon's pale sheaves
> As if by Ariadne's thread ...'

The woman's voice is pleasant, melodious, a girl's voice in a seacow's body. Immensely fat, bejewelled, she lies extended on a couch – yet with such elegance, such absolute repose! And her eyes: on each of us in turn, daring us not to remain timid Thebans –

> 'With serpents black the woodland seethes:
> The mother's rites are worshipped here,
> And Dionysus, in the leaves,
> Beckons the weary traveller near.'

Gazing at Chrobak now.

> ' "My twin!" he breathes, and on him wreathes
> The briony: berries of blood
> He crushes to the breast that seethes
> Once more with life's undying flood!'

She puts the poem aside, and I stand ready to applaud. But Chrobak's murmur breaks the spell.

'You do me too much honour, Baroness.'

'You deserve better,' a musical laugh, 'but as I'm sure you noticed, I ran out of rhymes.'

Breuer's glance alerts me. Wheeled machinery at my side, mocking the exquisite, serene apartment. I step forward.

'Baroness ... may I present Doctor Freud, a young colleague and Lecturer in Neuropathology, who has recently returned from a six months' visit to the Salpetrière –'

'Ahh ...' her face lights up, and she calls to me across the room, 'so you've been working with my beloved Charcot! Do tell me – is his wife still fornicating with hussars?'

Breuer and Chrobak, poker-faced; I match them. 'I failed to enquire, Madame.' A silence.

'Doctor Freud has brought with him some equipment modelled on the latest developments in electro-therapy, from Paris.'

'Indeed?' The Baroness beckons Breuer near. With serpents black the woodland seethes ... She whispers to him, eyes on me, her lips forming the word 'Charmant ...' Breuer straightens and nods to me.

As I tug the equipment along the floor, its wheels snag on tasselled carpeting. The Baroness laughs, this time like a fishwife; I feel as if I am towing towards her an immense mechanical erection. Unnerved by her mixture of elegance and coarseness. Chrobak steps forward.

'How is the arm today?'

She sighs. 'The arm ... is clay. Unfeeling. But the pain here, in my cheek, is gone.' Drawing a hand down her great jowls, slowly. 'I feel it like a slap, sometimes. A slap that stays, and glows.' Quietly now, 'A slap I may have deserved. But never received.'

Her eyes are on Breuer, as she extends her arm to me, fat easing to reveal an elbow. She and I study the limb like a foreign body.

'Strange ...' she smiles, 'last night I dreamt I was a statue. I'd forgotten. A statue of the Madonna: a plaster statue by the roadside.'

Hesitating, I wait for a cue from the two men beside me. None comes. 'If you will permit me, Baroness ...'

She nods, abstracted, as I apply the electrodes. 'And the Emperor rode by.' Once more she stares at Breuer. 'He had my father's face. And he raised his hat and I heard him say ... "Hail Diana, the huntress!"' The chuckle returns. 'It made me laugh to think of it when I woke up ... and yet –' I am waiting to switch on the current. 'There was something in his tone – it was my father's voice ... deliberate, mocking, as though there was some meaning in the *way* he said it. Diana.' Chill now. 'Die, Anna ...'

She looks at me for the first time.

'My name is Anna.' Holding my gaze. 'You may begin.'

In the *fiacre*, no-one speaks. Chrobak gazes out of the window, indifferent, as though counting patients. Breuer lights a cigar, without looking at me.

'She seems to like you.'

After a pause, the case history follows. Dispassionate: a rich, bookish, extravagant woman with thirty years of treatment at the hands of the finest doctors in Europe – Chrobak gives a faint, modest shrug – who succeed in relieving her pains, her paralyses, only for them to re-appear in some other part of her anatomy. As for the symptoms, and their endless variety ... after another silence, Breuer glances at me.

'You may charge forty gulden.' And quickly, to stem my gratefulness, 'But don't give her morphine, whatever you do!'

'A remarkable woman,' murmurs Chrobak. 'When in one of her trances I've known her to stick knitting needles through her arms ...'

We jog along; Breuer leans heavily on my arm.

'Between ourselves ... the husband is tired of her. After six children ...' He shrugs, eyeing me. 'I tell you so that you know.' Then, glancing at the gynaecologist, 'These things are usually born in the bedchamber. Eh Rudolf?'

Chrobak keeps his counsel, dour. At last a small smile.

'I know what I'd prescribe.' Still gazing out of the window. '*Penis normalis*. Twice a day.'

Breuer grins into his beard, avoiding my eyes.

The Mother's rites are worshipped here ... how was it that despite her ridiculous bulk, the Baroness could inspire such startling and obscene thoughts in me? And not only in me – in the cadaverous Chrobak! Her wit, her acumen, even the sumptuous room in which she lay, day in day out – were all equally provoking. She brought with her a distorted and distorting sexuality. I thought of Charcot: *la chose génitale*.

'Oh Saint Theresa ... oh sweet Jesus! Oh sweet Jesus ... I'm going to die ... help me – it's like nails ... in my side! Oh please ...'

I have been attending her all night. She presses my hand to her face.

'Can you feel my temples? They're on fire! Give me something to ease the pain ... I beg you ...'

I wrench my hand away, hurry once more to the medicine chest. Her voice pursues me.

'No alkaline water!'

'Some chloral hydrate –' I pour it out.

'Something stronger. *Please* ...'

Gazing at her, 'I dare not.'

'Oh God ...' The tears come again, and now a choking sound. 'Oh quickly ... I can feel it rising, swelling – in my throat! I can't –' She gags. 'I can't swallow! Help me!'

I rush to her and take her hands, helpless.

'Trust me. It will pass. There ... it's easing ...'

'Yes.' She holds me fast. 'Yes ... quickly –'

She frees me to fetch the chloral solution, suddenly calm again. As I turn, I see her eyes are no longer on me; she gazes at the dark windows. And the childlike, musical timbre returns to her voice.

'Look! Look ... in the trees ...' Giggling, 'The two of you –'

I stare, then turn back to her; both rapt, exhausted.

'Can't you see two men, hanging? In the trees?' Her heavy face crumples. 'It's you! And Breuer ...' Crying now, 'Oh God, what have I done ...'

I bring the glass, she drinks, slowly, like a sick child.

'Just now ... do you know what I thought? You ... with your soothing voice. Like Breuer. You're a match. You see?' She shivers, smiling. 'Pendants – hanging ...' A pause.

'You see? My mind is a better poet than I am.' She studies my expression, at length, sober. 'Am I not a worthless person? What I said to you the other day ... about Charcot ... only a worthless person would say such things!'

Or think such things as I thought, that same afternoon? Moments pass; I must speak. 'Believe me, it's not incompatible with an unblemished character – or a well-governed mode of life. Many of the finest minds, the most gifted and the most generous, have suffered what you are suffering.'

'A pretty speech.' A prompt and merited rebuke. Where can I find the tone? I am utterly unrehearsed for this; it's two in the morning. Her tender manner has gone, replaced by briskness. 'I'm hungry. Will you take some food with me?'

I shake my head.

'Some caviare?'

What would Breuer do? 'No. Thank you.'

'I want some.' Abruptly menacing.

'As you wish.'

I rise.

'Doctor Freud. Do something for me.' A moment. 'Fetch my children.'

'It's two in the morning, Baroness –'

'Fetch them!' She has begun to tremble. Something in the air between us begins to distort, I can feel us becoming different, like lovers trapped in the whirlpool of a murderous exchange, in the dizzy silences. 'Fetch my children! Do you hear me?'

I nod.

'Why won't you fetch them?'

Coaxing, 'Baroness –'

'Don't use that tone to me!' It is a shout. Her face is livid, our transformation complete. 'You peasant! You've stolen them! You've taken everything, you bitch ... husband, children – you've stolen everything I loved!'

I come to her, through thick air.

'I am not your governess!' As fiercely as I dare, 'Look at me!'

'Don't lie! You're not their mother! You're a spy, a dirty spy ...' I know: it is the truth. Her ranting turns to sobs, as she sees it in my eyes. Are we playing? Are we equally aware? 'Tell me the truth, at least! They've gone!'

The moment passes. 'Stop this! Your children are asleep, they're safe and well –'

A fresh burst of sobs, and the hallucination dissolves into an embrace. 'Hold me.' I take her leaden arms; clay. We cling like weary wrestlers, drowning, till her voice comes. 'I need a massage.' I knead her arm. Avoid her pleading eyes. 'Please ... a genital massage.' Girlish voice. 'I need something tonight.' Sly now, 'Breuer gives me morphine.'

I meet her eyes. 'No.'

Her face jerks to one side as if I have slapped her; I can feel the slap in my hand.

'Has the pain returned?'

She nods, grimacing. Now I have her.

'When I first came here, you said ... it felt like a slap.' She nods. 'And you said – it was like one you had deserved. But not received.' A moment. 'Tell me, is it possible that you once received one ... which was not deserved?'

Face averted, she shakes her head.

'Never?'

'No.'

She chokes as I squeeze her arms tighter. 'Please ... I'm going to be sick.'

'You are *not*. You will turn to me – look at me –' I wait her out. 'You no longer feel nausea – it's passing ... the pain, too, is passing, the pain of the slap. Close your eyes. And listen to me.' Oh, she is a ready subject. 'The pain is easing ... draining from your face. You feel relaxed, drowsy, free of tension ... There is no pain. There is no longer any pain: you feel sleepy.' We rock. 'When I tell you to open your eyes, you will do so, and there will be no more pain. Only the need for sleep. For long, long sleep.'

The rocking ceases. 'Open your eyes.'

A long pause, then she does so. Smiling, soporific.

'Is it better?'

'Yes.'

She settles back for the first time in hours. Shuts her eyes, contented. How my head throbs: I let my features slacken, released from her gaze, worn out.

The Baroness opens her eyes, glances smiling at me from the couch. Hopeful.

'Doctor. Do you play chess?'

'You wanted to see me, Herr Professor.' For several minutes now I have been standing silently in Meynert's study, watching him bent over paperwork, at his desk. He sits at an angle to the desk, uncomfortable, torso twisted round. Keeping me waiting. For what fresh humiliation?

'You're working at Kassowitz' Clinic.'

'Yes.'

Meynert raises his head; a faint smile. 'Anatomical work?'

'Yes. On sensory aphasia, at present.'

He returns to his paperwork, shifting in his chair as he does so. And giving me a glimpse of what ails him: a foot, propped up on a low stool behind the desk. He is speaking again.

'I understand from Kassowitz that you have nowhere to perform dissections, now that you've left the hospital. I'm placing my laboratory at your disposal.'

I stare at his bowed head in disbelief. At last he looks up, irritable, forcing me to find my voice.

'That's ... most generous of you.' We eye each other. 'Particularly in view of the opinions you hold about my other work – in the field of the neuroses –'

'Ever had gout?' His tone makes it clear: there is physical pain, real pain, and then there is neurosis. I shake my head. 'Keep it that way. You're treating the Baroness von Lieben, I hear.' Then blandly, 'Beneath your prim exterior, my friend, lurks an unmitigated rascal. Has she seduced you yet? Well?' He waves my protests aside, dismissing the subject. 'I shall tell my assistants to prepare a place for you in the laboratory. As from tomorrow?'

'Why?' I too can be peremptory; I will not be outdone. 'Why are you helping me?'

'I'm giving you a chance to remain a scientist.' Meynert waits for this to sink in. 'Besides, I like rascals. They get things done.'

Beneath the jocularity, some other emotion, some message from this irascible old man, pleads for recognition; and it eludes me.

My sisters, painfully corseted, occupy the sofa as if under review. But we await no matchmaker: it is Papa who is missing, and Sunday lunch is ready. His vagueness, his absences have become commonplace. Mamma meets no-one's eyes; Alexander lounges in an armchair. In the silence, I smile at Martha, embarrassing her. Willing or not, she is my ally here. I turn to Alexander.

'And how's the railway magnate?'

'A glorified clerk, I assure you.'

'But I understand you've procured Papa a free pass ... to travel anywhere in Europe.' He nods, faintly, 'You don't suppose he's decided to take advantage of it, today?'

I ignore Marty's warning look. Mamma coughs, brings out a handkerchief.

'He's simply gone for a walk around the Ring ...' She stifles further coughing.

'Mamma ...' Solicitous Alexander.

She smiles at me. 'One day you'll find me in your surgery.'

'You'll have to wait in line –' Alexander returns my fire, in time-honoured fashion. 'Won't she?'

'Some days. Other days ... I feel like the lion in the story: "Twelve o'clock"', a leonine yawn, ' "and still no blacks!" ' My sisters giggle. 'If it wasn't for my work at Kassowitz' Clinic –'

No-one is listening; the sound of a key fumbling in the front-door lock has breathed new life into the room.

'That'll be your father.' Lightly now. 'I don't suppose he has the faintest idea what the time is ...'

'I'll warn him.'

As I move towards the hallway, Mamma marshals the girls: 'To the table, children ...' My father stands, inside the front door, uncertain, as if in a strange house. Conscious of my presence, at the far end of the hall. He speaks, abruptly loud, to cover his embarrassment.

'Such a beautiful day ... a shame to come in, really.'

'Hello, Father.'

He works at the buttons of his coat, removes it as I come towards him. Hangs the overcoat, pats it.

'I heard your name mentioned at the Café Landtmann.'

I hesitate. 'Oh? Favourably?'

'What else?' He glances at me now. 'You were seen outside a great house on the Ringstrasse, descending from a coach and pair.' I picture the scene, the crowded café, the smiling acquaintance interrupting Papa's reverie –

'Rented.' I smile; he looks puzzled. 'The coach and pair.'

He nods. 'Your Uncle Josef had a coach and pair once.' With a warning look, 'Beware of borrowed finery.' He turns to go.

'Papa, lunch is ready.'

I guide him gently back towards the dining room. He comes, murmuring.

'Paid for it with forged banknotes ...' Then sharply, to me, 'But they caught him. They caught him!'

'It was my father's birthday ... of all days. We'd spent it at the lakeside, picnicking. I was five months' pregnant. Pregnant for the first time.'

Tears roll down the Baroness' face, her back erect, pressed tight to the upholstery, her legs extended on the chaise longue. She is in trance.

'I lay in the hotel bedroom, waiting for Georg. Reading.' A pause. 'Reading.'

In trance, absorbed, and yet distanced from her story by the telling. But the pain of re-enactment is new and overwhelming.

'Can you remember what you were reading?'

'Oh ... I was a voracious reader, in those days. Montaigne, Francis Bacon ... I read the same page again and again that night. Waiting. Counted the roses on the wallpaper. Imagined Georg drowning. Floating. Imagined lovers.'

A silence.

'When Georg came in, I pretended I was asleep. Pretended I

63

couldn't smell his breath as he climbed into bed. Then as the shame and panic of my dreams came back to me, I turned and put his hand on my breast. He saw my eyes were open, my mouth waiting for his, and looked at me. With hatred. "I'd rather make love to a sow in heat." His hand left my breast, and though he never touched me I felt him spin my head around, burning, against the pillow. Felt it like a blow: I couldn't cry, I couldn't move, I . . .'

Her voice breaks; she is shuddering. Enough.

'Listen to me. You are no longer at Aussee, at the hotel. No longer in trance. You are in your own house, on the Ringstrasse . . .' Her eyes open, find mine. 'On a fine May afternoon.'

She lets her head fall forward, sobbing now without restraint. I watch her, tenderly. Champagne waits, on the cabinet. Expensive goblets.

The Baroness glances round as I fetch them. Smiling, 'You've tired me out . . .'

She drinks, greedily. We sit, in the sunlight. There is no hurry.

'Can you remember what you told me?'

She nods slowly, studying me. 'Every word.' I know her shy glance – she discards it, serious now. 'Strange, isn't it . . . that I couldn't remember it till now. It seems so clear – familiar even –'

'What is the date today?'

'The twenty-fourth.' A sudden smile. 'Of May . . . my father's birthday. How did you know?'

'You mentioned it yourself, three days ago.'

She stares at me, and then away. 'He would have been eighty. It was his sixty-first birthday that day, at Aussee.' Handing me her glass to be replenished, 'Why do they hide from me, these memories? As if my life had been . . . chopped into pieces. Why?' I pour. 'I can remember once – when I was fifteen, propped up in bed, some childhood illness . . . my grandmother sitting beside me, reading to me –' I return the glass, grandmotherly; we smile, '– while I entertained instead . . . improper thoughts. And she shot me a look – as though she knew! And at once I felt such a pain, here . . .' touching her forehead, 'as if she had pierced my brain. It's as though I had the power to convert ideas into flesh. The slap . . . which never came, except in words. The nails I

64

sometimes feel inside, the ball that rises in my throat when I have to "swallow" something unpalatable to my mind, and even ... when I look at you, my dear, and once more think ...' smiling, '... improper thoughts ... I'm so filled with shame I feel dizzy.'

I hold her gaze: no need for awkwardness. I am a mirror.

'I've told you more things in these last few months –' she breaks off. 'More things than I care to remember. Sometimes I wake in the night and blush to think of what I've said to you the day before ...'

Silent; watching.

'Is it possible I might be free now ... of the slap? Or is it just another interval, at the play?'

'If other patients are anything to go by, you will be free. Of that particular symptom.'

'Why? Just by telling you ...'

'Not by telling me. By re-living the events.' Lightly, 'You've told me about the incident before.'

'I have?' She stares. 'Under hypnosis?'

'No, you told me calmly, of your own free will. Here in this room. But you told me without emotion ... embarrassed by the stranger you were telling. So you've forgotten it as surely as you did the night itself at Aussee. Then too – but far more powerfully – you withdrew from the experience, and left a poisoned thorn in the memory. Now at last you've drained the poison.'

No mockery in her gaze, no taunts. I feel Charcot's power in me; Breuer, gazing at me in pride and envy –

'And I told you before?' The Baroness extends a plump hand. 'And treated you like a stranger?'

'That was weeks ago.' Evade her hand; reach calmly into my dress coat. 'Today we've tunnelled deep. And I think I've earned a cigar.'

She studies me. 'Dear friend ... you know, you have been cunning with me – in more than one respect. You have rejected my love. I thought at first it was because I was old ... and worthless to you. Then I realized you were making me work all the harder ... to satisfy you with my memories.' A moment. 'But you know too that in my mind you are still my lover.'

Exhaling, 'I doubt if that's what Breuer means by the "cathartic" method ...'

Her fishwife chuckle rings out, and she rises slowly from the couch. It is the first time I have seen her walk; she knows it, poised, majestic, posing at the bookshelves.

'Once, when I was at a sanatorium in England, my doctor came to take me down to dinner – it was my first night there – and that night I found to my amazement, and his, that I couldn't walk ... for the pain in my right heel, a symptom I had never experienced before.' She picks a book, returns with it. 'It was only much later, when I had begun to learn the strange dramaturgy of my disease, that I understood the meaning of the pain. You see: I felt I was among strangers that night, in the motley gathering of that ... dreadful asylum. The other patients, the nurses, the doctors ... we were not on the same "footing", they and I ...'

I bow in acknowledgement of the elegant diagnosis.

'My foot understood: my right heel.' She hands me the book. 'But we two ... are on the same "footing" now. *N'est-ce-pas?*'

Smiling, I glance at the title page. 'Francis Bacon ...'

She clasps my hand over the book, to seal the gift, gazing at me, amused. 'The antidote, believe me – to improper thoughts ...'

I am thirty-five: *nel mezzo del cammin*. And at last I have found the true way, *la diritta via*. With the Baroness I am all things, father confessor, lover, friend. Sometimes I think I know her better than anyone in the world.

Marty turns on the pillow, to look at me. Have I been speaking aloud?

'Better than you even.' I turn to meet her gaze. 'Certainly better than myself.' And, seeing her expression, 'We don't have hallucinations to reveal our hidden fantasies. Or weeping fits ... confessional trances ... it's nothing to be jealous of, believe me.'

Faint light at the window. Five o'clock perhaps; and I've slept so little. Marty still studying me.

'In some ways I've learnt more from her than from Breuer – or Charcot. She understands the mind, its jumps, its lurid puns ...' Her foot understands. She cannot walk for those who are not on the same 'footing' ... but *we – n'est-ce-pas* – 'When the pain is too deep, too distasteful to be borne, the body translates.

But in code, to fool the mind – like soldiers writing home in code to fool the military censor. She's a true poet ... she gave me that image herself: the mind as censor.'

'And what have you given her?'

Father confessor, lover, friend. 'When I left her this afternoon, the pain had gone, from arms and face ...' Gone. And Meynert thinks he can offer me 'a last chance' to become a scientist!

As I take Marty's hand, pull her towards me, a sound comes, muffled. The doorbell. I push myself slowly upright, against resistant arms.

Sleepy, she moves after me as I leave the bed, and ends with her face against my pillow, eyes open. The image stays with me as I go to the door. Open it, and my heart sinks.

'Marty ...' I search the wardrobe; where are my clothes? Marty sits up, turns on the bedside lamp. Avoiding her eyes, 'It's the Baroness – her manservant ...' I must go to her at once. Acute pain, 'a relapse', fresh symptoms. Lies.

Cocaine dreams, cocaine lies. When the truth is, I am her drug, her fool, her puppet. *N'est-ce-pas*?

Angrily now: 'Where's my dress coat?' Fool!

Her coach awaits, in the street. A coach and four, liveried coachman at the reins, the manservant waiting patiently for me at the door. He bows, admitting me to the velvet interior. Only princes and doctors receive such deference. And sorcerers: the magus called for by coach at midnight. What had the Baroness called Chrobak? Gynaecologist and magus ... 'My twin ...'

Gaslight, cobbles. A lurch as we start forward. Crack, whip! Rattle, wheels, through the foggy streets. The magus comes.

THREE

'Papa?'

Someone was knocking, rattling at the door. A middle-aged woman enters. My child, Anna. My name is Anna ... you may begin. Did I name this child after the Baroness? Try to remember. After other Annas, perhaps. One should be able to remember.

'Papa. There's a patient waiting.'

Tense, in the waiting room; heart pounding, as for a lover. But no – there is no waiting room. This is London. Where do they wait, poor people? In the lobby, somewhere? Anna wants me to pay attention now. Turning the pages of my diary.

'She isn't due till ten.'

I find my voice. Mildly, 'They all come early now. Hoping I'm still alive.' The sound manœuvres its way past my tongue, through a cavern of metal, now stopping with a dry, sucking click, now tumbling on across my lips. But the humour survives; my daughter smiles, still studying the diary.

'I see you've put a ring around the date.'

October. Fliess' birthday. 'He would have been –' No voice; the metal palate slips, sticking. I press it back into my head. 'Eighty, today.'

'Who would?'

'You never met him. Wilhelm ...' Quick, press with the tongue. 'Fliess.'

'Of course I met him, Papa.' How angry they all are with me, impatient. A metal palate on a withered frame. 'When I was a child.' She is staring at me. 'You still celebrate Fliess' birthday?'

Celebrate it? I remember it; it's enough. Anna is still gazing at me. 'He was ... an unreliable person. But I loved him once.'

Time to begin, surely. My watch fights to stay in my pocket, as I fumble for it. It comes out at last.

'Are you sure you feel well enough to see this woman?'

'Thank you ...' Go away. 'I'll see her now.'

Reproachful footsteps; Anna leaves. Silence. The statuettes on my desk stare past me with indifferent eyes. So many of them, and in the cabinets beyond, more ancient figurines, more heads. How have they become so crowded? Even in this larger, London room, they throng like skulls in the catacombs. Those dreadful Catholic ossuaries ... altars made of shin-bones, candlesticks of vertebrae ... when we began in the Berggasse, there were no ghosts, nothing to distract me: bare leather on the couch, no draperies, no Turkish carpets, no effigies ...

'It's not much of a view.' Marty's voice. 'And you could do with a few more things on the walls.' She turns, from the window. Beyond, our unimposing back yard. Turns, with the bulge of her third pregnancy. Smiling, 'Would that be so bad? Something to look at?'

'They're supposed to look inwards.'

'I was thinking of *you*.'

The room, still empty, unkempt, an unfinished cell. 'Because I described the Monet in Charcot's study –'

She slips out of my grasp, still teasing; cheerful. 'I meant something more modest.' On the desk my papers lie in drifts. On top a parcel, sealed. 'You haven't opened it.' She finds the paper knife. 'May I?'

The aphasia book: six copies from the publishers. Does she think it'll make us rich? I sit.

'Fliess says I'd be a wealthy man, if only I went into general practice.'

'Is he so rich?'

'He has influential patients, which helps. And when you've studied under Lister and Pasteur, as well as Charcot – it gives you a good many strings to your bow. That I do envy him. And he's the best nose specialist in Germany.' Seeing Martha's expression, 'Don't underestimate noses – Fliess makes a fortune from them.' My head feels heavy with a sudden nausea. Pain in one corner, spreading, opening neural doors into my brain. I lie back; keep the voice steady. 'He also writes newspaper articles on everything under the sun, from medicine to astronomy. But then ... compared to me, he's a man of the world.' Is that what she wants of me? 'Apart from being a walking encyclopedia.' I glance at Marty, but she is busy unwrapping the books. Now

69

she looks up. 'It's true. He's written me a long letter about the latest developments in industrial steel tubing ...'

She glances back at the books, opens one. My left temple is on fire.

'What's the matter?'

I remove my hand. 'It's all right, it's passing.' Make it pass. I nod at the book. 'Note the dedication.'

As she does, I reach for my watch. Time to begin, surely.

' "To Dr Josef Breuer" ...' I rise, smiling. 'Why to him?'

'Come – I must smuggle you out now –' Moving her towards the little door. 'This is my secret exit ... patients come in through there –' the high doors to the waiting room '– and go out here, so they don't have to meet. Alternatively, *I* can slip out without anybody knowing.' She stops, pressed against me in the narrow doorway, and puts a dry hand to my forehead. I hold her gaze. 'Gone now.' Her fingers on my temple; I bring up my hands to rest comfortably on her belly, a circuit from my pregnancy to hers.

'Must you really learn about steel tubing?'

'Have no fear – I didn't understand a word.'

Usher her through the doorway. Adjust my appearance in the mirror. Ragged beard and moustache. And walk slowly to the waiting-room doors.

'Frau von Rietberg. Fraulein Elizabeth '

The girl's fists are clenched. Bow to the mother, as she helps her daughter to her feet. Elizabeth insists on entering unaided, glances at us both.

'Thank you ...'

She shuffles into the consulting room. I meet the mother's anguished eyes.

Fliess wrapped in his green cloak, against a chilly autumn. Beneath the pine trees, in the litter of dusty needles, a scattering of sponge-filled mushrooms, Bavarian ceps.

'It seems as if ... some mechanism can prevent us from acknowledging the pain of an event – if we're so disposed. But what mechanism? And it's only when something stirs the memory of that event, something quite trivial perhaps ... that the pain declares its presence. In that sense,' I glance at Fliess, 'the patient suffers from reminiscences. Like the rest of us.' The bowed, angry girl. 'And even when I do manage to remove the symptoms, for a while – the illness seems to bury itself more deeply in the system ... protected by some reticence – or grief. Or shame. As if determined to survive. And the patient insists he wants to be cured. But does he?' In the grass ahead of us, a dull grey head. 'The truth is ... since I got back from Paris I seem to have got nowhere. Thought nothing. Done nothing, except make children. And hypnotize women.' I halt. 'Excuse me ...' Squatting, I pluck the little mushroom, hand it to Fliess. '*Amanita fulva.*'

'*Amanita*, you say. Then it's a poisonous one ...' He taps it with a connoisseur's air, falling into my trap.

'Perfectly edible. And a favourite of ours at home.'

He grins, holding it up to study it in profile. 'It's already shedding spores. Curious, how the same shapes recur in such different natural phenomena. From this angle it puts me in mind of the cloud over Krakatoa, spreading out over the column of smoke above the volcano.' He watches me scan the surrounding grass for firmer specimens. 'Did you know that scientists are still arguing about the precise constitution of the cloud? I have a theory about it – concerning the ionization of the dust particles when they reach the upper atmosphere –'

Enough. 'Fliess – you shouldn't overestimate my knowledge of physics.'

He shrugs, satisfied; replaces the mushroom in the grass. Elegant, flushed with exercise. Frail features beneath the beard; I feel a bear beside him. His every gesture delights me. His glances of appraisal. 'I walk here every year,' he straightens now, 'and I've never noticed these.'

'They may not have been here. Such species remain dormant for years, until for no clear reasons ... they decide to put their heads up.' We take to the path once more. 'Like certain species of neurosis.'

'Only – for some –' Fliess grins, 'more readily identifiable.'

'Not really. The analogy holds up: what we see here is only the fruit – the organism itself is microscopic, spreading unnoticed through the soil. And there's the rub, for the student of the human terrain. We have no microscope.' He is silent now; I have my listener. 'Last autumn, I began to treat a young girl, Breuer sent her to me – clever, gifted, self-assertive ... if anything too much so. I imagine her father would have preferred a son, and consequently did his best to make her into a sparring partner, since his wife was no longer a companion of any sort. It's not uncommon, after all. Of course the girl becomes a willing substitute – so when the man falls ill ... it's she who nurses him, with a wifely care, through a protracted illness and a lingering death. Shocked ... and no doubt exhausted, she begins to display hysterical symptoms: cramps, sleeplessness, pains in the legs. As if out of a textbook. The family is already in disarray, thanks to the unhappy marriage of one of her sisters, and within the year another sister – the only happily married member of the household – dies in childbirth. The girl becomes virtually bedridden, unable to walk a step. The family has immobilized her: literally. And after two years she's still subject to acute pains – clinging to her sense of loss as though she felt herself responsible, as though she *must* carry the burden, like a guilty secret. Nothing physically wrong with her, needless to say.'

'You've tried electro-therapy?' I nod. 'And she doesn't respond to it?'

'On the contrary, she loves it. Result, one day she's released from pain, completely cured, the next day doubled up in agony, pleading for treatment. I tell you this: she's virtually an addict.'

'I know the kind.' Slyly, without looking at me, 'Sometimes it's the same with hypnosis – don't you find? Especially a certain kind of middle-aged woman ... almost certainly in love with her gynaecologist – receives a pack of doctors three times a week –' I glance at him; evidently, he too has his Baroness. 'And when you enter the room she's half hypnotized already!'

'You know – this girl ... she's the kind of eager, interfering young woman who's half in love with all the men in her family, without knowing it. What would you say if I suggested that – once we concede that hereditary factors are somewhere at play – all such cases, all without exception, find their impetus in the patient's sexual life?' A nod: a bland nod. 'You'd agree?'

'Wholeheartedly. But I admit, I have an interest in doing so –' Fliess breaks off. 'Why do you smile?'

'At your "wholeheartedly".' I think of Breuer and Chrobak,

smirking gossip in a *fiacre*, even Charcot disclosing it like a masonic secret . . .

'It's sincere, I assure you. My own work is increasingly concerned with sexual periodicity and the associated bodily phenomena – even the nose responds to menstruation, and to sexual excitement, in both sexes. And by treating the nasal passages I can dispel psychical disturbances as thoroughly as physical ones – anxiety no less than migraines –'

Quickly, before we lose ourselves in nasal passages, 'I'm saying, suppose it's the *invariable* cause. At first I took it for one factor among others . . . in certain individuals, plagued by memories of sexual abuse – but what if it's the single origin of every trauma?'

'What does Breuer say?'

Breuer, always Breuer. 'He's waiting for biology to make it respectable. Meanwhile . . . he sends me his unsolved mysteries. And I have too many mouths to feed, not to be grateful. Far too many. In the last month I've had to find somewhere else to live, somewhere larger. More expensive. This procreating must stop. Don't you think?'

'If you're sure –' straight-faced '– that won't lead to an anxiety neurosis . . .' drawing my laughter.

'Why not? I need more cases.'

We walk on, happy, silent. I brush against his arm beneath the cloak; we laugh once more.

'If I may say so –' his voice comes '– I think you should consider treating this girl as a case of nasal reflex syndrome. I have a theory, based on a number of my patients –'

'Tell me once more about the last days at Gastein . . . before you heard that your sister was dying. The day you took a walk around the lake.'

Even with my back to her, I sense her irritation.

'Why do you always come back to that?'

'Because you always resist it.' Turning from the window now, 'I know . . . it's been a tiring interview. Be strong. Just a little longer. You'd taken that walk with your brother-in-law . . .'

'And on other occasions. The three of us.'

Elizabeth studies me, attentive.

73

Sweetly, 'You may smoke, Dr Freud. I don't mind.' Enjoying her revenge. 'I know you're longing to.'

'Thank you.' The cigar can wait. 'But this time, on the walk, alone – you were dreaming about marriage.'

'Thinking about it, yes.'

'An unusual train of thought?'

She meets my smile. 'For me? Not really.' Gives me the fullness of her gaze. 'I've never met anyone appropriate, that's all. But that day it was no more than natural to think about it – when you see someone as happy as my sister was.'

'And when you're so unhappy yourself.' She stares back, unyielding; now the cigar . . . 'And you sat down to rest – and the pains came on.' She nods, more tautly. What were you thinking, when the pains began? Can you remember?'

'I don't know . . .'

'Try.'

'Probably . . . how unfair it was – for a person's good fortune to be threatened . . . by their very happiness –' She can hear it in her own voice; the lie. 'I mean Dolfi having a second baby so soon after the first one.' I nod. 'We were all anxious about it.'

'So . . . when you got home you took a bath to ease the pain – and at first it was soothing . . . the cramps relaxed . . .'

Light the cigar, relax the gaze. But nothing can prevent the mounting distress in the girl's face. Anticipated pain.

'And then, suddenly, they came on again. This time for good.'

I speak it gently, but Elizabeth hunches forwards, groaning, as if acting out my description.

'Why? What gave rise to it this time? Think.' Tears, as she shakes her head in answer. 'Look at me. Remember how it was: you're in the bathhouse, in the warm water, lying at ease, thinking about the day, the walk you took . . .' She calms slowly, meeting my eyes. 'About Adolfine and her baby. In the warm water, free from pain. Listen to me . . .'

'No!' Defiance returning, as she jerks her head to one side.

'Fraulein von Rietberg . . . must I repeat, if I'm to help you –'

'How? How is it helping?' Baleful now. 'If the pains are getting worse – this very moment –'

'And why do you suppose that is? You tell me.'

'Because you're tormenting me! Don't you understand how much I loved my sister?'

'I do. Believe me.' Come to her; slowly. 'Is it love that's giving you such pain?' Sit beside her. 'Come ... lie back on the couch a moment.'

She does, still writhing. Moaning faintly, rocking from side to side. I move to the chair beyond the head of the couch, where no sudden embraces can entrap me. Flick the ash from my cigar into the waiting receptacle, lean back, ready.

'Then put your head where I can reach it, rest it back. When I press against your forehead, you will try to clear your mind, clear it of all other thoughts, and think back to that afternoon.'

We sit in silence, faces averted from each other, yet connected through my palm warming against her brow, like a jointly reluctant blessing.

'What can you remember? When I press – hard –' A moment. 'Something, now ... the memory's coming ...'

'Only ... that I thought about my cousins. While I was lying in the bath. And my aunt Gisela.'

'Why about them?'

'They stayed in the rooms above, when they visited us.'

'And nothing else?' Patience. 'What are you thinking of now?' She hesitates. 'My mind was elsewhere.'

'Yes.'

'You could tell?'

'Just answer me. What were you thinking of?'

'The garden house ...'

'The garden house?'

'At Reichenau.' A moment's pause. 'Where Dolfi died.'

My hand on her forehead.

'And I was so upset ...' She is quite still. 'He wasn't there to meet us, at the station ...'

'Your brother-in-law? Why were you upset?'

'That was when I knew. I thought ... I couldn't move another step.' Her head, hotter; trembling. 'I'd seen it in his face, beside the lake ... how worried he was. And when they left, for Reichenau, he looked at me – to warn me ... that it would never be the same. That it was the end.' Tears coming now. I dare not touch them. 'Then the telegram, and the journey, in silence. And

75

when he wasn't there to meet us ... I was so afraid it was too late – that it had all come true –' shuddering, limbs stiff – don't stop '– that she was lying there – and he was all alone with her ...' I feel her eyes shut, skin tightening, in a spasm. 'And she was dead!' Shaking. '*Help* me ...'

'Fraulein von Rietberg ... don't you know that you're in love with your brother-in-law?'

A moment's stillness, then she pulls away from me. A cry.

Hunching in pain, 'No ...'

I move quickly round to her, seize her hands. Don't stop now. She stares, violent. 'How could you say such a thing?'

'Look at me – remember: when you arrived at last, when you came into the garden house, into her bedroom, and you saw her ...' Have I lost her to hysterics? Her face is wild. 'You thought ...'

'What?' She shouts it. 'What did I think?'

'*Tell* me.'

Gripping her hands, matching her fierceness.

'I thought ...' Ah, vengeful. 'Now he's free again ... and I can be his wife!'

A moment as she holds my gaze, then in the same raging tone:

'Is that what you want to hear?'

'Is it the truth?'

I match her, shout for shout. And now the rigidity vanishes abruptly; she begins to sob, I let her draw her hands away, and sit beside her.

'If it were the truth – why would I hide it from you?'

'For the same reason you hide it from yourself.'

Leave her to cry now. I move to the desk in silence, light a fresh cigar. The anger is still there in her glance.

'Do you think me so wicked ...'

'Is it wicked to have emotions, to be attracted to someone – even a brother-in-law?'

'It isn't *true* –'

'Your own words: you've told me so, yourself. You longed to be his wife. Is that so terrible?'

Bitterly, reproachfully, as though I were to blame, 'You think me without shame, then.'

'On the contrary. Why do you suppose you've fallen ill?

Because you *are* ashamed. And the force of your illness is no less than the force of your moral will – you may take it as a tribute if you wish ... to fend off immoral thoughts. The mind refuses them, but the body has no conscience.' Beginning to control herself now, as I too resume the doctor's voice, behind the desk. 'Thankfully. Or we should never suspect what others ... sometimes struggle to endure.' A pause. 'I've known for months.'

She makes no response. Then, 'Will you ... tell Dr Breuer what I said today?'

'Not if you don't want me to.' I know this ominous calm. 'He is your doctor too, of course ... and as such shoulders the same responsibilities as I do –' Glance at my watch; let her see the glance. 'Are you afraid he'll speak to your family about it? I can assure you –'

'I'll say you talked me into it. It's true! You did.'

Too late to tell the doctor. I remain silent. 'Tell me something. Where do you feel pain now?'

My tone gives her no choice. After a moment, 'Here ... in the thigh.' She touches her right leg. 'A little.'

I make a note. 'Only a little? Come – stand up, please.'

She does so slowly, as I come to her. Appraising, without comment, restoring her to patienthood.

'Remember this: what is said here is our concern and no-one else's. No matter how deeply we delve. Confessions, fantasies, denials – all alike. In this room you must cease to be afraid. And, please, be honest with yourself ... today we have breached the defences.'

Contained, 'You think so?'

'Next time we shall ease the little pain that's left. You'll see. Our victory will be complete.' Ah, the false intimacy; drawing her resistance once more, as I escort her to the door. 'Do you doubt me?'

She turns to face me, at the door. 'Why pretend? There are some things that can't be changed.'

'Some things, never.'

'Circumstances ... in people's lives. The misery it brings –' Searching my face, accusingly. 'And you admit yourself that can't be changed!'

Wait till she calms. 'But isn't it a kind of progress – don't you

77

think – if between us we can transform this misery into common unhappiness?' She looks a little shocked. 'You know about the man who owns a cockerel and a hen, and who can't decide which to kill, for the pot? Because if he kills the hen, the cockerel will grieve, and if he kills the cockerel, the hen will grieve, so he goes to the Rabbi and the Rabbi says, I'll think about it, come back in a week ... you don't know it? After a week the man comes back and says, "Have you thought about my problem, Rabbi?" "Yes." "What should I do?" "Kill the hen." "Kill the hen? But Rabbi ... the cockerel will grieve!"' A shrug. '"Let him grieve ..."'

Elizabeth's eyes applaud me, as I open the door for her.

'Till next week, then' she answers, quietly malign.

I bow, letting her walk towards Mamma's arms. Shut the door. Stand for a moment.

Then, gathering my forces. One discarded cigar on the spittoon beside the couch. Clamp it unlit between my teeth, and hurry to the cabinet, extract the bottle from the drawer. Now to the desk, the spoon, the glass, decant some water onto a spoonful of the bittersweet powder, draw pen and paper to me as I sit. Pen poised. More of an exorcism than a consultation, this time. Her words fresh in my mind. Put the cigar aside; drain the cocaine; begin.

Breuer sips at his drink. 'We need more cases. It would be most unwise to publish the result of a few inconclusive trials with a new method, which can only –'

'It's ten years since you began with Bertha Pappenheim –'

'A method, listen to me, which can only be expected to alarm patients and alienate professional opinion. You know that.'

I know his patient, badgered look. On his desk, my aphasia book. He hasn't even mentioned it yet.

'Sigi ... most doctors can't afford to spend hour after hour with their patients, discussing the most intimate details of their lives. They have no choice but to condemn it – by any means at their disposal. They'll say only the prurient would wish to engage in it ... they'll point out that only the well-to-do can pay for such extended treatment, and that because of it we have a totally unrepresentative sample.'

78

'The disease is common enough. And the treatment works, that's all that matters, not the time involved!' I reach the desk. The pages of the book are cut: he's read it. 'Imagine – if it was an overnight cure we were claiming ... imagine the protests then! What hypocrites they are ...' Breuer says nothing. 'Josef, surely we can publish a preliminary report!'

'Perhaps.'

Anything to avoid a fight. I hold up the book. 'You've been reading this?' He peers. 'My efforts on aphasia.'

'Yes. Yes, excellent.'

I hold the pause. 'You didn't think it failed to live up to the dedication?'

Smiling, 'My dear fellow ...'

'It won't sell fifty copies. But it'll get me a pat on the back from the neurologists. Won't it?'

'Well – there's controversial matter in that too.' Stroking his beard; a bad sign. 'But yes ... of course. It's very well written.'

'For someone whose mind is taken up with too much abstract speculation.'

'I didn't mean that.'

Unable to control my bitterness, 'This is my sop to science, Josef. You could at least applaud that a little more convincingly – if you're going to cavil at my "prurient" interest in the neuroses.'

'You must forgive me,' he gets to his feet, 'it's nearly eight o'clock.'

Without a glance to soften the snub, he moves to the cupboard, fetches a pack of cards. Scoresheets, pencils.

So: now I know where I stand.

I watch Breuer as he sets up the card-table. 'Sometimes ... I think I should move to Berlin. They have more stomach for controversy.'

'The more extravagant the better – to judge by your friend Fliess.'

Chapeau, Josef. 'Then you'd recommend the move?' In the silence he turns to me, with reproachful eyes. 'Or do you think his notions *merely* extravagant?'

'How touchy you are.' He brings chairs. 'Not at all ... but, Sigi, it's the same in Berlin as anywhere else: brilliant ideas must have an acceptable source. Why else are you so keen to have my name on a preliminary report?' He holds my gaze. 'Take Fliess himself, he's paved the way for years, built up a network of powerful allies –'

'Ah but that's where you're wrong! You speak of Fliess – he's every bit as much of an outsider as I am. But in Berlin, instead of patronizing him ...' Breuer's round stooping shoulders, bent over the card-table with his back to me, perfectly still. Why must I torment him? Chancing my tone, 'It's true. Fliess has no special title to acceptability ... other than his work. His father was a provincial Jew come to Berlin to make his fortune; and failing. Just like mine.' They even share a name: Jacob. 'The only difference is that while I fester here, he breathes a different air, less stale, less musty – but at least he understands my impatience! I tell you, after spending time with him I feel quite re-invigorated ... my appetite for work returns – I'm full of new ideas –'

Interrupting, 'Have you made any progress with the von Rietberg girl?'

I watch him for a while as he lays out the scoresheets and the little silver pencils. 'Yes. Yes, extraordinary progress. She deserves a whole book to herself.' Smiling at his back, 'But I'll settle for a chapter. The paralysis in the right leg is completely cured.'

A little nod. 'Congratulations.'

'The business with the brother-in-law finally found its way – kicking and screaming – to the surface.' For God's sake leave the card-table alone ... 'Have you read Weier's work on the mediaeval witch trials? You should.' Now he turns. 'The inquisitors are our true forebears ... and all those women, possessed by demons – in the carnal sense, of course, the unrepentant brides of Satan – they're still with us! Only we call it hysteria.'

Breuer is gazing at me strangely. Quietly, 'You say there's no more trouble with the right leg –'

'No – and what's so odd, comical almost, is how pedantic the disease is! D'you know that when she thinks of her brother-in-law it affects her right leg ... and when she thinks of her father, it's the left? We have yet to tackle that more delicate conjunction – but we shall. Exhaustively. I've found my vocation, Josef. As a witchfinder. And every soul I save I dedicate to you: the secret master of hysteria. The prophet!' Breuer is labouring to speak; prevent him. Lightly, 'Who else is coming tonight?'

'Oscar.' He shrugs. 'And Rosenberg. If his wife allows him to.'

'I have plans for Oscar! You know he's courting one of my patients – and with a little help from me –'

'Sigi ... answer me truthfully. I speak as your friend, and your doctor. Are you taking much cocaine? When I think of the hours you work –'

Cocaine: is that all? Amused, 'Why do you ask?'

'You know I prescribe it myself for external application ... Fliess' nasal treatment is of considerable value – but when it comes to internal use ...' He pauses. 'Remember Ernst von Fleischl.'

I meet his solicitous gaze. You and I are lost, Josef, if the best you can do tonight is try to reduce me once more to filial dependence. 'Josef ... Fleischl died of a blood disease contracted from a corpse. Not from the drugs he took. Besides: you know me well enough, I'm a habit-breaker by temperament, not a habit-maker.' Moving towards him, 'What you see is the intoxication of discovery ... are you really so embarrassed that I credit you with the lion's share? It's my sober judgement. I swear it!'

'If you're referring to the Pappenheim case –'

How ill at ease he is. 'And later, when you alerted me to the importance of the ... "secrets of the bedchamber" – that time with Chrobak –'

'I did?'

'Don't you remember? In the cab – after our visit to the Baroness.'

'In all sincerity ...' He stares, shaking his head.

'I was quite taken aback. But I soon learnt that you'd already fathomed the mystery of psychic illness: the age-old, erotic mystery.' He gazes back at me; I can feel shame beginning, shame at my old vindictiveness. Smiling, 'And I also learnt not to sit on a couch beside my patients ... while unravelling that mystery.'

Breuer hesitates. 'You too have encountered ... some problems in that respect?' Yes, I have touched a nerve.

A pause. Tenderly now, 'Josef ... of *course* ...'

'I wouldn't describe it as an assault ... it was merely – an initiation.' Herr Kaestner draws up stiffly, in the chair opposite me. 'Such as many boys of that age undergo, I would imagine. Among their schoolmates.'

'Indeed.' I check my notes. Civil servant; a man Breuer's age, looks younger. Nervous. 'And following this initiation ... you masturbated regularly, till the age of seventeen.'

Faintly, 'Sixteen or seventeen, yes.'

'And at the present time, do you continue, on occasion?' We gaze at one another; silence. 'To practise masturbation.'

'Infrequently. Yes.'

'How often, would you say?'

Sharper, 'Infrequently.'

'Once a week? Twice?' I make it perfectly matter-of-fact. 'More often?' Mulish silence. Very well. I make a note. 'Infrequently, then. Tell me ... the periodic depressions you experience – the bouts of anxiety, shall we say ... follow intercourse with your wife?'

'Not immediately.' Speaks of this more eagerly. 'Sometimes several days later ... I wake up feeling utterly apathetic – almost paralysed –'

'But the intercourse itself – has been unsatisfactory, I take it.' Pain at my right temple, again. I raise a finger, press against it. 'What is it that inhibits you from orgasm?'

'I'm not sure I could identify – precisely – what it is ... unless the fact of long familiarity ...' I have to shut my eyes an instant, now, despite his stare. 'Herr Doctor?'

'Please continue.'

'I was saying ... our sheer familiarity, allied to – the need to restrict our family –'

'You use a condom?'

He nods.

'And in order to combat these ... dispiriting factors, and to increase stimulation – do you perhaps conjure the images of other partners, during intercourse with your wife? Other women, or ... young girls you've encountered, and whom you say you've found increasingly attractive? Do you make use of such images?' He stares. A pause. 'Do you make use of them while masturbating?'

After a moment, 'I was warned to expect some unorthodox questions –'

Well? I hold his gaze, patiently. Pop-eyed civil-servant face, a little shocked, a little flattered. Explain to the man, *make* him understand: 'Herr Kaestner, when sexual desire is checked, the accumulated tension is transformed into anxiety. Paralysis, even. Do you understand? It's a simple, ordinary, human ... if you like, *mechanical* process. In all of us. And in order to relieve your condition, I must know what it is that obstructs the flow of sexual energy. And what it is that releases it ...'

Shock, and flattery; and vanity. Kaestner, why can't you *listen*! My head will burst.

As I open my eyes, the wad of cottonwool pulls free from my nostrils, a long strip of iodoform gauze. Dropping from forceps into a waiting dish. The nurse removes it, as I breathe in, through dizzying fire, through a clear nose.

'Thank you.' Fliess' voice. Beside the operating table, level with my head, a small sculpture, a model of the turbinal bones inside the nose, with its strange cavities. 'You can sit up now.'

His smiling face, above the starched white uniform. For Fliess, a routine operation; but the patient still feels shaky – every breath through my cocaine-tormented nose makes my head swim. Yet no trace of migraine now; I feel as if I'd slept a hundred years. Fliess turns to watch the nurse leave, shutting the door. Turns back, excited.

'I have some news for you! We exchanged love-tokens last night!'

I stare foolishly after the departing nurse. Fliess bursts out laughing.

'Not with Frau Steiner!' He sits beside me, whispers. 'With the divine Ida ...'

'Ah ... the divine Ida.' Can't he see how groggy I am? 'Love-tokens, eh? I hope her token was in proportion to her divine wealth.' Is it the heiress? Must be, from his expression. 'No need to look so sheepish. I suspected you hadn't come to Vienna just to treat my migraines ...'

Solicitous now, 'How is it?' I barely nod before he hurries on, 'Don't tell anyone yet – but I think I am shortly to be married!'

I try to rise, to speak. Reach for his hand. Head swimming. 'Congratulations . . .'

I feel him take my arm; I must sit up.

'Slowly, Sigi . . .' He holds me. 'How does it feel? The nose.'

I feel tears coming. 'The nose is . . . happily indifferent. It's numb – it's like breathing through cottonwool.'

'You were, till I removed it.' Tears; can't he see? 'And now that happy indifference should spread to your aching brain, along with the cocaine fumes.' He smiles, puzzled at my silence. 'Is it working already?'

'I was searching for words to express how delighted I am. For you and your heiress.'

I'm choking – can't he see – I try to stand, giddy, reach out for him in panic.

'Sigi –' Forcing me back to the couch. 'Do you feel dizzy? What's the matter? You should have warned me, if –' I grab him, hug him, trembling. Now he knows. I can't stop crying. 'Sigi, what is it?'

'Happened before . . . many times. Heart palpitations – and pressure – here . . .' Steady my head with both hands. 'It isn't the cocaine. Breuer says perhaps – myocarditis . . .'

Why doesn't he speak? With this wretched, weeping adolescent before him, pleading for his love.

'I shan't live long.' The words tumble out of me. 'I've known that for some time.'

Fliess draws back, stern. 'I don't believe a word of it. You're smoking far too much – I know *my* constitution couldn't stand it, and I don't suppose –'

'I keep dreaming farewell scenes –' Wilhelm – 'I *know* . . . I can't help it. Wilhelm, it's awful . . .'

'Stop this!' He takes my hand, at last; I am crying like a child. 'I won't hear this!'

Shuddering, like a child. Let shame come later; but I already feel myself calming, appalled. And Fliess, studying me. Yes, like a patient.

He smiles. 'I was thinking of our conversation in Munich, not so long ago.' My hand is still in his. 'Are there . . . sexual matters you haven't mentioned to me?'

84

Elizabeth's voice. 'And if I tell you it isn't so! I swear it!'

Haven't you noticed, Fraulein Elizabeth, that time and t again your most passionate denials are reserved for memor. that touch you most nearly? How the conscious mind ere defences against ideas too painful to be borne?

I can hear sobbing.

When he embraced you, on his sickbed, you felt his body against you: your words, Fraulein Elizabeth!

'*I* embraced *him*! He was dying!'

He loved you, with all his strength. With the desire that any man living or dying might feel, for an angelic creature –

'No! No! No!'

I shut my eyes against the screams.

I stand, formally dressed in overcoat and top hat, outside the old university building. It is dead of night. I stand as though rooted. The tall drab church façade to my left.

On the cobbles, a single table is set, candle-lit, with food and glasses, Breuer and Fliess sitting at it.

Breuer beckons. Affably at first, then with rising impatience.

Wilhelm too is gazing at me. His food is untouched. Breuer eats heartily, wiping his mouth, beckoning to me, draining his glass.

It takes all my might to approach them. Breuer beckoning, eating; Fliess motionless behind the candles.

Breuer follows my gaze, to Fliess, to the untouched food. He speaks, turning back to me.

'He died of a disease contracted from a corpse . . .'

'Marty . . .'

I can no longer bear it alone, in the darkness. One hand on her shoulder, I wake her gently.

'Forgive me.'

She turns, familiar with these vigils, stretching for the bedside lamp.

I wait till she turns back. 'I feel as if I'm throttling, as if I must get out of bed . . . out of the room, out of the house –' How to describe the night-terrors? When each attempt only reminds you of the distance between human beings. Dread of eternity; until it's gone and all you've got are words, and a relief so great that you forget the terror.

'Do you want to get up?'

I shake my head. In dreams, the other side of the coin: nothing but terrifying spaces.

'Tell me.'

'Agoraphobia.' As if the word could describe it.

'Just now – you said you had to get out of the house –'

And plunge into the fear. You understand?

'Explain it to me ...' A moment. 'This ... agoraphobia –'

'That was in the dream. It's gone,' I tell her. Marty nods, rebuffed; giving me strength, restoring me to everyday irritation. 'Don't look so anxious. Dreams tell us we're all neurotic – they don't distinguish the healthy from the sick. Unfortunately.' Do I believe that? Then dreams are no use to the doctor. She is still gazing at me, pained by my self-control. 'As to what it means ... I have a patient, an agoraphobic ... who leads a double life. Respectable family man – and night reveller.' I glance at her; *listen*. 'It isn't space that he's afraid of, so much as ... what he may do in that space. Who he may – indeed whom he longs to – visit. Prostitutes, no doubt.' She nods, but I have lost her. 'The man I'm thinking of – his family is riddled with disease. Have I not told you about him?'

'You used to tell me about all your cases –'

'I'm telling you now. A man who made a sensible marriage, happy, blessed with children ...' Marty – 'he and his wife practised *coitus interruptus*, for a time –'

'And now, when I ask about *you* –'

Sharply, 'You used to listen better.'

'I *am* listening.' Now she is hurt and angry; now it comes. 'But you'd rather discuss such things with others, I know that.'

Enough: I take her hands. 'I'd rather discuss them with you, believe me.'

'That simply isn't true. There are things it seems I cannot provide.'

'You must accept that.' Slowly, 'A particular kind of companionship, for instance ... that a side of me demands. A feminine side, perhaps. I can't put it more plainly ... do you understand what I'm saying?'

She nods, contained.

'Fliess himself believes that we contain both sexes – and for that reason, we need both sexes. Both.' Urgently now, 'Equally, I need more than male companionship, more than a sounding board . . .' drawing her to me. 'I've felt so listless now for months – unable to work –' I kiss her neck. 'Dull-witted, and wretched . . . and ill-tempered. Only you can help.'

No use; she pulls away. 'Last summer you couldn't work because you were too happy! You lacked the necessary misery to apply yourself –'

'The moderate misery. Not the necessary misery.'

'It's what you *said*.'

'That I was happy. We were making love then.'

She stares, in fury. 'Then all this . . . is my fault: your listlessness, your dreams –'

'Nobody's fault.' Must I always be the peacemaker? 'We agreed, not to take any risks, till you were stronger.'

'It's pregnancy that's dangerous. Dr Rie suggests –'

Now she quotes doctors at me. 'Oscar's a fool. I know what he suggests . . . and I tell you I've seen more than enough of the spiritual poisoning that comes with contraception and . . . other recourses! As in the case I was describing to you. No doubt . . . rather clumsily.' Marty is silent. 'Trying to draw attention to some of the . . . inevitable consequences of restraint –'

Rather, she's crying, silently; and remorse has its victim. I cradle her. 'Do I make you feel so useless . . .'

'No.' At last, 'Only sometimes it's as if *his* praise were nectar and ambrosia to you . . .'

'It is.' Still holding her, 'Don't you see? Fliess is the only one – the only doctor – who takes it for granted that my work is a serious scientific endeavour like any other, not just some . . . unsavoury obsession with erotica.'

She buries her head against me, unreconciled. 'Poor Breuer,' comes her voice at last, and she draws back. 'It's he who's loved you, like a father.'

Yes. 'Just so.' Loved and rejected, as she feels herself to be. Marty, come with me one more step. 'The truth is that for some reason . . . I've always needed the same two people in my life, over and over: an adored friend, and a hated enemy.' I meet her gaze. 'Sometimes in the same person.'

Fleischl, Fliess. And I had a childhood sweetheart once, called Fluess. Is my love merely alphabetical? Or did some genie whisper the fleeting syllables over my cradle? I watch Wilhelm, his glass raised to drink, frowning. He catches me gazing at him.

Quickly, 'It's nothing, just a migraine.'

'Right side or left?'

He grins at my ten-gulden-a-minute tone. 'Left.' And drinks deeply.

I glance around the café clientele. Busy with their food, their newspapers. 'Would it be tactless to ask a newly married man ... if there are sexual matters you haven't mentioned to me?'

The echo escapes him. Sombrely, 'I've always suffered from migraines.' Then, seeing my expression, 'Forgive me – I didn't mean to be so abrupt. And the answer is no: I have no complaints.' The liar brings out a cigar, grins at me. 'Except exhaustion ... and general debility.'

I shake my head, at the offer of a cigar.

'You've given up? Since when?'

'A week.'

He lights up, smiling. 'Then can I take it ... you've decided not to die?'

'For the time being.'

He contemplates me; how easily we switch roles.

'Any change in your ... domestic arrangements?'

'Only to the extent that we've had separate beds installed.' The news passes him by, I see him gazing over my shoulder, distracted. 'We're like the couple who go to the doctor to ask how they can best avoid making a baby, and he says: "Drink a glass of water." "Before or after, doctor?"'

'"Instead" ...' Fliess chimes in with the answer.

'Unless you can think of a better way –'

'There's someone trying to get your attention.'

I follow his gaze, turning to see two new arrivals at the door, making their way towards a table. One nods at me, smiling.

'An acquaintance?'

'A patient. Fraulein Eckstein.' I turn back, catching Wilhelm's greedy glance in her direction. 'Attractive girl. Advanced views on womanhood – and the battle of the sexes ...'

'Who's the chaperone?'

'It's her sister.' Lowering my voice, 'Emma has a peculiar difficulty. She can't go into shops alone.'

'She looks robust enough.'

'She is. A mysterious ailment, I thought – until we dredged up a forgotten memory –' The girls sit, by the window, and consult a menu. This beats Charcot's parades: Vienna is my stage now. Still softly, 'It's somewhat predictable: when she was eight, a shopkeeper forced his attentions on her ... but what *is* interesting is that she went back to the shop – she admits it – on subsequent occasions. It's not the incident itself that haunts her, but her own bad conscience.' I catch a waiter's eye, indicate further drinks. 'There are still certain somatic complications which I haven't been able to dispel, persistent stomach cramps, but ...'

Fliess, turned voyeur, gazes at Emma across the Café Landtmann.

'One thing I'm sure of: I believe there are two quite distinct responses to such an event. Hysteria develops from a passive submission to a pre-pubertal incident ... a sexual advance of some kind. And obsessional neurosis – like Emma's – if the advance itself is undergone with pleasure.'

Fliess doffing an imaginary cap, '*Chapeau*, Herr Doctor.'

'That's a recent discovery ... I tell you without fear of your repeating it – since no-one's likely to want to steal such an absurd idea.' Indeed, it seems absurd, as we watch Emma calmly ordering a coffee. A waiter stops by our table, refills our glasses. Fliess grins.

'You seem cheerful enough – despite your deprivations.'

I let Goethe answer for me: 'Sacrifice ... and further sacrifice, is the eternal counsellor's advice!' The waiter bows, sceptical, and retires. And yet, it's true: my spirits have risen, ideas flow – 'If I can do without cigars, I dare say I can forgo ... less important pleasures.'

'You may not have to. A propos your earlier question – there may well be a way to prevent repeated pregnancies, without having to substitute a glass of water.' We smile; I the celibate now, he the married man. 'I've been working on a theory of dual periodicity in sexual – and emotional – life: not only the twenty-eight-day cycle in the female, but a twenty-three-day cycle in the male. It's at an early stage ... but I'm convinced that intercourse can be perfectly safe at certain stages of the cycle – provided the dates are carefully observed.'

His turn, modestly taken, putting me to shame. 'But if that's true ... my dear Wilhelm! If you could establish a reliable gauge of fertility – you'd free us all. There'll be a statue to you in every city –'

'One will do.' Eyes on Emma, humorous. 'Preferably on this very spot.'

'I'll pay for it myself. I mean it ... you have only to choose the marble ...'

'In that case, we must go to Carrara and inspect the cliff face at dawn, like Michelangelo ... to make sure the marble is as flawless as my theory!'

Bravo! Raising our glasses to each other, while the Eckstein girls survey us from their table, a little bemused.

'My reputation suffers just as much as yours!' Breuer battles to keep up with me, in the pelting rain. 'Not that you notice such things. I've argued the significance of sexual factors as passionately as you have – but I will not concede that every single psychic ailment derives from them! I'd like to know what gives you the authority to disregard all other causes ...'

'My own experience. Mine, Josef! Don't you realize: in this field self-knowledge is worth a hundred patients! Delusions ... nightmares, depressions – I've suffered amply from them in the last twelve months ... there have been days when it was more than I could do to cut the pages of a book – d'you think I don't know why?'

Breuer huffing and panting. But I need air.

'And when I find you sick and wan, at home, staring at a hand of patience, d'you think I don't know why *that* is? D'you think your wife doesn't know why? Will no-one guess that impotence has invaded the Breuer household?' He slows, silent. 'The dreadful secret!'

Breuer stops, wiping rain from his moustache. 'Really, one cannot talk to you in this mood.'

'One cannot talk to *you* in any mood ... you're growing senile. In the head.'

He broods; I cannot help him.

His voice subdued, 'This ... this was not what I wanted to discuss with you –'

'You astonish me.'

'Herr Hartmann has written to me from Egypt – very anxious about his health ... it appears that dysentery has supervened.'

'Nonsense.'

'He was already showing symptoms –'

I walk on. 'The man's defecatory problems were entirely hysterical. *You* had to go and send him on a sea voyage!'

'No doubt ...' anger spurs him after me, 'you resent my having deprived you of a patient ...'

'Not in the least. As far as that goes, my work at the children's hospital is tiding me over nicely at the moment, thank you.'

It is the worst rebuff. We walk in silence.

'There's also ... the matter of Fraulein Eckstein.' Breuer ignores my glance. 'I understand that Fliess has begun to treat her, at your recommendation.'

'He shares my view that her abdominal pains are connected with the sexual trauma – and further, that the haemorrhaging may coincide with menstruation. In his opinion – a classic case of nasal reflex syndrome.'

He shakes his head: 'I should only like to warn you of a recklessness that ... others have observed in his approach –'

Recklessness! 'I should have thought you'd be the first to celebrate if the man can find a way to cure neurotic patients without having to ... hunt the minotaur through the labyrinths of puberty!' Bitterly, 'Such distasteful labours!'

Breuer is silent for a time. Then, 'I can see you're not well.'

'You don't trust me, you don't trust Fliess – worst of all, you don't trust yourself! You should stick to dissecting pigeons.'

In the quiet of Kassowitz' Clinic, I review our conversation. Children file in one by one, some naked, all mute, all aphasic.

I have been intemperate, hysterical. Approaching forty, and

experiencing adolescent passions as if for the first time. 'I can see you're not well ...' I blame him, I blame Marty, I don't know who to blame. And all the while I'm in a ferment of discovery, like a diver grasping at underwater treasure.

At home a letter awaits me: 'My dear Sigmund, with regard to our unhappy meeting the other day, I have no doubt you've had time to consider your words at greater leisure. I know I have, and I can only offer this conclusion: that while you continue to play the rebellious son, I have no option but to play the aggrieved father. It isn't only neurotic patients, you know, who undergo a giddy transference of their emotional needs, onto the person of their confessor. It happens between friends ...'

' "Nonetheless ... I must concede one thing: I am getting older. It is time I put my head on the block. So, my dear immoderate friend – I acquiesce. Let us publish our endeavours ..." '

Marty listens as I read the letter to her. Her smile of delight matching mine.

' "And may the public never know how close we came to destroying our precious collaboration ... your devoted – Josef." '

She hugs me. Then, drawing back, 'How did you do it?'

'I shouted at him.'

My mild tone makes her laugh. 'You can't fault him for magnanimity ...'

'So long as he doesn't change his mind. But I shan't give him time – I'll work on the book at Schloss Bellevue, if needs be ... it'll be a pleasure.' I take her hands. Cautiously now. 'Perhaps it'll bring in some money. And – who knows, before too long ... if you were feeling stronger ...'

Marty's expression barely changes. But she makes no answering sign.

Guests in the sitting room; patients, many of them. In short, a normal Viennese tea-time. They chatter, at ease. On the sofa next to Martha sits Anna Lichtheim, fortyish, operetta voice. Telling Marty where to buy the best Gugelhupf; Marty catches my eye. Anna looks up. 'Oh – doesn't your husband like cake?' All the best doctors like cake.

I spot Dr Oscar Rie, ogling the widow Lichtheim, and I sidle up to him.

'You must come and visit us this summer, at the Bellevue. Bring Anna.' He glances quickly at me. 'Just a suggestion, Oscar ...' Rie says nothing.

'Tell me ... do you think Martha's well enough to withstand the rigours of another childbirth?'

'I wouldn't presume to advise you, Sigmund.'

Rie, pince-nez, precise. Does he come here to ogle my neurotics?

'But you advise her. As her doctor, you can give her the necessary reassurance.'

'And you'd like me to?'

Someone knocking at the door. 'Come in.' I nod to Rie, 'Yes ...' Still no-one enters. 'Come in!' Gently launching Rie towards the sofa, 'Don't let Martha monopolize the lady – or we shall have invited her in vain ...'

The pince-nez quivers. 'Sigmund, are you advising me to ... pursue an arrangement with a patient of yours – who is still undergoing treatment?'

'Why not?'

The door has opened to reveal Mathilde, our eldest. Eight years old this summer. For a moment she stands dumb, like my aphasics at the children's hospital.

'Papa ... the telephone.'

She follows me down the corridor, eager to see the instrument in use. I shoo her back; to me it's a monstrosity. And the voice in the earpiece is full of fear and anger, as a telephone voice should be. 'Who's that? Speak louder!' Mathilde, laughing. 'Rosannes?'

Dr Rosannes: once a giggling student, tense with stomach cramps. I can still see him in the throng of the laboratory, gulping down my cocaine. Now an officious, stuffy-looking fellow, greeting me at the door to the Eckstein apartment, with a cold stare. Now a doctor.

Inside, Emma stands rigid at the end of the hall, braced against a piece of furniture like an animal at bay. Her sister Sophie at her side. Emma lets out a moan, begins to stalk from side to side in pain, eluding our grasp till the three of us force her at last into the drawing room, half carrying her. She struggles to stand, her back pressed against a wall.

'Does this hurt ... here ...?'

Rosannes probes, palps, in vain, while I pinion Emma's arms. 'Emma – hold still –'

She writhes.

'Hold still. *Please*.'

'Is it here? Tell me!'

She nods, blindly; it hurts everywhere. 'And in my head ... oh god, the pain –'

'If you would only lie down, Fraulein Eckstein ... for a moment.'

'No –' turning from Rosannes to me, 'tell him ... explain – I mustn't lie down, it's so much worse –'

Rosannes hurries to his bag. Emma fights to get free, seeing the metal instrument emerge. I hold her fast.

'It will make the examination easier, Emma ...'

'No!'

'Now *please* ...' Rosannes glares '... if you would put your head back. Just for an instant.'

'Be strong,' I repeat helplessly, 'be strong, we'll soon find the cause.'

He pries her mouth open, adjusts the torch. Gaping jaws, like a snarl. Rosannes turns his attention to her nose. When he turns back to me, he looks pale, the ailing student once more. Then, abruptly, 'Some cold water!'

Sophie stares. 'Some ...'

'*Cold water*. In a basin.'

The girl hurries out; ignoring me, Rosannes takes hold of Emma, lifting her off the floor before she can protest. Lurching with her towards the sofa. Across her screams, 'I must insist that you lie down!'

'What is it – what's the matter?' Emma gazing at Rosannes. 'I'm perfectly able to stand!'

We force her onto the sofa.

'Lie down! You'll be all right, just lie quietly!'

I take her hands. 'Do as he says. Be strong ...'

She lies, sobbing, defeated. Rosannes is rummaging in his bag again; now he sends me an angry, beckoning glance.

'It's as I warned you,' I whisper to him as we confer, 'she has a history of psycho-somatic pains –'

'I am familiar with the case.' That officious stare again. 'When did Fliess operate on her nose?'

'A week ago. Ten days perhaps.'

'And returned directly to Berlin? Without waiting to see the effects?' Seeing me ready to reply, 'Is it true that one of his patients ... had her nose entirely rotted away, by a cocaine necrosis?'

I stare at him, in silence. 'It's *you* who've been talking to Breuer ...'

'Sigmund: have you ever heard of a qualified doctor leaving an entire length of cottonwool inside a patient?'

Contemptuous words rise to my lips: who hasn't? Then I see it in his furious gaze. Emma. 'It isn't true ...'

Sophie returns, behind us, with the basin. And Rosannes breaks away from me, forceps in hand, to dip a cloth in the cold water. He brushes past Sophie, towards the sofa. I follow, taking the basin from her, unable to comfort her, to speak at all.

'Quite still, please,' Rosannes kneeling at Emma's side. 'Head back.'

He bends over her. I can barely watch. I dip the compress in the basin, squeeze it dry and place the cloth across the girl's forehead, her upper nose and eyes. She must not see.

Slowly, Rosannes extracts the strand of bloody gauze from Emma's nose. Pulls, till a metre and more of tissue dangle like a hideous conjuring trick; like a string of clotted blood, like bleeding ectoplasm –

A moan. Mine, or Sophie's? Emma lies deathly silent. Seeing me totter, Rosannes turns to deposit the cottonwool in the basin. Fliess' face, as he pulls the gauze out of my own nose, smiling ...

A gasp from Emma, then a sudden cry, and a rush of blood from her nose. Rosannes pulls the compress down to staunch the flow, it stains blood red across her face.

Rosannes glances up at me, then round at moaning Sophie.

'A cognac.' He waits till he has her attention. 'For Dr Freud.'

Pulling the cloth from her face, Emma sits up abruptly, gazes at us, panting, with a grisly smile. A sudden, second rush of blood. She ignores it, looking straight into my eyes. A mocking, clotted noise comes from her throat.

'Be strong, he says ...'

The cognac comes, too late; I am going to faint.

Elizabeth's voice. 'Poor Father ... he was so lonely, sometimes I read to him all day – Mama couldn't do it, she had eye trouble then. Shut away in a dark room. I could see the pain in his face. But he never complained. Except at night, in sleep. They made up a bed for me in his room, so I could stay with him ...'

Yes. Go on.

'And at night, when he cried out – it was unbearable. I had to comfort him, and lie with him, without waking him ... and hold him ... hug him tight.' Softly, 'You understand?'

Emma's face. 'I dreamt the Devil came to me, when I was asleep – and I pretended to be fast asleep, but I could see him ... he was so well-dressed, just like in stories. He had pearls in his lapel. At least, I thought they were pearls, until he took one out – it was a long pin ... then he took my hand and stuck the first pin in my finger. There was no pain. Then he took the others out and stuck them in. I kept quite still. He took the pins out – there was a drop of blood on each spot ... and from his pocket he took some little sugared sweets and put them on my fingers, covering the drops of blood.'

And then?

'That's all. I must have woken up. What does it mean? One other thing – I heard a word ... I'm not sure when, inside my head. During the dream.'

What word?

'Tri- ... tri- ...'

Widow Lichtheim, trilling. 'What am I to do? I can't sleep, I can't eat – I only break out in a rash ... and no matter how often we talk, the nightmares still return! I can't go on like this ...'

You should do what all your friends suggest, Frau Lichtheim. Marry Oscar.

'Marry ... Oscar?'

Why not?

'Dr Freud! After all these months, all this heart-searching ...
physical tests, visits to spas – is *this* what it comes to? Marry
Oscar?'

You reject my solution, Frau Lichtheim?

Emma's face. 'It was ... such a *peculiar* word –'

Try to remember.

'Tri- ... mythel ... methylanin. Is that a word?'

It's a chemical. I can only think ... Dr Fliess may have mentioned it to you. It's a hobby-horse of his – he believes it could
be the sex chemical.

'The sex chemical? Can one buy it in chemists', Dr Freud?'

'Marry Oscar? Is that all it comes to?'

'Poor Father ... you understand?'

'And from his pocket he took some little sugared sweets ...
white powder on them ... and he put them on my fingers,
covering the drops of blood. That's all. I must have woken up.'

Emma's voice. Emma's face. 'What does it mean?'

'It's past seven, Mathilde!' Marty calls through the open doors
into the garden. Warm air, clean air, surrounds the Schloss
Bellevue, wafting in. Holiday air.

The child walks slowly in. Then runs to me, to press herself
against me, winningly. I shake my head, nodding towards our
guest. 'Say goodnight ...'

Oscar Rie smiles at the hesitant child, gets to his feet. 'I must
be going too.'

No-one demurs. The evening has been full of silences.

Rie gives Mathilde a brief kiss on the head; glances at me. 'I
have a rendezvous.'

I watch Martha bend forward in discomfort, to kiss the child
goodnight. Since the onset of this pregnancy, nothing but pain
and demonstrations of pain.

'Before I forget ...' Rie opens his bag, brings out a luridly
coloured bottle of liqueur. Marty and I avoid each other's gaze.
'I brought you this.'

'Oscar ...'

'Just a few sips, last thing at night, and you'll sleep, believe
me –' As Marty shakes her head, smiling, 'Is it so bad?'

'It's always bad.'

97

Mathilde is still watching from the doorway. I wave her away, up to bed, and rise to take the proffered bottle. 'Thank you.' Rie bends to kiss my wife's hand.

'We'll see you at Marty's birthday party, I hope . . .' I lead Rie into the hallway. Quietly, 'Anna Lichtheim sends her regards.'

He nods, non-committal. 'We went to the Burgtheater, on Friday.'

'I'm just in the process of writing up her case. For publication. Under a heavy disguise, of course.'

He stops. 'Isn't that a little premature? She's far from cured, you know.'

'Really.'

'In my opinion.'

Under Rie's stare, I lift the bottle, unscrew the cap, and sniff. Pleasantly, 'What are you trying to do to Martha? Poison her?'

'Well . . . she doesn't have to drink it – it's for both of you –'

'I see: you don't mind poisoning *me*.'

He takes it with the utmost seriousness.

'Sigmund . . . I feel I must tell you this. Frau Lichtheim is as ill as she was two years ago. If not more so.'

'Of course. She's still in love with you.'

'With me?' Taken aback.

'As you are with her. I've told her – no more visits to the Burgtheater till you're man and wife.'

The pince-nez nearly falls off his nose. 'Yes . . .' he gropes for the door handle. 'Well, that's one way to destroy two lives at once!' A moment. 'Goodnight!'

I lift the bottle, sniff the cloying stuff once more. No question: it's a marriage made in heaven.

Alone, in the little sitting room. Papers heaped on the writing desk, under the lamp. I can still smell the sickening liqueur. I breathe in at the open window.

A little orchestra somewhere, in some garden, drowns the other night sounds. A waltz, rising and falling on the wind.

The ballroom is crowded. Rosannes is there, and Rie, and Breuer. I search for Fliess' face in vain.

Emma, in her café suit, strolls among the guests. She lets me catch up with her. Applause comes, as the music ends, and the musicians put aside their instruments.

'If you still get pains,' I murmur, 'It's your fault . . .'

We walk on, greeting guests. She speaks without looking at me.

'If you only knew what pains I've got now – in my throat.'

I guide her, one hand under her arm, towards a corner of the room. The ballroom guests ignore us. But when I turn back to Emma, Sophie stands there in her place.

'Show me,' I say.

She hesitates.

'Show me, please.'

Sophie opens her mouth a little. Gradually wider and wider. I lean forward to peer inside. To my horror, her mouth contains strange curly structures: the turbinal bones of the nose. As I draw back, Emma closes her mouth. Emma's face.

We are surrounded by a group of doctors, now pressing and probing an unresistant Emma. Rie, and Rosannes, and Breuer.

'Quite still please. Head back.'

'She has a dull area,' observes Rie, 'down on the left. You see? She's far from cured, you know.'

'Quite still please. Head back.'

Breuer studies her closely. 'There's no doubt it's an infection. Now dysentery will supervene . . .'

Emma writhes, under our hands, head back, mouth open. I am trying to shake her awake but she grows more ecstatic. I am struggling with Martha, fighting to subdue her pregnant belly. She claws at me, enraged. I hold up the syringe and plunge it into her, dissolving her. Plunge again: into the Baroness. Into Anna, Anna Lichtheim.

Breuer, watching me. The scream is Fleischl's, as the band strikes up once more, drowning his cries. Breuer, beside me, has suddenly changed: he is beardless, sickly, ridiculous.

The thin arms of the girl in front of me, the arms I grip with both hands, are naked now. The arms of a naked child in the children's hospital. She tips her face up to me.

The face comes up. It is Mathilde's face. I stand rigid with fear as she presses against me. Unable to let go of her. Shuddering. Rising excitement on her face. A word comes: trimethylanin. She speaks. Try! Taunting me:

'Tri ... Tri ... Tri ... Tri ... Tri ...'

I wake with the terror still vivid. And lie, for long minutes, holding the mosaic together in my head.

The shocks, the petty mysteries, the trivia of the past few months have drifted together into a single constellation, every detail in place.

I glance across at Martha in her bed. Her shallow, painful breathing brings back the gruesomeness of the dream. Pushing back my covers, I slip silently out of bed and find the door.

The lamp is still burning at the desk. I put it out – no need for hasty notes, I have the dream intact, the diver's treasure.

Soft night air, outside the front door.

My dear Wilhelm ...

My dear Wilhelm: by one of those accidents to which we are all happily prone, the unfortunate business with Emma's operation returned to haunt me last night – most fruitfully – in dreams. One day, perhaps, a statue matching yours will be erected at the Schloss Bellevue! If not, at least a plaque: believe me, I deserve it. I had already recognized that we were all neurotic in the inverted, nocturnal world – but now I see that the dream only reveals what lies concealed during the day – in all of us: the primitive, unbridled, sexual megalomania of the instincts. The dream is simply wish-fulfilment.

Warm grass brushes my ankles; above me, constellations.

Dear friend, if Martha has a boy, we shall call him Wilhelm. If a girl ... I've been thinking – of the women in my dream I already have a Martha, and a Mathilde, after Breuer's wife. Why not ... Anna? Like Anna Lichtheim, and the Baroness. That way, true to my dream ... I have them all!

FOUR

'Hello? Anna!'

The corridor is empty. Why is it that when I want silence the women shuffle around like monks at prayer, but when I need someone –

'Is something the matter?' Anna, on the staircase.

'The doorbell – didn't you hear it?'

'No.' She comes, touches my arm. 'I'll go.'

Someone up above, singing. Humming. I move to look, into the stairwell. The house is full of strangers now, I come across people I've never met, they stare, bereft of words, as if I were a ghost. In the Berggasse they stayed in the waiting room. Now all these benighted stairs.

I gaze up. Minna, on the landing, staring down at me in her ridiculous hat.

'Papa . . .'

The singing has stopped.

Anna's hand on my arm, as I begin to climb the stairs. 'Mother's gone out, Papa. And Aunt Minna's asleep.' Let go: I turn to look at her. 'She's not well. The doctor says she needs another operation on her eyes.'

Why am I climbing these stairs, then? I let Anna support me, as I come down again.

'There's no-one there, at the front door.' She tugs. 'Come.'

Down the corridor, towards my room. The front door is round the corner.

'She was like an Amazon. An Amazon painted by Rubens.'

The bright hard voice, at the front door.

'I'm here! Hello – Marty! I'm here!'

'Minna –'

Marty rushing past me. As I turn the corner, they are embracing, in the doorway. I had forgotten how much taller she was. And the hat! The plumes are bedraggled and sticky with rain.

A cabman stands behind her with the luggage, gaberdine dripping.

'We were expecting you tomorrow –'

'I got fed up with Prague. In this weather . . . even window-shopping palls.'

Martha hugs her again. 'How good it is to see you!'

The cabman waits, heavy-moustached; Minna reaches into her bag.

'No no . . .' Marty glancing at me. I pass her my wallet, and advance on Minna to exchange kisses.

'How splendid you look.'

'I?' She removes the hat, pats her hair, finding the mirror. 'I look like a stork caught in a thunderstorm.'

A stork? We have enough babies. The cabman leaves, and I pick up her suitcase, as she turns to me.

'And you – let me look at you.' Drily, 'Every inch the man of means.'

'I've put on weight, you mean.' Now her carpet-bag; heavier still. 'What have you got in here?'

Behind us, fresh mealtime plans are being laid.

'Marty . . . I don't eat lunch.'

Nonsense, the stork must eat: Marty ignores her. Minna sweeps the bag out of my hand.

'I know the way. Come – I'm used to carrying it. It's full of books.'

I follow her. 'How long can you stay?'

'We'll see.'

She drops the bag onto a sofa, gazes round the apartment, pleased. Another appraising look. 'You *have* put on weight. A good sign. You're prospering.' She smiles. 'Despite what Marty says.'

'Why. What does she say?'

Minna shrugs, walks around the room, taking possession.

'I understand we're all your patients now – even the children aren't safe from your scrutiny. She wrote that you're causing a scandal.'

Mildly, 'I hope so.'

'Good. I want to hear all about it.'

She pauses at the window, gazing out. I hadn't remembered

her so tall; or so provocative. Years as a governess have made her eccentric, it would seem: the eccentric spinster, not the sad one. The heavy carpet bag full of French novels? I see the old, quick boredom on her face. She hunches her high shoulders, shivering.

'Horrible old Vienna. How can you stand it?'

'When we set out to form an opinion about the causation of a pathological state such as hysteria, gentlemen, we find that a thorough analysis carries us further and further back in the patient's memories, towards the source of this manifold condition ...'

Some movement in the audience. Passing something along the row. A folded note.

'... so that, no less than Schliemann laying bare the seven levels of ancient Troy, the doctor is confronted with an archaeology of personal experience.'

Let them scribble!

'If his work is crowned with success ... the discoveries are self-explanatory: the ruined walls form part of the ramparts of a palace or a treasure-house, the fragments of columns can be filled out into a temple, the numerous inscriptions will in time reveal an alphabet, a language ... and undreamed-of information about the events of the remote past.'

The note has reached Breuer. Expressionless as he reads it, and bends to pen his answer.

'Our esteemed colleague, the late Maître Charcot, insisted that a predisposition to neurosis lay hidden in the womb of heredity: an intangible region, denying the archaeologist his precious evidence. But tonight I propose to argue that the decisive source lies in a no less mysterious but less remote territory – and consists of real events in the patient's own life. Gentlemen, the predisposition to neurosis derives from sexual shock, in childhood.'

Now I have their full attention.

'I myself have recently treated seventeen cases where, by gradual deciphering, the illness can be traced to a sexual assault during the earliest years. In the main, by teachers, nursemaids, governesses ...'

Doctors, too. They know. The hall bristles; and I see the

folded note, passed back along the row, has reached its original begetter, tonight's ring-leader.

'*Saxa loquntur!* Like stones the memories of childhood, mute for so long, speak to us ... and the thousand-year-old question of the origin of psychological disturbances can at last be answered. Gentlemen, we have found what Charcot sought, the true source of this many-watered Nile!'

I stand with Breuer, in the marble lobby. Like a jilted bridegroom with his intended father-in-law, watching the embarrassed guests depart. To say the least, uncertain of each other.

'I saw Krafft-Ebing have a word with you,' he murmurs, impatient at my silence. 'Well? Where does he stand?'

With the asses, naturally. Old wives' psychiatry ... ' "A charming scientific fairy tale, my dear colleague ..." '

Breuer grins. 'Surely he means a bedside story.'

Ah. Am I supposed to titter? He studies me.

'You didn't mention fathers, in your roll-call of seducers.'

'One shock at a time. Don't you think?'

A passing face, trapped by our smiles, nods his congratulations.

'Thank you ...'

Breuer turns. 'Why isn't Fliess here? We could have done with his support.'

'I can fight my own battles. He knows that.' And if I cannot bend the Higher Powers, I shall stir up the Infernal Regions ... 'What did Jauregg's note say?'

'Just ... foolishness. I wrote back that your work would outlive his efforts.'

I feel tears coming, and dare not look at him. His loyalty puts me to shame. And then, as we follow the last of the departing audience, down the staircase, I hear him whisper:

'All the same – I don't believe a word of what you said tonight.'

My dear Wilhelm ... as you anticipated, my infantile seduction theory met with a frigid reception from the Society of Physicians. I shall not lecture there again ...

The Berggasse, dark and empty. A corner of an exhausted

city, with its heavy face of stone. Would it be different, anywhere else? I'm part of it now, I have my refuge, let them come to me.

... In short, dear friend, my isolation here is now complete, and I must gather my forces for a long and solitary journey ... rather a pleasant prospect, were it not for my current state of mind. My father is failing fast; at eighty-two he has little heart for the fray. This last illness is dreadful to behold – and is evoking unforeseen turmoil, inside me ...

In, under the heavy archway. Up the stairs. Two sets of footsteps: on the landing a woman passes me quickly, avoiding my gaze.

... And our household has been further shaken up by the arrival of Martha's sister, who presents herself as something of a free spirit ... and regards our settled routine with a humorous eye ...

I let myself into the apartment, into the smell of furniture polish. Floor polish, books. Discard my hat, and coat, and scarf.

... She says I'm growing fat. She means bourgeois. If only she knew ...

Before me, as I open the door, Martha and Minna side by side on the sofa, looking up at the same moment. There will be time enough, to tell them about the lecture. 'Herr Baumann's entertaining again – on the stairs I passed the most entrancing creature ... not the oriental one ...' But they do not respond; I follow Marty's gaze; a figure rises, grim-faced, from a chair. 'Alexander?'

Once more I am the witness. The listener, while my father talks and talks, dying. Talking as if to keep death at bay. His strength is draining with the light: it won't be long.

'Oh, they ... ransacked the place, tore up the floorboards ... and the chairs, ruined the chairs ... hunting for the money. And the women – the girls huddled crying ... you were at school, thank God. What a noise the women made.'

The money; still the money. I sit beside him in the dying light, beside one more averted head. Is there to be no grief? Nothing at all?

'We had to throw out the chairs. You never even asked what had happened ...'

Quietly, 'Mother told me.'

'Hunting – everywhere – looking for the banknotes: Uncle Josef's forgeries. He said . . . they weren't his . . . may he rest in peace. He couldn't bear to be poor.' His face turns to me; but he doesn't see me. 'We never spoke to him again.' A small, childish noise from his throat, and he begins to cry again. 'Help me . . . I don't want to die here.'

He doesn't see me. I can feel it now, I can feel the fear.

'If you only knew . . . how I miss the old town, and the woods. Even the mud . . . the mud in winter. Remember – the Lubina, and our bridge. The floods. The water.'

Yes.

'Do you still think of it?'

I nod. His gaze, running with tears.

'You know . . . my father was a harsh man.' I watch him struggle with self-pity for a long dreadful moment. 'I hoped I would see you . . . secure, that's all. You never tell us – but we know. You've always antagonized people.'

'We're all right, Papa . . . we're managing all right.'

But he has turned back to the ceiling, eyes closing. How much more? His voice comes, strange.

'That stupid woman . . .'

Silence. 'Who?'

Dry coughing racks his body, and once more I move to calm him as he tries to sit up. Blood comes from his mouth. My father, staring at me.

'Put on your boots! We must get you to the doctor's.'

I wipe the blood from his chin. He won't lie down; shouting now.

'Put your boots on! Philipp will help you –'

'Papa, it's me . . .'

He reaches out to touch me like a blind man. The spasm is gone, he lies back.

'Little blackamoor. You were born with a head of black hair . . . she swore it was a sign. And your mother believed her!'

'Rest now . . .'

'The witch . . . she took our money, too. Stole from us.'

'Who did?'

His gaze is vacant. 'I forget her name . . .'

Time passes; God knows how long, in this darkened room. My hand still clenched in his.

'Promise me ...' The voice is different. When I turn to look, his eyes are clear. 'Promise you'll make professor – even if it means ... bowing the head.' I nod. I can feel anger rising. 'No matter *what* it means.' Anger; but his clear eyes address me now, for long moments. At last, 'You were a cruel child. Your mother ... left me the others. But I loved you.'

Before I can speak –

'Help me ...' With all his might.

The door opens, behind us. He wills me not to turn.

Her voice, 'Sigi, please ... you'll only tire him.'

Mamma, in the doorway; and beside me Jacob wrenches free in rage, head rising from the pillow.

'Go ... away!'

The shout echoes around the room, for the whole house to hear. My mother stands, motionless, with the light behind her. I cannot see her eyes.

I am helpless, absent before their violence.

Please, God ...

In order to understand –

In the same dark wintry light, I sit beside a patient. His face too is averted, as I speak.

In order to understand, in order to rid yourself of the confused emotions which haunt your adult life, you must go further back, back to a time when your very presence threatened to destroy your parents' love, and when your demands made a lover of one and an enemy of the other ...

Is he listening? Does he understand?

... This inexorable family drama returns, disguised, in adulthood: a landscape peopled for the grown-up boy by figures of threatening authority and reincarnations of motherhood; as it is for the grown-up girl by jealous maternal counterparts, and likenesses of her father; a landscape of ghosts.

My mother, perfectly still in the doorway. I can't make out her face. Jacob, on the pillow, in a silent rictus. He whimpers.

Humiliated, a child again, 'I've wet the bed.'

I turn back to Mamma.

'Wait there.' She hurries away down the corridor.

He's dying.

We sit in darkness. The patient has found his voice:

It was the first time I'd heard my parents shouting at each other – I'd come into their bedroom late at night, my father ordered me back to bed, and I could hear them shouting, from my room. I felt . . .

Yes?

Such excitement . . . fear and pleasure, mingled –

Exultation. Terror.

Papa stares up at me, dying.

We move across the field, spread out, like hunters: my small tribe on a Sunday walk. We shout our mushroom finds. Each one making his own slow progress through the grass.

'Where's Martin?' Minna, trying to shepherd us. 'Mathilde . . . where's Martin got to?'

'He's gone home with Liesl.'

'He has not gone home with Liesl . . . Liesl's over there, with Sophie.' I see her, pointing irritably. 'By the trees.'

The housemaid, with a small child, ducking into foliage at the edge of the field. She waves.

Pleasure beyond words, in this sunlight, just to walk at a child's pace, apart, watching them. Just up ahead, Oliver burrowing; Marty bends to help him.

'I can't see Martin.' Even Minna's dress makes an angry sound, in the grass.

Marty straightens, unperturbed. 'He's over there.'

Minna sets out, crosses my path without a glance. Now Martha, running after her.

'Minna – leave the girl, she's *promised* to keep an eye on him . . . *I'll* go.'

Minna gives up, stands staring: all around her, sunstruck idiots. She watches me approach.

Vaguely, 'Martin's run off again . . .'

'You'll get used to it.'

108

We stand, in the sweet mountain air.

'She lets the girl do as she pleases with the little ones.'

'Yes, I know.'

Minna gazing at me, vexed. 'A little strictness does no harm.'

We walk a little. If she wants *my* mantle ... so much the better. Her stride certainly matches mine.

'Really ... Martha can be so feckless ...'

'The children seem all right to me.'

Peaceable Sigmund. Minna gazes at her sister, over in the distance, no longer searching but attending to another child.

'Of course, *she* was a thoroughly obedient child, perhaps that's what it is.' To herself now, 'Never ran off; never stood up to anyone. Perhaps that's what you liked in her. I often used to wonder.'

Did I hear right? 'What did you use to wonder?'

'Why you chose her.'

I stare. Smiling. 'You mean, instead of you.'

'Be serious.'

'I loved her.'

Nothing daunted, 'And now?' She bursts out laughing, at her own effrontery.

I smile back. 'Now I'm married to her.'

'And sooner or later you'll take a cab ...' Seeing my puzzled expression, she recites: ' "A woman is like an umbrella ... sooner or later you take a cab." That is, if you haven't already found one.' A pause. 'I'm indiscreet, aren't I. But you tell me so little.'

We have reached the path; I help her over the stile. Footsteps, behind us. Mathilde runs up, holding wildflowers, and stands gazing at us. Minna smiles.

'Oh, they're lovely ...'

Are they for us? But for which of us? Mathilde holds them against her chest, as though uncertain herself. I nod at the little shrine beside the stile, with its peeling Madonna.

'Put them there, with the rest. Then everyone can enjoy them.'

The child obeys, placing the flowers in a small heap at the statue's feet, and runs off without a backward glance.

'They were for you,' Minna teases. We walk on; she is still studying me. 'Sigi ... d'you want your daughter to honour the Madonna?'

'*I* did, as a child.' It catches her unawares. 'It's true ... my nurse was a Catholic. When my parents were away she used to smuggle me off to church in Neu Titschein – I can still see her squat, ugly bulk before the candles.' Minna amused. 'Yes, she taught me all about her Catholic heaven, and above all about her Catholic hell. And a few other things besides, she taught me.'

'Oh?'

How quick she is. I nod.

'Until she was dismissed – for stealing. That's something I've only recently discovered: Mamma ... filled in the details. Teresa was her name.' Deathbed images, recurring; I shut them out. 'I've been remembering more and more about my childhood.'

'Including these ... other things the woman taught you.'

Smiling, 'She filled me full of ambition, told me I'd become a great man – and on the other hand ... made me feel very clumsy. In a different department.'

'And you remember all this?'

'It's coming back. I'm beginning to believe that dreams consist of ... things we've seen in infancy – while fantasies derive from things we've heard. And neurotic behaviour from the kind of sexual assault that I'm ... increasingly concerned with.' Quickly, 'Of course, that could all be nonsense. D'you think?'

My serious expression forces a laugh.

'I?'

'I should like your sincere opinion.'

She stops, and eyes me closely, almost as though I'd made some unprovoked advance.

'My sincere opinion isn't worth a damn.' Gazing back down the path, 'Come – we've lost the others –'

We start slowly back. I feel suddenly at a loss.

'You know ... what you were saying just now, about Martha – I want you to understand: it's very important for me to have someone ... who can bring me back to mundane things, very important. She's the centre of my life.'

Minna nods. 'She says she's going to Hamburg shortly ... for a week or two. Why? I mean, why now – before your father's funeral. It seems a little strange to me.'

'It isn't strange at all: your mother isn't well, they haven't seen each other for a long time ...' Her eyes on me; I know this won't do. 'Besides, I'm not very easy to comfort at this moment. I have no use for it.'

She is silent. I've failed to make things clear to her.

'You should also understand that ... certain aspects of my marriage have been fully amortized.'

'Amortized?' She grimaces at me. 'What a word to use ...'

'It's the word that fits: amortized. Obligations paid, on both sides. To our mutual satisfaction. It's perfectly possible to make one's peace with sexuality.' I hesitate. 'As I'm sure you'd agree.'

Minna gazes at me, expressionless, as Liesl and the children clamber over the stile, coming towards us.

The fields return, in dreams. The woods a little denser, the grass coarser. With nephew John, I stalk his sister: we ambush her on the crest of the hill, crawling up it like cats hunting their prey, to fling ourselves on little Pauline and wrestle her to the ground, stealing her flowers.

The shadow looming over us is stern Teresa. Hugging Pauline to her apron. Under the cloth, in her basket, a loaf of black bread and a knife. She cuts thick slices, comforts Pauline with the first slice then holds our slices out before us, one in each hand, till we crawl to her, penitent.

A bite each from the bread still held in her hands like communion wafers.

Teresa sings softly as she pours water into the wooden bath, steam rising. Gaslight in the sweating hut. As I step forward, hands on the bath's rim, to watch her add the salts, I see the bathwater, a dark forbidding red.

The salts glisten in the red water, sinking to the bottom: coins. Teresa lifts me up and lowers me towards the water.

The coffin slides to rest in the grave, then lurches, bobbing faintly, in the rain-filled trench. It floats, as though weightless.

I am drawn down the corridor, towards the sound. Stop at the door, listen. As I look in, I see Minna beside one of the children's beds. She finishes the lullaby and glances up at me, one finger to her lips.

'Where did you learn that song?' I keep my voice down, as I follow her back along the corridor. She shrugs. 'It's Moravian.'

'Is it?' Minna pauses, by the sitting-room door. Do we enter? 'While I was working in Bruenn, then, possibly ...'

A moment, then she goes into the room, switching on the lights. The curtains are already drawn. I follow, watching her.

'Have you finished work?' When she turns to me I realize I haven't answered. A silence. 'You don't mind me singing to them?'

'Mind? I hope you'll stay as long as you want. I speak for Martha and the children. You know that.'

She walks to the cabinet, raises a decanter in invitation.

I nod, coming to join her.

'Especially the children. All the best people had two mothers ... a no less loved and influential foster mother, at any rate.' She pours, ignoring this. 'Leonardo, for instance. Oedipus.' I have reached her. 'Myself, of course.'

She glances down, puzzled to see my hand on her wrist. When I do not remove it, her smile turns interrogative. But there is no coyness there.

'What are you doing?'

I remove my hand. 'You know the story of the bereaved husband discovered in the arms of the housemaid, on the day of his wife's funeral – "Emil! How could you!" – and he answers ... "Do I know what I do in my grief?"'

Minna smiles curtly, takes her drink towards a chair. Why did I have to say 'the housemaid'? Not a happy choice. She studies me as I fetch my drink.

Level, 'Do you feel grief?'

'No. Not even today. Nothing.' The coffin, bobbing. 'For so long I've felt only – impatience ... and contempt. Contempt for one's father ...' How can she understand? 'No grief; but I still feel torn up by the roots. It's a matter of ... the way my whole life has been going, not just the loss of Papa. As if a void was forming around me – professional *and* personal. There's been no-one I can talk to, except you, and Fliess.'

Her gaze invites me no further; I sit, opposite her. We sit in silence. Must I obey the old conventions, make nostalgic speeches?

'My best memories of him are when I was a child ... taking me to the woods, up into the mountains. It was a good time, and yet ... my childhood was peculiar in ways that only now – begin to fall into place. My father was old enough to be my grandfather; he had sons my mother's age; they had children my age. Imagine what that means. She could have been my sister.'

'Your mother could?'

'She was the same age as my step-brothers. And my playmates were my niece and nephew, the same age as me. A topsy-turvy world.'

Yes: no wonder I felt I was the centre of it, the gravitational force, among all those misplaced labels, mother, father, brothers ... nephew, niece – all too young, or too old, for their status in my life. I was holding them in orbit.

I can see Minna thawing slightly now, smiling. 'It's curious – I've always thought you were a little afraid of your mother.'

'Possibly. Is she so frightening? What makes you say that?'

'Your expression, when we go to lunch on Sundays.' Slyly, 'And your stomach-aches, before we go ...'

'That's because I know her cooking.'

'And because you know that she's waiting to hear – news ... of fresh glories. All the things your nursemaid promised –'

I shrug. 'Like any other son. Unless he's a professor he's a failure.'

'You admit that much.'

'And when I'm a professor, you'll see: she'll still cook badly.' Then, changing tone, 'I might as well not bother ...'

But she turns back to her drink, unmoved.

'What does it take, to become a professor?'

'Ah ... to become a professor – you must be popular. And sound! And if the Faculty votes for you, then the Minister submits their application for the Imperial signature and then – unless you have the misfortune to be a Jew with obscene ideas ... he signs. And you get rich.'

Laughing, 'And does that matter to you?'

'No, not the money.' After a moment, 'D'you know why money doesn't make us happy? It's because we never wished for it in childhood.' I pause. 'Simple, isn't it?' If I could only make her understand – 'All our deepest desires, the ones that could afford us happiness ... derive from infancy.'

She breaks my gaze, understanding only too well. She knew: as she looked up at me in the children's bedroom, from Teresa's place, beside my children.

'If not the money, then ... the fame, at least. You wanted that, in childhood.'

'I was taught to. Yes ... I shall apply for the professorship. And go on applying.' I can see: it's what she wants to hear. Smiling, 'If my constitution can stand it. Like the old Jew on the way to Karlsbad ... who gets thrown off at every station because he hasn't got a ticket, and they say "Where are you going?" "To Karlsbad ... if my constitution can stand it ..." You *do* realize: baptism is the ticket. If I were to join the pitiful crew rushing to the cross – even Mahler's doing it now, for the directorship of the Opera ...' Breaking off, 'I'd rather starve. Than crawl to Rome.'

Minna shrugs.

'Oh, I don't know ... you've got a zest for martyrdom, it seems to me: that's one qualification –'

'To be a Christian? You think? To be Christ, certainly. But that's quite different.'

No; she too wants the professor in the family. Well, she must pay. Carefully now:

'I do fear poverty. From childhood. Like the wild horses of the pampas – I remember reading about them when I was a boy – once they've felt the lassoo around their necks, they retain a certain nervousness, for life. I really thought – this ... most recent development ... the seduction theory ... would make my name. Far from it. Even the patients are nervous of it. And self-analysis is hardly profitable ...' Rising to re-fill our glasses, 'I have a banker, a distinguished neurotic ... who's fled from me, just as he was about to re-enact the crucial scenes – that's what makes it so difficult at the moment: trying to complete a map of childhood, with the help of grudging adults. If I could make you understand – you could help me.'

I pause.

'No-one's explored it, I have no authorities to guide me through this jungle, these ... primaeval stages in which all kinds of sexual zones, which are later prohibited, hold sway: the mouth and throat; the anus. In time we learn to "turn up our noses" at certain things, faeces for instance. We feel shame and disgust – our sense of smell is recruited to a new, moral universe.'

Minna nods. Unperturbed.

'But at what precise stage? What I'm certain of is that somewhere in this journey through our sexual prehistory, what overwhelms the ego and creates a psychosis, rather than a mere neurosis ... is sexual abuse by adults, before our psychic and moral apparatus is complete. Unfortunately, my patients' memories are rarely exact when it comes to the stages of infancy. My own are just as hard to date. However ...' glancing at her, 'if it were possible to investigate children's own reactions, at different ages ...'

'How could you do that?'

'Quite simply. It would involve testing their responses – without alarming them.' A moment. 'Of course, when I spoke to Marty about ... using our children, she was appalled. I thought perhaps – you might feel differently.'

Staring at me, 'If I understand – you mean ... present them with –'

'With faeces, say, at a particular age – yes – or rather, simply observe –'

'No.' Hard. 'Not while I'm here.'

She takes her drink, sits for a long moment without looking at me. At last she glances up at me, amused, her old self. I shrug.

'Then I shall have to go on ... trying to remember, myself. Using what inspiration I have to hand.' The furrowed brow and pointed stare force her to smile; I turn to the sofa and stretch out full length. 'Sing me the song. The lullaby.'

Minna shakes her head, still smiling. She knows.

I press my glass against my forehead, stare upwards.

'You can't imagine how ugly Teresa was! Like a fairy-tale witch.' A comfortable silence now. 'D'you know ... I've found the explanation as to why witches "fly": can you guess? Their broomstick is the great Lord Penis ...'

Her laughter rings out.

... Of course, you can still see witches' covens, their secret gatherings, their dances, any day of the year: on the streets where children play ...

Before me, instruments of mediaeval torture, each more horrible than the one before. Above them, on the walls, illustrations of their function.

... And à propos my would-be 'experiments', the ones you shrink from – did you know that the gold which the Devil gave his victims, according to mediaeval confessions, regularly turned into faeces?

I move on to the next exhibit. That Nuremberg, of all places, centre of ancient, homely crafts, should contain this treasure-house of morbid artifacts. Even the most innocent of men, faced with these racks and spikes and thumbscrews, would feel they were designed for him; justly, for him. What was it the churchmen decreed, to make Galileo recant? 'Only show him the instruments ...'

... If only I could work out why the Devil's semen is always described as 'cold' ...

Impatient footsteps, at my back, bring me to myself. Realizing it is Minna I have been addressing, in my head. I call out, beckoning –

'Look at this repulsive device!'

Fliess answers dully, his voice swallowed by the tall, echoing chamber.

I point up to the illustration. 'They're searching with needles – you see – here – for diabolical stigmata. The inquisitors. Probing, searching ... while the victims pour out their gruesome stories. Both parties re-enacting their earliest youth; both possessed.' I turn. 'In fact, the very theory of possession resembles the splitting of consciousness –' Gazing round, 'Wilhelm?'

He is nowhere to be seen.

We sit outdoors, at the café, our cups of coffee growing cold. Too warm, the weather. Whereas we ourselves –

'Tell me: does Martha ever complain, when you ... come away to these "congresses" of ours?'

'Not in the slightest.' No; but now it comes ... 'Why? Does Ida mind?'

He smiles.

'Yes. A little.' Silence falls. 'I wouldn't have suggested a meeting in Nuremberg if I'd known we were going to spend half the time staring at engines of human destruction.'

I say nothing.

Fliess studies me: 'You look tired. Why don't you take a holiday – away from the family ... go to Italy ... I spent the most enchanting time there, when I was convalescing –'

'I don't want to go to Italy.'

'Very well.'

He changes tack.

'Did I tell you about a patient of mine, a woman, who persistently hallucinates enormous snakes ...' A pause. 'The meaning requires no explanation, obviously, but – I thought that through her case my idea of bisexuality might shed some light on the whole question of repression –'

'Yes. Indeed.'

'I've been meaning to write to you about it.' Undeterred, 'And also – send you some novels by C. F. Meyer. Do you know him? The bisexual theme is very strong in his work ... also incest, between brother and sister ...'

'Oh?' I turn now; is the man psychic?

'Meyer.' He seizes on my attention. 'The novelist.' A moment. 'I would say he owes more than a little to Nietzsche – the idea that certain individuals can transcend taboo ... I understand it derives from experiences in his own life. And it's made me sensitive to certain resonances in my own.' Confidingly, 'After my sister's death I simply blotted out all my childhood emotions towards her – until Ida came along ... it was like a reincarnation. Perhaps you guessed. I never felt able to tell you ...'

I nod, ashamed of the way I've been treating him.

Fliess grins. 'He too makes too much of the Italian landscape ... in particular Lago Maggiore –'

'Wilhelm, I've told you: I don't want to go to Italy. I want to stay here; and suffer. And God willing, solve the problem of repression.'

He meets my smile.

'By personal suffering?'

'If needs be. But the last thing I want is to be surrounded by *more* symbols of repression – all those churches ... those dreadful saints and martyrs glorying in their pain or carried up to heaven for denying their simplest instincts: to love and war and wallow in what life offers us. God knows it's brief enough.' Have I said too much? 'That's all holiness is ... saintliness ... the residue of sacrifice! I refuse to call it beautiful.'

'You're talking about mere piety ... Italian *art* is one of the glories of mankind –'

'And what does it amount to – those upraised suffering eyes beneath their haloes ...' I strike the pose. 'I'll tell you: the disguised blood-lust of persecution – persecution of any other race or creed that refuses to join them on their stations of the cross. The cross! It leads inexorably to the rack ... those instruments we were looking at ...'

He gazes at me, pityingly.

'You don't suppose that for once you could ... surrender to the transcendent beauty of the images? Just that. Go to Rome – to Orvieto –'

Fliess –

He ignores my warning look. 'And instead of analysing it ...'

I gaze through him, like a man who wakes to find he's married an idiot. Silence returns.

'Sigi ... I realize things are going slowly for you at the moment – in the field of theory. But if patients are relatively few just now, then surely –'

'My theory is fine. My patients are fine.' I reach for my coffee. 'I'm perfectly all right.'

He sits, abashed. Cool coffee suits me very well.

There are patients who are such intolerable bores, you could kick them down the stairs yourself.

... Doctor, it occurred to me since our last meeting – you remember the business with my childhood dream ... about the black fellow I was chasing through a strange landscape ... and couldn't catch – it came up when we were discussing how my mother had been unable to make up her mind about her second marriage, and how I myself had difficulty with ... important decisions – well – I think I understand the connection now. The black man was perhaps ... a 'Kaffir' ... and as soon as this occurred to me I saw that 'Kaffir' was really '*Que faire?*' *Que faire,* you see? Meaning – 'What shall I do?'

Take strychnine.

... Am I making progress with your methods, Doctor? '*Que faire*' ... you see, I briefly had a French nursemaid; my first love, so to speak –

Who no doubt seduced you.

... Seduced me – physically, you mean? Physically, Herr Doctor?

And patients who know everything; patients too willing. All too willing.

... I began to feel jealous – when I saw the way he treated my brothers. Physically, I mean. The way he sat them on his knee, caressed them ...

Willing, educated ladies.

... whereas with me he was always cautious and reserved. It was left to me ... to make the advances. Of course, I didn't know *why* I was doing it, much less that it was wrong ... and for years I've succeeded in – "repressing" the memory. It's only here, with you, that I can talk about it – without feeling guilty. *Tell* me ... am I making progress?

The door opens. Minna, coming towards me, tray in hand. She places the tray on the desk, stands for a moment.

'Marty's gone to bed.'

I nod.

After a time, she takes her cup, and is halfway to the door before I realize, and speak.

'I've made a serious mistake. No ... more than that. I've made a fool of myself.'

She has stopped.

'I don't believe in my seduction theory.'

I watch her move slowly to the couch and sit, obedient.

'The patients do. They feed on it. They're manufacturing stories for me. Like the devil-worshippers they are.'

She holds my gaze, 'All of them?'

'I don't know. No, of course not. But if I can't tell truth from fiction –'

Her gaze: mocking? Or what? Why doesn't she speak?

'Perhaps I'm taken in by everybody –' Everybody. 'Everyone I meet.'

'It's possible. For a psychologist you're a surprisingly poor judge of people.'

Ah: yes. I burst out laughing, the burden lifted. 'Yes. A poor judge of people. Yes: quite right. No doubt that's why I make it my profession – just as poets are often those who find it hardest to express themselves. I'm well aware I don't – hear ... others. So I have to listen twice as hard. And I may miss the obvious, but I hear things the rest of you have missed.'

She smiles at this mercurial vanity; but I could hug her.

Instead, 'You don't seem convinced ...'

'It's rather a convenient explanation, that's all. You wouldn't go to a concert by tone-deaf musicians, all trying especially hard –'

'*I* would.' Gleeful. She laughs, against herself. A long pause. 'I've decided: I'm going away for a month.' Her reaction is well under control. 'To Italy.'

'With Marty?'

'Certainly not. With Alexander. Marty doesn't really enjoy sight-seeing – at my pace. And the great thing about Alexander is that ... as a railway employee – he's good at time-tables.'

Her silence is gratifying; a long silence. I search for words.

'Thank you for being brisk with me. I mean, about my work. Besides ... it's nonsense, the seduction theory's perfectly good. I'm just so tired I can't even trust my own ideas.'

Minna nods. Another pause.

I lean across the desk, 'Have you read this? It's a novel by Meyer.'

'Which one?' She comes slowly towards me, sees the title. 'Yes. I know it.'

Of course – I should have realized; the well-read governess. As she takes the book, a smile. She knows it – and its incestuous theme –

'Ah. Do you? It's ... remarkable. A fascinating subject.'

She eyes me, and replaces the book on the desk. Mock solemn, 'And where are you going, in Italy? Lago Maggiore?'

'No – no ... to Rome, I suppose. I haven't decided yet. But – à propos Rome – I *have* applied for the professorship.'

She nods, standing close to me now. In open invitation, surely. My equanimity returns.

'And in Rome I shall be surrounded by Madonnas. I shall tell myself that, after all, she did belong to our race. A Jewish virgin.' I glance at Minna. 'Like you.'

She smiles, standing over me.

'"In the bottom right-hand corner of the Crucifixion fresco, dressed respectively –"' Alexander turns the page, '"– in red and gold against a gesso ground, we can see standing among the crowd Signorelli himself ..."'

He glances at me to make sure I am paying attention. I turn my eyes to the fresco, along with the knot of tourists who seem to be using my brother as an unpaid guide to Orvieto's cathedral.

'"... next to Fra Angelico Beato da – Fies – "' He stumbles on the word.

'Fiesole,' I supply. The gigantic fresco fills me with tedium. Stiff, unconvincing figures, with identical faces. Angelico da Fliessole, next to the Blessed Sigmundelli, wizened observers, gesturing foolishly. Still, better than the bloated flesh of the Baroque, like massed choirs of acromegalics.

'"Fiesole,"' Alexander resumes, '"his predecessor whose work on the frescoes was interrupted by his death."' Gazing round his tourist audience, humorous, 'Well, that *would* interrupt his work.'

We move on, in eager Alexander's wake.

'"In the next fresco, the Anti-Christ can be seen, performing his false miracles ..."'

No question as to who the Anti-Christ is. Fra Angelico – or perhaps Signorelli – has painted me erect with one hand pressed to the forehead of a sick woman. The False Healer. Behind us, in colours fading fast, rats invade the temple; and the horsemen of the apocalypse announce the coming of the Last Judgment.

A knocking at the door. At last, 'It's me ...'

'Come in.'

Alexander enters. Trim, smiling, flushed with cultural endeavour. His face falls as he gazes at my face and sweat-stained shirt; at post-cards, maps and letters from home strewn beneath me on the rumpled bed. Am I sitting on Michelangelo? So sorry. He turns, walks to the shuttered window.

'My God it's hot in here –'

'Leave them shut.'

He turns to look at me, bewildered.

I murmur, 'I'm sick of the sound of bells.'

'It must be for vespers – they'll soon stop –'

'They *never* stop. Reminding the faithful that every instant ... is a guilty instant, that the end is near. That God's church owns them body and soul as it owns the streets and buildings ... even the hours of the day!'

He stands silent for a time, cowed.

'You must learn to put up with it, Sigi. It'll be worse in Rome.'

'We're not going to Rome. Not tonight.'

Alexander stares.

'Why not?' A moment. 'We've booked the rooms –'

'What kind of a Jew are you?' The little room shakes at my shout. 'I know why you want to go to Rome! To visit the whores! Or did you want to attend "vespers", in Rome?'

'What's the *matter* with you? *You* wanted to go to Rome –'

'Another time. As our great predecessor might have said ...'

Exasperated, '*What* predecessor?'

'How slow you are! Our Jewish predecessor. Hannibal!'

'Hannibal was a *Jew*?'

'Of course! He was a Semite!'

I can see it in his eyes: my brother's mad, the man's demented. I shrug, 'According to one theory.'

He turns away, shaking his head; while I pick up one discarded letter. Turn it over in my hands. Must I explain: to *him*?

'When Papa was dying ... all he could talk about was Freiberg. You remember? The beauty of it – the woods, the mountains. Even the mud.' I pause. 'And all I could think of was the day some good Christian knocked his cap off in the street – we were walking along, the man spat at him, pushed him and sent his cap flying, into the mud. D'you know what he did? I can still see it. He cringed. Stepped down, fetched the cap, wiped it ... and came back to me. A cringing Jew.'

I climb off the bed and come to Alexander, with the letter.

'There ...'

Head for the door. As I turn back in the doorway, he is still gazing at me, with the letter in one hand.

'Read it. They've turned down my professorship.'

Anger, boredom, fear. A witches' brew, begetting visions. I patrol the streets: each one seems to lead back to the Cathedral, with its towering mosaics. A different kind of gaudiness, Byzantine; less oppressive. Around the base, carved figures of the damned entwine. '*Sovegna vos* ...'

Cavete, felices: beware, ye happy. *Sperate, miseri* ... look up, and live in hope, ye miserable!

I find myself standing once more before the false Messiah. Peering closely: not rats but locusts, devouring the temple beyond. While the Anti-Christ cries doomsday on the unbeliever, in my own, mocking tones.

Enough!

... Seeing them alone, at night ... I had no choice but to confess their splendour ...

I turn to the true cross, the crucifixion peopled with familiar faces. I stare.

... but my dear Wilhelm, there was nothing transcendental about these images! Nothing pure, or abstract. Nothing!

Fliess and I behold the miracle, the fruit of suffering.

... I saw at last what had been hidden from me for so long. The scales fell from my eyes: when I turned in shame from my own image as the false Messiah, to the crucifixion and the grieving women ...

The sorrowing mother; and Mary Magdalen. Martha and Minna –

... the effigies that had pursued me since my arrival here began to speak!

Dizzy, I turn from the frescoes – and the images that crowd the Cathedral, in paint, plaster, and stone, multiply before my eyes.

... Madonna and Child: Maria Lactans, baring the breast at which human desire and hunger meet!

Mother and child. Virgin and child. Amalie; Teresa; Minna –

... Pagan images, Wilhelm! Not Christian icons – pagan images, surviving like a brazen code. Mother-lust: the universal longing for the mother: the universal fantasy!

Voices thunder. The images declare my life, my passion, recorded everywhere –

... Had no-one ever wondered why the infant Jesus is depicted not as a baby but as a tiny man, a supernatural man-child gazing up at the Virgin with adult eyes? Why had it taken me so long to understand? It is the child who lusts, like pagan Oedipus, for the sublime erotic union! Not the parent who abuses the innocent child ...

Myself the Christ-child now, the true Christ, not the false Messiah. Glutted at the breast, the source of wisdom and delight.

... the lusting infant at the breast – was I myself, the pagan anti-Christ in every child, mocking the pious gaze of civilized humanity!

Teresa lowers me towards the bath, into baptismal blood. Her face is Minna's face. Her voice the thunderous choir.

... When I woke up ... it must have been at Breslau, in the middle of the night ... I could see the gaslights, on the station – I remembered the journey when we left Freiberg for good. I was barely four years old ...

The jolt awakes me, as the train comes to a halt, jarring open the door to the adjoining compartment. I rise from the narrow bed, to close it.

... It was the first time I'd seen such lamps, and with old Teresa's stories still vivid in my mind – they made me think then of burning souls, in hell ...

Before I can shut the door, I glimpse a figure on the bed beyond. Seated, naked, with an infant suckling at her breast.

... It was on that journey, in fact, that I first saw my mother naked ...

'And as I now realize, of course ... desired her.'

Martha and Minna sit before me, silent, over afternoon tea. But not even their evident discomfort – to be precise, Martha discomforted; Minna embarrassed for her – nor the dreary musty smell of the Berggasse can dispel my mood. The visions of Orvieto remain with me, inspiring me. And the hallucination on my northward journey, hurrying to confide in Fliess. Or was it a dream ... the train halting

'She was occupied with little Julius. My brother. Poor child – how I hated him! His death sowed the first seeds of guilt in me ...' I smile at the women, defying them. 'Which have been flowering gloriously, in recent months.'

Neither stirs.

'By the time I reached Berlin I was in a state of high excitement, as you can imagine – even confusing Fliess with little Julius, my childhood rival. I gave him short shrift, I'm afraid. But he'll recover.'

Three figurines, trophies from Tuscany, stand funerary witness on a small table beside me.

'I wish you could have both been with me there, in Italy. Orvieto was my ... road to Damascus! I feel like the founder of a new religion ...'

I adjust the figurines: father, mother, and child.

'They're Etruscan. Grave gifts – a family portrait, in terracotta. D'you like them?'

'They're beautiful ...' Minna's voice breaks the silence. Marty nods; I catch her eye.

'And relatively inexpensive.'

She smiles, and gets to her feet.

'My dear, forgive me ... it's bath-time –'

'Marty ...' Apologetic Marty. 'Don't go, I've got more to tell you.'

She hesitates, and Minna rises to go in her place. A moment, then Marty shakes her head, one hand on Minna's arm. They sit, together. I am permitted to continue.

'Best of all ... I've come to understand all the distressing feelings towards my father that – burst on me when he died. With all the force of the unthinkable. And they were only a mask ... for a greater, long-lost rivalry: for possession of my mother.' Smiling at them both, 'I'm already beginning to like him again.'

Minna's gaze is discreet. It doesn't fool me.

'You see – no wonder Oedipus Tyrannos is the greatest of all dramas of destiny: every member of the audience was once an Oedipus! And it's still there, all around the Mediterranean, in every house and every street where the Queen of Heaven is depicted – Regina Mater, nursing her son! Can you imagine how I felt, in Italy for the first time, bracing myself against the banality of the image … shielding my eyes. With good reason. There, painted all over Italy, was the most primitive, the most licentious of heathen images … not only permitted but sanctified by the Church and venerated by the faithful! So obvious you could miss it altogether, like all the best hiding places. Like the churches themselves built on pagan sites, Minna-sopra-Maria – ' quickly '– that is … *Minerva*-sopra-Maria …' I could laugh out loud at the slip; but I see their faces. 'It's a church in Rome …'

'Oh …' Mock disappointment. Minna comes in sweetly, 'I thought they'd finally dedicated a shrine to me.'

'Naturally … I was confusing you with the goddess of wisdom.'

This doesn't entirely help. A moment, then Martha's attention is drawn to the door, where Liesl looks in.

Martha rises, 'I'm coming.'

Her eyes linger on me. As gently as I can:

'Does it distress you – what I've been saying?'

She shakes her head. 'It's all right for you. As a mother, your ideas make me feel … aghast.'

'There's nothing you can do about it, Marty. Except feel properly aghast.'

The door shuts behind her, and we sit in silence, as remote as the figurines. Minna avoids my eyes, and starts to load the tea-tray with empty plates. More grieving, sorrowing sisterhood.

I come to her, select a biscuit, and munch it while she adds the plate to the rest. Ready now to take the tray out.

Instead she looks up, releasing her anger. Then sits, at last, watching me. I stroll back to the chair.

'D'you know what Fliess said … when I told him all about it? "Don't let the artist in you overwhelm the scientist …" I didn't expect that from *him*.' Turning on her, my patience snapping, '*You* understand, don't you. We've found the key – the *matrix* – older than Athens, old as humanity itself – the single destiny that still directs our passions, despite all the sentimental fables of the pulpit and the schoolroom. It's my supreme achievement: a discovery fit to rank beside electricity, beside the wheel – nothing less!'

126

Still no response; she looks disgusted at my vanity. As if the vanity mattered.

'Aren't I to be allowed my moment of triumph?'

Here, if nowhere else. Minna hesitates.

'From what you've said ... it seems to me you've turned all your work on its head. Now it's the children who are the seducers ...'

'In their imaginations – yes. In a passion play we all try to forget: but it surfaces again in every one of our adult attachments. The mirror of our childhood drama.'

'How can you know, if we've forgotten?'

'Because I've lived through it again, been a child again, these last few weeks – in dreams. In waking dreams, too. Seeing childhood rivals in my dearest friends. Renewing childhood loves.'

A moment, before she breaks my gaze. 'How can you talk about your feelings that way – as if this were another of your cases ...'

So; she knows. And her anger releases me. Lightly now, 'It's my only case. And I've been astonished to find how carefully one hides the really intimate things – from oneself as much as from others. It comes to the same thing: since we're strangers to our instinctual selves. As an animal among others ... sharing natural desires, things we've learnt to call perversion. Incest, sodomy, murder. No wonder we're so angry with ourselves.'

She smiles, guarded.

'And are you going to tell the world they're natural?'

'Yes.' I pause. 'But not that they should necessarily ... act on them.'

No, you can pay civilization's price. Earn its bitter rewards. Be satisfied.

'On the other hand, suppose I were to argue that in the absence of God ... revealed as a pitiful fantasy – there was nothing higher than enjoyment?' I wait her out. 'Shockingly immoral? More so than ... virtuous renunciation? I've seen the rewards of virtue: they terminate in my consulting room.'

Minna still silent.

'The Tarquins prophesied that he would conquer Rome, who first ... should kiss ... the mother.'

I give her my best smile.

'Metaphorically speaking. Of course.'

Alois Pick looks up from his cards. There's always one who doesn't really want to play. Tonight it's Pick. He grins.

'I had a dream last night. I was in Prague – not that it looked like Prague, but that was where I knew I was –'

Koenigstein has closed his eyes, in despair.

'– and I was walking with Count Thun, of all people. He had some fascinating gossip to impart . . . about Czech politics . . . I only wish I could remember what it was!'

'*Please* . . .' Koenigstein opens his eyes, 'tell us later, about your dreams. Not while you're playing cards.'

'Especially not while playing cards with Freud.' Oscar Rie meets my eyes, always happy to score off me.

'That doesn't usually stop *you*' comes Pick. 'Sigmund's the one who never lets us eavesdrop on his dreams.'

We play. Rie takes the trick.

'Very well. The other day I dreamt I was climbing the stairs in a state of undress –'

Laughter interrupts me.

'Really?'

'That's quite enough . . .'

The hand comes to an end, the silent reckoning begins.

Climbing the stairs . . . to come face to face with stern Teresa. A mocking stare. I look down at myself, then back at her. The mocking eyes repeat: my clumsy little blackamoor . . .

Pick breaks in:

'*I* know what Count Thun was telling me! It wasn't about Czech politics – it was about Turkish politics –'

'Oh do shut up, Alois!'

They're ganging up on Pick again; it'll be me next. 'No . . . I find it interesting.' I glance at Pick. 'I have an hour free on Wednesday . . .'

Koenigstein chortles; Pick deals, silent. Oscar studies me, as the cards go round.

'Sigi . . . is it true that a patient of yours – recently put an end to herself? The nonsense people talk . . . it's said you were too busy to see her.'

The others examine their cards.

'Is that what you've heard?'

'I heard she hanged herself.'

His gaze, all innocence; eager to scotch the rumour.

'*Not* for the reason you mentioned. D'you really think I'd refuse to see a patient? You know me better than that.'

'I *said* it was nonsense –'

'The poor girl was demented.' Beyond help; and beyond your vicious gossip now. 'Who told you all this?'

Pick's blather rescues us from the icy silence.

'People everywhere ... they're all committing suicide – at least that's my impression. It's turning into an epidemic. Last week in our apartment, a young chap ...' he hesitates, 'cut off his member. Bled to death. Apparently the neighbours heard him shouting, "Nature! Nature!"'

Koenigstein, revolted, '*Please* ...'

'It's an epidemic ...'

Koenigstein catches his eye at last.

'It's your bid.'

Pick obeys; but the cards are a blur to him. 'You know ... when I was in Turkey, I was often struck by their extraordinary attitude to death. The Turks. They seem almost ... completely indifferent to it. After a certain age, that is.' Seeing Rie's expression, 'No, it's true. Once their active love-life is over ... as far as the Turk is concerned, his days are numbered.'

Wise Turks. We bid in turn, judicious, non-committal Viennese. Koenigstein glances at Rie.

'A propos numbers ... have you read the reviews of Fliess' book?'

'The one I saw described it as a new Kabbala ... I suspect *his* days are numbered.'

They wait for me to rise to it. Polite, 'Have either of you read the book?'

'I've dipped into it,' Rie smiles. 'You'd have to be a mathematician –'

'Or a necromancer – all that numerology! Provided you make love every twenty-three days –'

'More often, if you're left-handed ...'

I bide my time.

'All in all, it only lacks a dedication from the "Faust": "A distant land . . . awaits me in this secret book, from Nostradamus' very hand! Now shall I read the starry night –" '

'You've missed out a line, Oscar.' He stares at me. ' "Nor for a better guide I look . . ." No wonder, since a better guide is what *you* lack.'

Caustic, 'A significant omission, Sigi.'

He glances at Koenigstein, grinning.

Turning back to my cards, 'And it's "starry pole", not "starry night". I wonder why you got it wrong. Could it be that as an unremarkable family doctor of Polish extraction – as a Pole whose starry fortunes pale into insignificance beside the gifts of Wilhelm Fliess –'

'Oh come, Sigi –'

Rounding on him, 'Or are you trying to draw our attention to some other difficulty you're experiencing – with your own "pole"?'

From the silence that follows, I wonder whether I haven't hit the mark. Once again I've used a blunderbuss where a pea-shooter would have done the trick. Fliess' book is half-baked; and I know it.

'Really . . .' Pick tries to conciliate, 'is there nothing you won't twist into some scurrilous meaning . . . nothing perfectly innocent?'

He shrugs, seeing my expression.

I bring out a cigar. Mildly, 'No no . . . I often ask myself the selfsame thing.'

They eye me.

'And the answer is: yes. Sometimes –'

'Even Homer nods,' Koenigstein murmurs.

'– on certain occasions . . .' ignoring him, 'a cigar . . . is only a cigar.'

I smile at them, serene.

She sits on the floor in the children's bedroom, surrounded by toys; making a pile of the ones our children have outgrown, to send to the hospital. No point in keeping them now.

'Marty . . . I wish you'd come with me.'

'You know I can't.'

I meet her glance.

'You can. We'll go as slowly as you like.' Teasing, 'No more than two museums a day.' A pause. 'And one cathedral.'

Marty smiles, unyielding.

'Alexander swears he won't go anywhere with me again – unless I sign a document, promising to catch the appointed trains ... we make appalling travelling companions, two berserk wills in head-on collision ...'

She has turned back to the toys.

I hesitate. 'You can understand why I want to go back, before the summer's over and patients start returning – God willing –'

'Of course ...'

She glances at me.

'Go then.'

Busying herself with the toys. I nod.

'I thought perhaps ... since Minna's never been to Italy ... I haven't spoken to her yet – but if you can spare her –'

After a time, 'By all means.' Silence. 'Ask her.'

I wait for her to meet my gaze.

Minna turning to me. The piazza beyond is almost empty, the buildings in shadow. The days are drawing in. No mockery in Minna's gaze. She sips her drink and turns back to the view, replete.

Cavete, felices. Sperate, miseri!

FIVE

Voices in the corridor, approaching. Shuffling feet.

I close the book in my lap. They've dressed me in my Sunday best, for Minna's birthday.

Anna helps her into the room: a mumbling old woman. Marty looks young beside her. Minna stops for a moment, searching for something with her failing eyes. Do I too look like this, like an old tortoise peering from its shell? She turns to Anna.

'Where's our Sigi?'

A moment, then Marty answers quietly, 'He's here.'

Marty's eyes on me, pleading. I can only stare.

'Papa's here.' Anna escorts Minna towards the table, laden with expensive cakes. And presents. 'Come.'

'He can't come up so I must go down.' She pats Anna's hand. 'She's a good girl . . .' and with a sudden chuckle, 'but we'll never get up those stairs again.'

'Of course we will.'

Minna stops, in the middle of the room.

'Where must I sit?'

'This way – it's only a few steps.'

I feel Marty beside me, she takes the book and helps me up. Under her breath, 'She's not so good today.'

I take back the book from her and place it on the table, before some officious person can bury it in the bookshelves where I can't find it; it happens all the time. We sit.

I see Minna staring at the table, overwhelmed. She's going to cry, I know it.

Bewildered, 'Linzertorte?'

'And Gugelhupf.'

Anna pushes the cakes towards her.

'Gugelhupf . . .'

'Aunt Minna –' Placing a present under her fingers. 'Happy birthday.'

Minna gazes round us; she can see me, behind those blind old eyes. Hands working at the ribbon on the present. Then she pushes it back to Anna.

'You do it, I can't any more.' And with a welcome flash of wickedness, 'Sometimes I think I'll see better when I'm dead.'

A scolding sound from Marty. She reaches for a plate, begins to slice.

'Birthdays.' Minna falters. Now the tears come. 'It's to laugh.' Anna takes her hand, but she shakes her head, controlling herself. 'It's my fault, I shouldn't have come down . . .'

Marty rises quickly, goes to put her arms around Minna. Anna too. Only the Christ descended from the cross is missing. And I still cannot speak. None of them look at me. I can feel the old rage rise to choke me.

Yes! Everyone! We hate them, fear them, love them – out of the same source. Wanting to possess them, afraid of losing them –

I can see Jung standing before me, silent, accusing. The old pompous Jung of the war years. The condescending Jung.

– hating our dependence, loathing it, loathing *them*, it's all the same emotion, my dear Jung: drink at that well and you drink it all. Don't moralize with me – there are no good emotions. Only civilized behaviour, between friends: at best. I never promised unalloyed approval. Not to you, not to anyone!

He speaks: 'But we must come on bended knee, with daily proof of our devotion . . .'

'To the work! Not the man. The *work*. I warn you . . . this house isn't a refuge for the godstruck – for benighted orphans whose father has failed them.'

Jung smiles. 'I don't come here looking for a god, believe me. My eyes have been opened. And I tell you this, as a friend: *you* lack the civilized virtues, when it comes to potential rivals – allies, I should say, but you don't know the word. You treat grown men like impudent puppies to be smacked down when we go astray. Pats on the head, and punishments . . . and you complain about *our* childishness – our "father complexes"! You talk of loving and loathing us as though that were perfectly natural –'

'It is.'

'– while you dangle the purse-strings, controlling our livelihoods, doling out patients to the faithful, threatening excommunication . . . you of all people! You who know so much about repressive fatherhood – who've seen its devastating effects in your patients, who've described it in all its vindictiveness . . .' He shines with sweat. 'Well, let the others quail, I'm not afraid of you. And I will not submit to a one-sided partnership. You expect us to confess our complexes, our secret weaknesses, you brandish them over our heads. What I demand is the same openness from you –'

'What you demand! The bully shows his face.'

'You know quite well what I'm referring to.'

I see the hatred in his face. The joy. Now it begins. I rise, slowly.

'I've come here to beg you to open your heart . . . don't turn away from me –' He blocks my path, ferocious. I can smell him. 'Whatever else, I've tried to behave like a friend.' And then, lethally quiet, 'God knows you've needed one.'

I am shaking. 'There! At last! The condescension of the Gentile to the Jew!' Naked, in his stare. 'Go home. You are no longer welcome here.'

I walk past; and then he breaks. Sitting, weeping, noisy tears. I think of Breuer: so long as *you* play the rebellious son . . .

He speaks, without looking up. 'Now I know how Fliess must have felt.'

I am beyond your cruelty. Cannibals, all of you; you all want pieces of me.

And now the anger comes. I turn on him: '*You* wanted this!'

Flowers clinging to the scree. We climb, above the tree-line. Glorious, heady air.

I can hear him struggling behind me. No cover here. Why won't he tell me the truth any more?

'It's the poets who've known all along. That's why I take it as a compliment when people call my dream-book "fiction" . . .'

'What I've read has been – highly complimentary –' Fliess' voice comes, conciliatory.

'Give me insults every time. After all . . . it's the same resistance one meets in patients.' I pause beside a boulder, eyeing him. 'The dragon guarding the gold!'

'Could we stop for a moment?'

'Of course.'

He catches me up, stands, ignoring the stupendous view. Achensee glittering beneath us.

'We hear the same thing privately, of course – from Marty's friends. "Poor Frau Doctor Freud, her husband was such a promising neurologist. Now she finds herself married to a disgusting freak."' I watch Fliess wheeze. 'Aren't you going to sit down while you've got the chance?'

'I'll never get up again.' He smiles, watching me wipe dirt from my palms and fingers. 'D'you want a handkerchief?'

I shake my head; he mops his brow and folds the piece of cambric carefully again, replacing it. My hands, still streaked with crumbling dirt; and a memory. And shame, at the way I have been tormenting him.

'I remember somebody ... my mother, I think – when I was a child – rubbing their hands together to show me the little scales of dirt. Dead skin. Telling me that's what we were made of, scraps of earth.' I glance at Fliess. 'What a lot of fuss we make.'

He smiles, grateful.

'I do think ... you protest too much, about the book. How many copies did Darwin sell?'

'Ten times as many. But then – he didn't use "high-flown obscurities". I'd like to write the whole thing again, from the beginning.'

'Nonsense! The style is quite lucid enough.' Under my gaze, 'The writing is excellent.'

Ah, Fliess. Cheerfully, 'But ...?'

He gazes at me, innocent.

'Wilhelm. You've been feeding me lukewarm compliments all day. I can't take any more of it.'

He grins, and comes to sit beside me.

Carefully, all too carefully, 'Speaking purely for myself, and since ... you know that I'm committed to your work – I have to say that I can see a certain element of danger in it.'

'Danger? Who to?'

'I mean: the danger that, no matter how cautious, no matter how objective he may be ... the mind-reader – I mean no offence – may inadvertently read his own thoughts into a subject's mind.'

135

'Of course.' The *mind-reader*?

My mildness gives him courage.

'While your work was concerned with childhood seductions, these were events that could at least be verified, in many cases, but now with fantasies and dreams ... reflecting a childhood *desire* ... you've crossed the line between what can be tested and what can never be more than an inspired guess. At least in my opinion. No-one can doubt that you've made great discoveries ... but to speak with the authority of science you must be sure that you're not merely choosing – or inducing – the evidence that suits your purpose.'

Fliess studying my face for a reaction.

'I see.' Quietly, '*Et tu, Brute.*'

'Sigmund –'

'Science – what you call science! – would not exist without inspired guesses: *you* know that if anyone does. You know quite well that you can make your numbers fit anything you like – the fact is you *believe* life marches to a rhythmic drum, you're certain of it, and you work from that hypothesis. You find a woman's twenty-eight-day cycle doesn't work for men, so you come up with the twenty-three-day cycle – and if that doesn't fit the case you multiply the two together, subtract five, and if needs be add the number you first thought of!'

'Not so ...'

'Not so? *You* are the scientist, then?'

Faces mock me, Koenigstein and Rie; I wear their sneer. This isn't what I want to say. Fliess hurt, defensive. But I won't be lured into a slanging match.

'Wilhelm, what I've propounded is neither science nor art ... at least not yet. One day I shall have proof to satisfy the pedants. Bio-chemical proof. All I have now is the fruits of observation. Must I resist them because I'm a "scientist"? Observation suggests that the human psyche leads a devious life – we've made it devious, to protect ourselves from the sexual anarchy within. We cling to our blindness, to our precious fear and anxiety, we use all the cunning at our disposal to put the hunter off the scent – like you, just now – like every patient protesting when the inner sanctum is threatened: "You're imagining it, doctor!" and it's then that I know I have it!'

Fliess hesitates. 'And you dismiss my reservations for the same reason? I'm not your patient.'

'Nor you're a doctor. You should know better.' Seeing his expression, 'But do you know *why* you're a doctor? Or rather ... do you *want* to know?'

'I know perfectly well –'

'Do you *want* to know why you're a specialist in one field rather than another? Where did you first encounter the diseases of the nose? At your father's sick-bed. And no-one could help him; no-one could cure the suppuration ...'

Patiently, 'So I become a rhinologist. To compensate.'

'No. Not to compensate. Not out of loving grief. But in revenge for his hold over your mother ... and your sister Clara.' His face, expressionless for a moment, like a man in shock. 'And now you have him on the operating table – day after day –'

At last: a look of pure hatred.

'You go too far ...'

Mildly, 'You see? You *don't* want to know.'

Fliess rises blindly to his feet, dusts himself down. I extend a hand to help.

'The irony is ... I'd already have more of your so-called proof, if I had your good fortune.'

'My good fortune?' His tone rejects all friendly gestures.

'To have an infant son to study. Mine are all too old – and too devious. They know my tricks. What I know of the stages of infancy I've learnt from your observations. It's true.' Fliess turns away, unsoothed. 'In fact ... it's about time I did some original work of my own. I've been planning a new opus – to be called "Bisexuality in Man". And woman, needless to say.'

'Bisexuality ...' He stares at me.

'Another "unscientific" thesis?'

'Hardly – I've been arguing for it myself, for years now – as much to you as to anyone!'

'You have?' The man is glaring at me now; this is beyond a joke. 'You're not calling me a plagiarist ...'

'After the way you've dismissed my work, my whole vocation – it'd be a mild reproach!'

He turns furiously on his heel, sets off across the hillside, alone.

'Oh come now ... Wilhelm –' I give chase, succeed in halting him. 'It's *that* way ...'

He follows my gaze. Curtly, 'I'd rather not attempt the cliffs today, if you don't mind.' A moment. 'They're altogether too steep for my liking.'

Does he know what he's saying? I try and laugh it off.

'And you're afraid I might push you off – in order to obtain exclusive rights over bisexuality?'

We stand in silence.

He speaks, quietly. 'What is it that makes you say a thing like that? Will you tell me?'

'Your expression.'

'There's nothing in my expression ...' ignoring my smile, 'except the desire to get back to the hotel, before Ida arrives.'

My turn to stare: so this was all foreseen ...

'Her Highness is joining us? You didn't tell me.' Foreseen, forearmed. 'Don't look so peevish. Her dowry was a princely one. Though I admit, it's her exalted *manner* –'

'I must ask you not to call her that to her face, in future. Or to mine.' Another silence, and a sundering. Formality, merely. 'She's coming on the express.'

Fliess turns, and continues down the path.

The Berggasse, my oasis. I put down my suitcase, inhale the odours. Muffled sounds from the children's quarters.

'I'm home!' I walk towards the sounds, louder as a door bursts open. Martha emerges past wrestling children, and we kiss.

'How was Wilhelm?'

Yawning, 'We nearly climbed the Hochschneeberg. He's fine.'

Children tugging at me.

'The dreadful truth is ...' I can't suppress the smile, 'we *did* discuss the whole bisexuality business – last year. I've even found it in his letters. And I'd completely forgotten.'

Minna, head bowed, listens without comment.

'Mind you ... there's always a reason.'

She glances at me, then bends back to her embroidery. I rearrange the linen compress on my forehead, and extend my legs once more.

138

'Between the two of us, bisexuality might be said to be ... a delicate subject. No doubt that's why I suppressed the memory. But the worst was yet to come: in the morning when I made my way down to the dining room, for breakfast, they were already up, he and Ida – dressed to the nines, no rough walks for Her Highness; eating away. There was only one other chair at their table, for some reason. And Fliess had put his cloak over it ...' The green cloak. 'Not just hanging over it – he'd put the cloak around the chair, covering it! We said hello, I stood beside them for a moment. Silence. Finally it was Ida who said, "Willi ... your coat. Sigmund wants to sit with us." Can you imagine?'

Minna studies her pattern.

'One of us always outgrows the other ...' Then, trying to fight off my own mood, 'Perhaps he was of no great worth in the first place.'

I hear her mimic me, drily: 'Now it starts ...'

'Well, I don't know. I'm a poor judge of men – you've said so yourself. It's true. They frighten me.' Seeing Minna's smile, 'Yes, I know – I frighten them. It comes to the same thing.'

I lift the limp, warm cloth from my face. She puts down her embroidery and comes to fetch it, dipping it in the basin. I watch her, leaning back.

'It's among my worst qualities ... a certain contempt for others. Whether they frighten me or I them. In the depths of my heart I can't help feeling that my fellow men are as morally ... untrustworthy as I am.' She ignores me. 'But I fight against it. I fight against it!'

'Don't fight so hard.'

She squeezes out the cloth, dips it again. Shall I tell her?

'You know what migraines signify?'

She nods. 'They signify an excuse for me to come and keep you company.'

'Well ... like all symptoms, they *are* directed *at* somebody. Above all at that first, prehistoric love, who can never be equalled.' I wait for her to look at me. ' "*La donna che non si trova* ..." The true love who is never to be found.'

Scathing, 'Does this apply to migraines in particular?'

'No ... I have a patient who whimpers in his sleep, in order to be taken to his mother's bed – to the mother who died when he

139

was two years old. No –' careful now '– migraines in particular, I think, represent a forcible defloration – the wish for it, that is – as a result of a fantastic parallel equating the head with ... the other end of the body.' I hesitate, seeing Minna stock still, with her back to me. I add weakly, 'Hair in both places ...'

To my relief, she laughs, turning. Holding up the compress.

'I can't help thinking what a disappointment this must be, then ... for the other end of the body.'

I hold her gaze. 'Yes.' Now; speak now. 'You know the "Bride of Corinth" ... where Goethe makes the young man fall in love –'

'Yes ...' harshly, to stop me.

'Not with the sister who is his intended Christian bride but with the other, pagan sister ... "A youth to Corinth, whilst the city slumbered, came from Athens: though a stranger there –"'

'Sigi. Enough.' Her gaze is fierce.

'Prose then. Have you read Merechkovsky's book *The Antichrist*? It's about Leonardo. When he meets his Mona Lisa, her smile re-awakens a memory – the smile of rapture on his mother's face as he suckled at the breast.' I pause. 'But – instead of making love to her, he paints the picture ... and pays with self-denial for the world's applause.'

I wait; the choice is hers.

'On the whole ...' I prompt her, 'I prefer Goethe's hero. He has his cake and eats it. Better than painting it – but then ... he's a simple Athenian. He doesn't aspire to great achievement.'

The bitterness of 'aspire' galls her, I know. I see it in her face. She holds up the compress, angrily.

'Do you want this or not?'

I shake my head, she squeezes out the cloth and leaves it folded on the basin's rim.

'Minna ...'

'You've got letters to write. I'll leave this here –' drily, 'in case the pain returns.'

She crosses to her embroidery, picks it up, and walks on.

'Don't go.'

The two of us could live the truth, and let the world mock at my work. Need they ever see it? Minna pauses, but without turning. Leaving me no choice.

'I do aspire to some achievement – when I'm not blinded by self-pity.' Scanning my desk, 'Don't go yet '

I find the letter; a folded double sheet of paper. And bring it to Minna. She takes it in silence, starts to read. Glances up at me.

'It's from a psychiatrist called Stekel ... with a number of other signatories – I don't know any of them.' Drily, 'One's an oculist.'

But she is already reading, absorbed.

Finally, 'When did you receive this?'

'A few days ago. A week, perhaps ... I haven't even answered it.'

I submit to her chiding look. No; not chiding; something more devastating. Tenderness and contempt. She starts to read aloud.

' "We have read your book on dreams, with its revolutionary vision of the human unconscious. Thanks to you ..." ' Minna glances at me, ' "the secret forces of repression which have tyrannized us privately and publicly can never go unrecognized again. We believe that you have set us free –" '

' "– from the posturing of consciousness." ' I succeed in stopping her. 'A handy phrase. I think I'll steal it.'

Minna returns the letter, studying me at length.

'Why haven't you shown me this before?'

Doesn't she know ... how I've enjoyed my isolation? How I've used it? I shrug.

Meekly, 'Last month Elise Gomperz offered to campaign for my promotion ... her husband is a favoured friend of the Minister's. I even turned that down.'

Two Romes. Minna-sopra-Maria, the Rome of Madonna Minna; and imperial, professorial Rome. I smile at her, conceding.

'Perhaps it's time to set out my wares, in the market-place. And pay the piper.'

... My dear Herr Stekel: I confess myself greatly flattered by your letter. And I welcome your proposals, which come at a time when I truly believed myself to be alone in my endeavours. As a result ...

At seven-fifteen, the barber. At seven-thirty prompt, breakfast.

... You find me the prisoner of a fixed and somewhat solitary – even rigid – routine: my only forays into public life are my visits to the tobacconist next to the Café Landtmann. My days are filled with patients, whenever possible until nine o'clock at night ...

Patients till one, lunch, exercise, more patients. Finally, correspondence. Then begin work – writing, that is.

... Might I suggest a Wednesday evening for our get-togethers? If my last patient is not fully analysed by eight o'clock, I shall send him out half-cooked into the night, and make my quarters ready for you.

Four of us at first on Wednesdays. Stekel: desperate to impress, loves the sound of his own voice. 'As any student of psychoanalysis knows ...' or 'Only this morning I saw a patient of this kind ...' This recurring figment is now known as 'Stekel's Wednesday patient'. Reitler and Kahane: not much better. Adler, the former oculist, the only one who's any good.

... Dear Adler: You must be aware how much I value your contributions to our 'Wednesday Society', and I particularly welcome your offer to read us a paper on 'Sadism and Neurosis', thereby expanding my own work on the sexual perversions, which as you know has attracted more than its fair share of attention. Havelock Ellis, I'm glad to say, speaks well of it in this month's *Nature* ...

'Meissl.'

The monosyllable is squeezed out like an order. The man, a total stranger, halts me in the street, detaches me from wife and child, without a word. Now we stand facing one another, on the empty, rainswept Ringstrasse.

I nod in acknowledgement. 'Herr Meissl ...'

Silence, then at last he speaks.

'I should like to take this opportunity to tell you ... what a depraved and filthy-minded man you are.'

If he has more to say, nothing comes.

'Thank you.' I nod once more. Released, he turns on his heel and strides away.

I rejoin Marty and Ernst, and we walk on.

'What did he want?'

I think she knows. She glances down at Ernst.

'Oh – like the others . . .' I shrug, 'a chance to congratulate me on the professorship.'

Professor Freud is fifty. The beard is trimmed now; and the moustache must shortly follow, till I look like a true academician; or a prosperous chemist. Six years have passed since the day at Achensee when Fliess shunned the cliffs. Too steep for his liking. Now Mind-Reader Freud has his own band of outlaws, and they sit here in my waiting room apeing the Grecian busts above them. Solemn faces, listening for their cue. Sipping coffee, puffing smoke, waiting for the last few speeches. Then at last informal chatter, and more coffee, and jokes. We are a Jewish assembly. Otto Rank puts one hand into the urn to choose the next speaker, brings out a slip of paper with the name on it. Rank: owlish, eager, even obsequious. Why not? I have four daughters.

Unfolding the slip of paper, 'Dr Federn . . .'

Federn sips his coffee, peaceably. Stroking his fine patriarchal beard, as Breuer used to do. The beard says: peacemaker. The beard means: fear-my-temper.

'I have no comment to add.'

Rank reaches into the urn once more, brings out the next slip. 'Dr Adler . . .'

Adler crouches lower in his chair, a toad about to spring. And spring he will. Neck muscles hunched. The Anthropophagi . . . and men whose heads do grow beneath their shoulders –

'Well . . . I feel I must say this:' Adler begins, 'I think that Dr Tausk has adhered somewhat too slavishly to the concept of the latency period in childhood. No-one here questions the concept. But we cannot ignore the fact that certain developments – sexual in their consequences if not in their nature – affect the individual between infancy and puberty.'

He grants his victim a friendly look. Young Tausk ignores it. Others glance at me: have I detected the heretical note? Adler continues, and I make no sign. I am the basilisk.

'The child is increasingly subject to the spirit of competition during this time, in forms that recapitulate, we may say, the passionate contests of the nursery. Nevertheless, he is learning to compare himself to his fellows, both socially and physically – whether for better or worse. And surely these experiences will also mould his attitudes to his fellows in later life ... *and* his sexual responses.' He pauses. 'To mention only one aspect of the pre-pubertal struggle.'

'Do I have the right to reply?' Tausk glances quickly at me.

'Of course.'

Tausk hesitates, hearing around him murmurs at this break with convention. For a moment he loses the thread; how vulnerable he is, another dilettante. Adler's mocking stare restores him to the logic of his anger.

'But this is mere ego-psychology ... the di-phasic nature of our sexual evolution, entailing a *resumption* of the sexual life in puberty, is precisely what distinguishes our psychic development from that of animals – it's the seed-bed of neurosis ... the gap, the lull in our development –'

Something must be done. I reach for my notepad.

'– and to imply that such ... surface influences as playground squabbles could be seen as decisive –' Before Adler can demur, 'It isn't enough to make passing reference to "recapitulation"! There is nothing but recapitulation! The sexual stage is already set. In infancy.'

How well he's learned his lesson; too well. And as my note passes around the gathering, towards Otto Rank, I see Tausk falter. Eyes following the note, unnerved.

'Erotic attraction for another person ... manifests itself between the ages of two and four, though – I would submit that the height of the Oedipus complex is frequently delayed until five or even six ... by which time the "competitive spirit" is surely thoroughly engaged, on the level of the ego – and will be mastered or not in the light of earlier, Oedipal confrontations. Rather than the other way around ...'

As the note reaches Rank, Tausk's nerve fails.

'I hope the Herr Professor will be prepared to share his comments with me later – no matter how derogatory they are.'

Shocked silence: no-one pulls the Herr Professor's beard, not even the favourite son. It's the best of Tausk, and the worst. I turn to Otto Rank.

'Read it.'

The owl opens my note, peers at it, reads.

'"Let's ... dispense with this business of the urn, if it makes the younger members nervous."'

Tausk unable to meet anyone's eyes, least of all mine. Only Adler has the gall to press the point home:

'I agree, especially if people are to be allowed to answer back – not to say interrupt!'

I intervene, 'Are we all finished?' Rank nods, glancing into the empty urn. 'Very well, then. If Otto would be kind enough to see to our replenishment ... we can regard the formal exchange of views as terminated, and insult each other quietly.'

Noise rises quickly; the place sounds like a café, and I almost have to shout –

'There is one other matter I feel I should report to the Society ...' I wait them out. 'I have been in correspondence with two ... members – inmates, I was going to say ... of the Burghoelzli Psychiatric Hospital, in Zurich. Bleuler and Jung. Two leading lights, I should say, among the staff there. Bleuler I'm not so sure about ... he wants us on his own terms ... but Jung, I think, is genuinely impressed with our work.'

No one speaks.

'As an adherent he would naturally be an asset – he seems to be an experienced and cultivated man; but as a campaigner on our behalf ... his contribution would be beyond price.'

Viennese, they stare at me; experienced and cultivated in their own right.

'I say it without apology. We are Jews: a fact not lost upon the world. And if our efforts are not to be labelled a "Jewish science", easily derided, we must have allies.' A small smile, 'Even among the Swiss.'

No-one demurs.

'Do any of you ... have any knowledge, professional or personal, of the man Jung?'

Already he stoops, in the lobby of the Berggasse. But nothing can disguise the physical man, the military mien; not even the little steel-rimmed glasses with their false humility. Even stooping, Jung towers over me. Insisting on examining the whole apartment. I see it anew, through his eyes, his nervous aggression.

'To tell the truth ... this is not what I think of as typically Viennese.'

I smile. 'No?'

'No offence to your compatriots. But their taste in art –' he gazes round. 'Usually so garish ... you don't mind my saying so?'

'Not in the least. But I warn you – be tactful with my colleagues here. They pride themselves on their good taste.'

We stroll into the waiting room.

'Of course – I defer to them. As scholars. Many of them I admire. Others, if I may be frank with you, are not of the highest calibre. Fanatics ... decadents, in my opinion. Amateurs.'

'We are in Austria. And an outcast science attracts eccentrics.'

He smiles uncertainly, under my gaze. Transparent face and eyes. Thinking now: I must show how normal I am.

'Adler has some interesting ideas,' I add. 'The pig finds truffles. Alas ... a socialist pig finds socialist truffles: the truffles of envy.'

Quickly, 'There is much to envy ... for a pupil of Freud.'

'Enough to go around, I hope.' God save us from normality. 'Beyond our little circle. What we need now are advocates ... translators ... we need ambassadors. The English are ready to hear from us, I think, provided they can understand it. The French – I'm not so sure about.' I usher him towards the inner sanctum. 'The Germans, certainly, will understand it. When they're told to.'

Jung chuckles obediently.

'Please ... come through. You don't by any chance have contacts with the Kaiser?'

He looks startled. 'Forgive me? Herr Professor, I'm only a lecturer in psychiatry –'

'You might have treated one of his relatives.' A moment. 'My study's in here ...'

Is he shocked by my opportunism? I haven't got his measure yet. Now he turns, hanging back.

'Will you excuse me for a moment – I won't detain you long.'

He hurries back towards the lobby, all arms and legs, an

146

overgrown farm boy. I check my appearance in the little mirror. Still the chemist; less so if I frown. His voice comes, bellowing

'I'm afraid I have no contacts on that level ... socially speaking ...'

I stand, waiting, behind the desk.

'Besides ... I am a heretic! Like you – by nature –'

He gallops back in, a book in one hand. My gaze stops him.

'Do you always shout so, in Switzerland? We are rather quiet here.' Then, seeing him abashed, 'Shut the door.'

He does so and approaches, speaking normally once more.

'I've brought you my book. On *dementia praecox*. I believe it shows for the first time how severe mental disturbance may be understood in terms of your own theory of neurosis ... if I'd had the temerity, I would have dedicated it to you. Reading your work has brought about a re-birth in my approach to medicine, though until you've read it I realize my veneration will seem hollow –'

Enough. 'My dear Jung, you make me thoroughly uneasy with your compliments.' A pause. 'I'll tell you why. We both know that a Christian and a pastor's son finds his way to me only against great inner resistances. And those resistances ... express themselves in several ways. Bravado. Self-abasement. I've no doubt you're aware of this.' Silence. 'So ...' I gesture at a chair, 'tell me about your work.'

His expression does him credit. He sits.

'My ... doctoral thesis is in the psychology of the occult – it was this subject which turned me towards psychopathology. As you know, I am a senior physician at the Psychiatric Clinic –'

'And what made you take up such a despised field?'

He smiles, regaining composure.

'While I was at university, I read a psychiatric textbook by Krafft-Ebing ... at the time my courses were in anatomy and histology, but since my parents were unable to support me financially in my ambition to become a specialist, I had to resort to general practice: I was lucky enough to get a post under Bleuler, at the hospital. As a psychiatrist. It is a despised field, as you say. But Goethe puts it well: every great man inherits an age of ignorance.'

Talks well. A creditable background; and one must not despair of a farm boy who quotes Goethe. Voluble now:

'Until recently you could say the work largely consisted of tabulation – itemizing symptoms in the crudest possible way: "The patient displays such and such contortions", "The patient doesn't speak", "The patient speaks nonsense ..." No-one asked, what happens *inside* the severe cases? For me, illumination came with *The Interpretation of Dreams*; for Bleuler too. Of course as Director he does not wish to appear sectarian ... but the more we interpret psycho-analytically, the more meaning we find in psychotic symptoms which had seemed quite senseless. Recently I've been experimenting with word association – using a stopwatch.'

'A stopwatch?'

'To compare the intervals between the questions and the patient's answers – as a means of grading the sensitivity of the material. Measuring the resistance.' A moment. 'I've brought some detailed figures with me – if we have time –'

A stopwatch: like a good Swiss. Still, he seems diligent.

'... and I found that I could only communicate with her by means of a strange charade: I was her son. Every day was Mother's Day, in the ward – I had to bring her presents ... imaginary ones, of course –'

Listening to Jung, I realize I am quite wrong. The man is far from merely diligent; he is original, erudite, charming. Before lunch, in the drawing room, he holds the women spellbound with his anecdotes. How he talks! Now they cannot move him, despite heavy hints, towards the dining room.

'... But during these interviews she was completely rational. An illustration, I think, of the way in which mental disturbances are also an attempt – I'm sure the Herr Professor will bear me out – to reach sanity; an expression of the desire for sanity; an attempt to escape the disease.'

An optimist, however. I smile, 'And to protect it. After all, you were her prisoner.'

'She was the prisoner. Though I admit – she was a tyrant when she was sane. A martinet with a deep, deep voice. A classic example of the failure to keep the two halves of the personality

148

in balance: masculine and feminine. Just as the man must not deny his feminine side –' Jung is not above a teasing glance at each of us in turn '– so the woman must not deny her masculinity, or it will compensate in startling ways. As in this case. Our shadow-self is not to be denied.'

More than once, I see him study Minna, curious. In the circumstances I would be doing the same.

'Does he get this from you?' Martha turns to me.

'No ... but –'

'The two must be in harmony within – like a well-matched couple.'

Jung's graceful, deferential glance, taking in Marty and myself, is interrupted by a vulgar creak from the woodwork behind us. Minna turns.

'The bookcase disapproves.'

Almost at once, a second creak, and we burst into laughter. As they subside, 'I think it's telling us it's time to eat ...'

'Of course –' Jung stands. 'I've kept you far too long.'

'On the contrary. Sundays we keep for visitors.'

Marty rises. 'But we only feed the interesting ones.' Minna beside her, moves towards the door.

'If you'll excuse me, Herr Doctor –'

Jung bows, watching her leave; then turns to peer at the bookcase.

'Does it often make such sounds? It's my ambition to live in a haunted house.' He catches my expression. 'I'm serious – don't you believe in communication with the dead? Who lived in this house before you?'

Marty smiles, pleased by such frivolities; they make a change. 'The house isn't old ...'

'Perhaps not, but there must have been one here before.'

'The previous tenant was an old schoolfriend of mine, I can tell you that much: Viktor Adler – now a troublesome politician, and *very* much alive.'

'Viktor Adler? Then you have a socialist spirit in your bookcase!'

'My bookcase is entirely apolitical. Look at the books ...'

'Well then: no wonder it's complaining.' He laughs, holding the floor. 'Surely you don't dismiss the supernatural? Admittedly

– like the science of dreams – it's a subject still treated with contempt by official science. But that will all change. Telepathy, graphology, astrology, even alchemy ... these will soon be acknowledged once more as legitimate areas of aspiration. The human spirit seeking to rise above its material prison.'

He has forgotten his efforts to seem normal, thank goodness; but forgotten other things, as well. I catch his eye.

'Religion, too?'

Minna returns, unobtrusive. It is enough to break the moment. Martha turns to her.

'He insists the bookcase is possessed!'

'I say such things occur. Fraulein Bernays, come to my aid –' But Minna is busy with silent signals, concerning the meal. 'You think they don't? Why not? Once you admit that life is full of lesser mysteries – coincidences, moments of clairvoyance –'

'Coincidence I grant you: things happen to us by chance ... just as nothing happens *in* us by chance.' Holding his gaze, 'For the superstitious man it's the other way around.'

The women gather at the door.

'Are you saying you've never experienced anything ... *in* yourself ... that you couldn't explain away?'

I feel their gaze on me, and hesitate. 'Once, perhaps. When I was a young man. In the streets of Paris – I was convinced I heard my name being called. By my beloved Martha.'

Marty stands quite still. Expressionless, like Minna. I shouldn't have said it.

Quickly, 'But I count that as hallucination. As for clairvoyance, if it exists it's physiological, not psychological. Besides which, the impulse to cheat must always be a factor ...'

He jumps in. 'Isn't that precisely what is important – psychologically? The *need* for such manifestations!'

'No.' A moment. Coldly now; enough frivolity. 'All these things ... while they remain subjective, unproven, offer us little more than speculation. They might as well be fairytales – since once proved, they're no longer very interesting: they take their place in the natural order. And our "need" for some communication with the spirit world ... as you should know, is merely Oedipal despair. A childhood cry – "Are you there, Father ..."'

Jung smiles. A gracious glance at his hostess.
'Or *Mother* ...'

It is late. How one begins to tire, at fifty; and how tiring it is to listen. The man has proved his point: he is the first to bring his own authority to our movement. I feel relief, and gratefulness, and something more ... a foretaste of release. I can rehearse my own death, at peace, watching his tireless animation. Twelve hours have gone by, a day of talk; my study, usually so quiet, seems exhausted too. And still he talks.

'... I think the only difference between us, on the matter of childhood, is that you can go further still! Not only does adulthood recapitulate the earliest stages of infancy – childhood itself rehearses the infancy of Man, the primitive history of mankind. I'm convinced of it – that during the first months and years we live through a kind of animism ... totemism – with perhaps even darker prehistoric forces, around the cradle: Stone Age figures. Stone Age dreams ...'

'Perhaps.' I rise slowly. 'In that regard you are far better read than I.' He looks at me, startled. 'Oh yes.' I search for a glass. 'You know ... tonight at dinner, my family were treated to a novel experience: I was made to listen. It's been many years since I came across such an impressive range of interests –'

Not since Fliess. Bury the thought. Jung studying me, puzzled by my mood. Is Freud surrendering, begging the coup-de-grâce? Or issuing a reproach, in his devious way, for insufficient deference?

'For me too ... this has been a memorable day. Just to be here – among these photographs ... the whole history of our science seems to unfold: Charcot ... Breuer ...' Jung seems genuinely moved; but still one wary eye on me. 'So much has changed – within your lifetime. Even the illnesses. You must find it strange ... there are so many fewer cases of hysteria, in the old sense – don't you find? With fainting fits ...' he nods at the photograph, ' "*Grande Hystérie*" ... fewer cases than we were taught to expect.'

Ah, must I shuffle offstage now?

'Every age has its diseases,' I reply. 'They move on, like everything else.' I hold up the decanter. 'Are you sure? You never drink?' He shakes his head. 'Less so in your field, I should say: true madness has no history.'

He watches me return to the desk, and sit.

'I could never have become a psychiatrist.'

I sip my drink in silence.

'You know,' I look at him, 'I sometimes think psycho-analysis is only any use ... to the kind of people who barely need it. People who can understand, who can learn how to help themselves. How to free themselves.' Jung nods. 'People of some worth. With at least a glimmering of culture.'

He nods once more. I see it in his face: people like you and me.

A shout of triumph, over on my left, beneath the trees. Young Martin has found one. But so have I, a prize specimen. I drop my hat over it, issue a shrill blast on the whistle, and my mushroom-hunters come running.

... My dear Jung: I cannot hide my delight at the news that you plan to abandon Bleuler – and set up on your own. Do not go back on this. You feel a traitor to the man, I know ... but remember: without some criminality there is no achievement ...

Oliver too has a selection of delicate *russulas*; Martin brings his find. The girls bend down to our basketful, disputing the five-gulden prize.

... All the same – I did not mean to influence you so precipitately, when I came into your life. Do you realize we spoke for thirteen hours – non-stop – the other day? And I do not have a reputation for being garrulous with my colleagues ...

The children are unanimous: I have won five gulden.

... You may be grieved to hear: I've sorted out the business with the bookcase. Our caretaker – an unlikely exorcist – informs me that the water pipes are responsible. When the warm water comes, the wood expands in answer. So I now confront despiritualized furniture much as the poets did Nature once the gods of Greece had passed away ... A propos: I only wish you could be here to celebrate the coming of *boletus edulis* with us. These are precious weeks – when the children are outdoors all day and I can enjoy them freely, without feeling that I'm snatching time from the few creative years ahead of me ...

Exhausted children, straggling back behind me to the hotel. In the mountains I still have the energy of a young man, and people gather to stare. am I so comical?

... Happily, my appetite to return to Vienna has been whetted by the arrival of a remarkable new patient, a Russian nobleman with more symptoms than the Czar has mistresses. At our first meeting he politely offered to defecate on my head ...

No; the staring crowd by the hotel have come to bury, not to praise elderly Jews. Here, of all places! The bolder ones begin to shout their slogans, as the children reach me. I usher them in, and turn. Beating my alpenstock to right and left, raining blows on them. Yes! Blows, from a Jew!

... You will see: the case provides a classic instance of the infantile origins of neurosis. I shall rout Adler and his minions! In any case, it is just as well that we are leaving shortly. An unpleasant incident outside our pension reminded me that even in the most idyllic surroundings, malice and hatred spring up like poisonous fungi ...

'It was night, in the dream. Winter. My bed stood with its foot towards the window: outside, I could vaguely see the walnut trees. Then suddenly the window seemed to open of its own accord. I couldn't look away. Outside – only a few feet away – were six or seven white wolves, sitting in the nearest tree. White ... with their ears pricked and tails like foxes.'

My wolf-man falls silent. I write; and hear him shudder, on the couch beside me.

'They sat quite still, in the branches on either side, looking at me. Their whole attention riveted on me.' He holds still. 'I think it was my first anxiety-dream, I was three, perhaps four, at the time –'

'How did the dream end?'

'I screamed ... and my nurse came running. And I – tried to describe the dream to her.' He pauses. 'They were so lifelike, the wolves ...'

A silence, then he turns his head to look at me.

Sweetly, 'Shall I draw them for you?'

'The idea that the wolves represent the source of childhood fears

– the boy's father – may be plausible enough ...' Adler, on the attack. 'But we are asked to accept that at the same time the wolves also represent the boy himself! In their immobility, watching him ... that he is the watcher, as well as the watched ... that the dream masks a memory of watching something terrible – his parents making love, in the manner of beasts, *a tergo*, while he was younger still.'

He pauses, gloating.

'*Why*? Why *wolves*? Why six or seven? Why *white* wolves? Because of ... the white of the bedclothes under which his parents – seemed to be struggling? This I find fanciful, to say the least ...'

Federn, my marshal, tries to quell the noise; since we abandoned the ritual of the urn, everyone speaks at once. Pandemonium, after the calm of the consulting room. And my poor wolf-man, my poor prize mushroom, is torn to pieces now by ravenous theories.

'If I may be permitted to answer' Federn roars. 'It is of course not only fanciful – but fantastic! As befits the iconotropy of dreams. How else can they escape the censorship of the mind, except in code? In puns, inversions, outlandish similes ... every one can be deciphered – and in more than one way: because the issue here is not whether this particular interpretation is correct, but whether it leads where all the other trails lead, to the heart of the patient's condition, his fear of a bestial assault, in infancy.'

'Where all trails must lead ...' Adler breathes it, with muted sarcasm. Thinking me passive; thinking me beaten.

Tausk too, perhaps. Glancing at me. Now he takes up my cause.

'The patient himself recognizes his fear of the father – surely that is the common thread –'

'I have never denied this "thread".' Devious Adler. 'I have never denied it! But it is here and now that the patient recognizes it! We have no way of knowing for certain whether these are genuine memories that he provides the analyst – or merely the fantasies of adult life ...'

Now his allies join the hunt, emboldened.

'Can we be so naïve as to ignore the way a patient uses the past, to put us off the scent of present troubles?'

'Precisely: it can be an evasion of the truth, one of the many faces of resistance —'

Voices rise. Battle is joined.

'I think we can agree that this is a matter of emphasis, not dogma —'

'It is not a matter of emphasis!' Tausk, struggling for my attention. 'The natural scientist is a dogmatist: he lays down a principle, and declares ... that is how it is!'

Adler now, 'We are not alone in our opinion! Even the infallible Jung has suggested that the pathogenic cause may lie in the present circumstances ...'

He doesn't look at me; but the others do, wondering at my restraint. The jackals, Stekel and Wittels, exchange glances.

'And no wonder ... he is at pains to obscure the source of his *own* neurosis.'

'What neurosis? The Swiss have no neuroses! Mountain air suffices to dispel them ...'

Amid laughter from his party, 'It's no laughing matter! The man who declares himself without neurosis has no right to be an analyst!'

Hard not to laugh outright, at Wittels' purple face. And my bewildered Federn snaps at last.

'Enough of this! How dare you speak of an absent colleague in this fashion? Would you say so to his face? But you say it in Freud's presence and expect us to permit it – you who are completely unaware of the aversion you create in everyone around you!'

Federn's rage is terrible, compounded by my silence. We can all see that Wittels is near to tears.

'Perhaps ...' Adler fixes him with a poisonous stare, 'it is time for those among us with a "brother complex" to declare their interest in these proceedings.'

Wittels hides his face, pushing back his chair. For a moment I fear he will fling himself at my feet like a flagellant. Then he looks up.

'So I do ... willingly ... but I will not hear the cornerstone of Freud's work treated as a subject for derision!'

'If we could return to the matter at hand ...'

Federn has retrieved his trance-like calm. But he is too distraught to carry on, and Stekel picks up the baton.

'It seems to me ... that Dr Adler does not dispute the importance of the primal scene in the foundation of the patient's neurosis – this being the "cornerstone" in question: fear of the father, which goes hand in hand with the child's jealous passion for the mother. Adler merely wishes to draw our attention to the way in which the man's present condition has activated, shall we say, the crucial memories.' He pauses, judicious. 'In essence, his view of the case is substantially the same as Freud's.'

Bless him, the hypocrite. I lean forward at last.

'Unfortunately for this conclusion, Dr Stekel, there are two people here who do not share it.' I meet the toad's eyes. 'Freud, and Adler.'

Silence. At least they know a Rubicon when they see it. Voices begin to rise, Federn can no longer control the gathering. Adler sits silent, while his followers rage; and Tausk turns on Stekel. Amid the noise and the gesticulating figure, one voice shrieks: 'You accuse *me* of disloyalty! Freud is my Christ! And I am his apostle!' Darkness reigns.

... A group, my friends, is an obedient herd which cannot live without a master – who must possess a strong and imposing will which the group itself, having no will of its own, can accept from him. It is only through the influence of individuals ...

... who can set an example, and whom the masses recognize as their leader, that they can be induced to perform the work and undergo the privations upon which the existence of civilization depends!

I slow up for a moment; even Jung's long legs must flail to catch me. Then, resuming a Swiss pace:

'One thing I do insist upon, through all the accusations and ... vilifications ... we must not abandon the discoveries, simply to make them more palatable to the rabble. We *must* stand by the primacy of sexuality. That above all' – I turn to him – 'promise me that! No matter what refinements of technique you bring us ...'

At a corner of the Ringstrasse, an elderly man approaches us, with a middle-aged woman beside him. I stare. Jung follows my gaze. With recognition?

I hurry Jung across the road.

'One other business I wanted to discuss with you – I've been invited to speak at Clark University, in Massachusetts –'

Jung glancing back, bemused, in silence.

'It seemed to me we should present an international front, with yourself and perhaps Ferenczi, our Hungarian champion ... I think the Americans will like him, don't you? Let Adler stew in his own juice, for a while ...'

Minna's soft tapping, on the door.

'Yes?'

She looks in, sees me at work.

Less peremptory, 'I must finish this.'

She nods.

'I came to tell you ... Marty's eyes are bad tonight. I'm going to read to her.'

I study her. *Is* that what she came to say? Or, rejected ... We smile.

'Good.'

My gaze stops her from leaving.

'I did a shameful thing today.' I rise from the chair, and walk. Minna says nothing.

'We met Breuer and his daughter in the street. And I didn't even greet the man.' A pause. 'Jung says coincidence follows him everywhere. Perhaps he's right ... it came just as we were discussing the core of our wretched disputes.'

Silence. She will not let me off the hook.

'I've asked myself whether I did it ... so as to forgo an opportunity to show off my new disciple. But that won't do ...' I hesitate. 'I simply shrank from the encounter. Like a snail into its shell. Jung saw it. He was quite taken aback. D'you suppose he understands?'

Do *you*? A moment.

'The sadist is a masochist at heart ...'

Ferenczi eats like the Hungarian he is, with napkin spread across

157

his ample front. Loving his food to death. Smiling as he devours it, reaching for more.

By his expression, Jung pines for a nice clean plate of meagre lentils.

'Are you insured against the journey?' Ferenczi munches. 'I am.'

Jung glances sidelong at me, then back at Ferenczi, amused. 'How much?'

'Ten thousand marks. And you, Herr Professor?'

I nod, embarrassed, and confess: 'Twenty thousand.'

Ferenczi guffaws and refills my glass with wine. 'It's only right ...'

Jung's glass of water is untouched. What have I done, inviting these two? Ferenczi eyes Jung, wipes his mouth. I catch his eye.

'If I know Carl, he hasn't insured at all. He trusts in God to deliver him from the whale.'

'In God?' Ferenczi leans towards the expressionless Swiss. 'I'd been told you were a mystic, but –'

'A *reformed* mystic,' I put in hastily. 'In psycho-analysis he has eaten of the tree of paradise, and acquired knowledge!' I must have taken too much wine; first I cast the man as Jonah, now ... 'A metaphor which renders *me* the serpent. But let it pass.'

Ferenczi grins at Jung.

'Let me be the serpent ... *one* glass – won't you join us?'

Jung shakes his head politely.

'In the process, he has given up the pleasure principle entirely ...'

Jung ignores me, turns to Ferenczi. 'A scientist should never drink.'

'On the contrary – he must drink! Science is the most complete renunciation of the pleasure principle known to man. If you couldn't drink –'

He breaks off, seeing Jung's expression. Time to change the subject; time to broach the matter I have reserved for this, our last evening before the flood. Before departure. I'm not used to drinking so freely. Ferenczi's fault.

'Surely ...' I rise. The guests around us in the restaurant

ignore me; birthday capers ... 'We should at least toast our venture – in whatever liquid we choose –'

'To America!' Ferenczi raises his glass.

'To our new continent ...'

We drink. I sit, still holding their attention.

'Not the least of the pleasures this voyage affords ... for me ... is the opportunity to see you learn to know each other better.' Addressing Ferenczi; my gaze coming to rest on Jung, 'Psycho-analytically speaking, this is my son.' And, before Jung can speak: 'I have said as much, to Ferenczi, on earlier occasions. He knows that when the empire I have founded is orphaned, you – and you alone – will inherit.' A moment's silence. Turning to Ferenczi, 'Like Joshua, he is destined to explore the promised land which I am only permitted to view from afar ...'

A longer silence. Have I spoiled it, mishandled it? Maudlin tears in my own eyes. Ferenczi too drunk, Jung too vexed? But surely the man could say *something* ...

I lean towards him, with the bottle of wine. 'Come – you must take one more bite from the tree. Come.'

He submits, as one who might say: very well, now ask no more of me, this is enough. And sips the wine.

We sit, unable to find words. Tender Ferenczi can see my state, and Jung's.

'I understand ... that a primitive form of wine – was among the last things consumed by the unfortunate victim of the Bremen bogs ...'

What? What are you talking about?

'... it's a local curiosity. A man from the Stone Age or there-abouts, I don't know exactly, preserved here in the peat bogs. They have the corpse in the museum now.' Ferenczi, casting Jung as Stone Age wine-drinker? As Stone Age corpse? *In vino veritas.* 'I thought we might visit it, tomorrow, if there's time. Have you ... been to the city before, Herr Professor?'

'Once.' My voice sounds strange to me. 'With Fliess,' And fainted: I'd forgotten: in this very hotel.

Jung and Ferenczi avoid each other's eyes. I glance at Jung. Still nothing. Must I be your Lear? He speaks now.

'I have seen the bog corpses. They are very interesting – one in particular. And you are right, Ferenczi, he was given wine before he died.'

I feel my head throbbing. 'And got so drunk he fell into the bog? Really, is this a conversation for the dinner table?'

'He did not fall into the bog, Herr Professor. It was a ritual execution ... the man in question, the best-preserved specimen, was garrotted and then placed in the bog.' Jung continues, relentless: 'The rope they used has decayed, but you can see the marks around his neck – the body is intact. So much so that an analysis was possible, on the contents of the stomach – establishing the man's last meal: wine, some seeds, a kind of gruel ...'

'I have no desire to hear any more. You two can ... discuss it afterwards, if you find it so interesting –'

'But it is. Uncommonly interesting. Thanks to this one find, we know as much about the prehistoric inhabitants of this region as we do about their mediaeval counterparts. We have the clothes, we have ... some pieces of incised bone, reindeer bone, used in worship –'

Why can't he stop – what is this morbid rhetoric – 'I said, enough! Must you go on about it?'

He stares, baffled.

'I don't see the harm ...'

It bursts from me: 'What is it, then – can't you wait? You want me dead too!'

I can feel myself swaying, Ferenczi's arm outstretched, a glass spills, I'm falling.

Ferenczi's voice.

'Help me – for God's sake –'

Hands under me. Faces staring, as I rise, and meet Jung's gaze. I take my seat once more, amid a silent restaurant.

'Thank you ...'

Chairs moving back, around me, to their tables. Conversation resumes. I drain my glass, with a confused head.

'Shall we go upstairs?'

'D'you think Jung has jumped overboard? He didn't come down to breakfast.'

'Not while I was there, certainly.'

Ferenczi smiles at me across the cramped cabin. Now I know why I brought him. He is a dear, sloppy Hungarian.

'I owe you both an apology ... about the other night – not a very auspicious start to our voyage of discovery.'

'Too much excitement –' Loyal Ferenczi.

'You know better than that.' I pause. 'Some ... portion of unruly homosexual emotion, I dare say. Still awaiting the proper cathexis.' Ferenczi makes to look startled. Perhaps he is startled. 'Allow me that much honesty.'

He lies back in the bunk.

'I too have a confession to make ... last night I dreamt about my mother.'

His broad smile comes too, as I erupt with laughter.

'How good it is, to find an analyst who dreams about his mother! My dear Ferenczi ...'

A faint rap on the door, and Jung enters, like a walking cadaver from the bogs. He stoops under the lintel. The cadaver speaks.

'Good morning.'

We answer in kind as he supports himself against a table. Ferenczi can barely disguise his glee.

'You've been up on deck?'

Jung nods, faintly. 'I was ... on the way back to my cabin, but I thought I must inform you – a most remarkable thing –'

'Another coincidence?'

He turns his pale eyes on me.

'On deck I met my cabin steward. He was sitting reading. I thought: lazy fellow.' He pauses. 'The book ... was *The Psychopathology of Everyday Life* ...'

He too smiles, at my delight: 'This isn't a coincidence – what do you say, Ferenczi? It's an omen! Cabin stewards versed in my work ...' I make room for Jung on the bunk. 'Come, sit with us ... you've earned your place, my boy.'

He approaches, dislodging things.

'You think this ship is altogether safe?'

'On board ship everything creaks, believe me. Sit here. We were discussing our dreams, just now.'

'I confessed *my* dream,' Ferenczi smiles. '*C'est à vous ...*'

'Very well ...' But I am too elated; turning to Jung, 'A cabin steward! Did you talk to him?'

'I was too amazed. Besides –' he gestures, 'the motion ...'

'Never mind. My dream ... was a most pleasant one – rocked in this little space. I was a child again, in Freiberg, picking flowers. Two beautiful clumps of celandine. Just as it used to be. A dream ... with that sense of reality that always signifies unusual importance.'

They look thoroughly foxed.

'Perhaps simply ...' I hint, 'that only childhood itself is real.' A pause. 'And sexual adventure – which is childhood revisited.'

Now they study me in earnest.

Jung, at last, 'Is your dream, then, concerned with sexual adventure?'

'Possibly.' Dear God. *Two* clumps of celandine, man. And this is the fellow I've elected Crown Prince of psycho-analysis. 'Yes ... with the desire to obtain pleasure, without cost. For once. You see?'

He eyes me.

'But surely ... obtaining pleasure is not necessarily identical with sexuality –'

'Really? Beware ... you will become a little Adler unless you're careful: and the Prince will turn into a toad.'

Once more, Ferenczi has to break a silence.

'Your turn now, Carl – tell us your dream.'

'I can't oblige.'

We stare at him. What dangerous Swiss dreams is he denying us? Then he shrugs, shame-faced, 'I was up all night ... with sickness. The Swiss are not good sailors. Especially after wine.'

I dare not meet Ferenczi's eyes.

'... And I believe our founder, Jonas Clark, would have been proud, as proud as I am today, to welcome to Clark University the founder of a school for pedagogy already rich in new methods and achievements ... leader among the students of psychology and sex, of psycho-therapy and analysis: Sigmund Freud of the University of Vienna ...'

I rise to cross the podium, with our host's words ringing in my ears: the University of Vienna indeed. Mercifully, only Americans are present. In their hundreds, a sea of faces. And the applause, which has begun modestly, swells instead of waning.

There are students standing at the back; dress-suited scholars rising to their feet – their wives, I note, remain seated – to cheer me. I stand at the lectern, but they will not let me start. Why this ovation? Why here, of all places – here among Europe's bastard, rebellious children? Cheering this elderly alien, this student of psychology and sex.

I can see Jung and Ferenczi applauding with the rest, flushed and moved. I am crying too.

The quiet of the Berggasse; the small noises of cutlery on crockery. Martha and Minna transferring dishes to the tea-trolley in harmonious silence.

'America is gigantic . . . a gigantic mistake.'

They smile at me, tolerant. I know: this isn't what they want to hear.

'The greatest experiment in the history of mankind, and it's a failure. Jung says it went wrong when they started to kill the Indians . . .' Vaguely now, '*I* don't know. Perhaps they didn't kill enough.'

The truth is I feel tired, to my bones.

'Did you visit Coney Island?'

I nod. 'They showed us everything. They took us to the cinema, to restaurants . . . they don't know how to eat at home, these people, they're still immigrants – they can't find the time. Which is understandable, since they've forgotten how to cook.'

Imagine: a country without wild strawberries.

'Still . . . they seemed quite pleased with *us*.'

My mood upsets them: they both glance with relief towards the door, hearing the doorbell.

'That'll be the photographer –'

'Let him wait a few minutes.' I sip my coffee. 'I need to prepare the photography face.'

Is there a glance between Martha and Minna? What schemes have they been hatching, while I've been away? Minna goes to the door.

'I'll show him in next door.'

I sit beside Marty; we sit in silence, while she studies me.

'I hope that isn't the photography face.'

'No.'

It's the face of ...

'You look tired.'

I nod, grateful. She has given me my cue.

'It comes of running about with younger colleagues.' A moment. 'Marty ... when I return, from the International Congress – I think I shall need a holiday.'

By now the words carry a precise meaning. No trace of anger in her answering look. She nods, all acquiescence.

We stand before the Moses. So familiar now, his face wearing my own revengeful mask. Like meeting oneself coming round the corner ... an augury of death, in the old doppelgaenger stories.

'From this side ... there's more pain – less anger and contempt –'

Minna follows me, still gazing at the statue.

I walk up to him.

'This is the real Moses: coming down from Mount Sinai to find his followers abandoned to the dance, around the Golden Calf. Smashing the tablets in his rage. But from there –' I turn to where she stands, 'you can see the hands. You can see that Michelangelo's Moses will *not* destroy the tablets. See how he grips them! He will not surrender to the wild dance in himself.'

The eyes – and the hands ... the conscious, moral self and the vengeful unconscious, in mortal combat. Torn between understanding and seeking to act –

'The mob have turned back to their old, illusory idols. Rejoicing. But he will not destroy the tablets. He will not!'

We walk, through empty Ostia, after a night of rain. Tall columns, and a green, troubled sea before us.

My hectoring is done. I am not Moses, I am driftwood.

'After all these years alone, the truth is ... I'm unfit to be a leader. I'm too jealous of the long years spent struggling with the work myself. What I wanted was ... for people to flesh out my first attempts – to shore them up ... not tunnel off in every direction. The whole structure will collapse, and the seam will be lost. Like a dead mine with "Danger, Keep Out" posted above it.'

We gaze around.

'They all want quick results. Psycho-analysis must be a factory, turning out normal people . . .' Walking on, 'I think of the occasions when I can say: I've cured a patient. Removed the symptoms. They're usually the least fruitful cases, barely worth recording. And must I feel proud? Suppose chemistry has its way and neuters us all in the laboratory . . . what would we be, then? And when I listen to speeches, reports of therapeutic triumphs in my name, I want to cry: analysis isn't a kind of aspirin! It's a lifelong pursuit, for the self-styled healthy *and* the sick – it's a philosophy or it is nothing! They don't seem to be able to understand that, the Adlers and the Stekels . . .'

Her glance reminds me: I'm complaining again.

'The *public* do. They know that what I've done is to remove the human animal a little further from the centre of creation: just as Copernicus took away our cosmic arrogance and Darwin our claims to a miraculous body – so I have challenged the last of our shibboleths, the mind. In its vanity – the arrogant posturing of consciousness –'

'*Stekel* said that.'

I shrug. 'He's forgotten. Too busy now, saving souls. But people aren't fooled – they know there's nobody to run to any more. We must turn and face our demons, without cant . . . and live with them as best we can. Without destroying ourselves. People know it, even in their despair, they know it.'

Minna brooding at my side. Something in the seascape afflicts her too; brings stormy, sluggish silences.

At last, 'And they think that's what you're telling them? I doubt it.'

'No, what they *think* is that it's something shocking, to do with sex – as the Americans call it. And it is shocking . . . because I'm saying that we must liberate ourselves from the secret tyranny of sexuality: then and only then can we place instinct at the service of civilization.'

'By suppressing it . . .' she mocks.

'Remember, we talked of Leonardo once. Transforming his

desires.' A pause. 'It was the same for Michelangelo, whose passions were homosexual. Don't you remember our talk?'

'I thought then ... what a hypocrite you could be.'

She walks beside me, without looking at me.

'I've heard you say that homosexuals should be shipped off to South America.'

'Nonsense. Not because they're homosexual. *Any* man who cannot learn to keep his sexuality within bounds – no matter what the object of his lust: that's what I meant.'

Silence. Yes: within bounds. I glance at Minna.

'You know quite well I'm not shocked by perverse emotions – or perverse acts. But as for criminals – they should all be sent to South America and quickly too. And I'd pay for Adler to go with them.'

I have forced a smile from her.

'You wouldn't believe what lengths I had to go to, to persuade him to accept Jung as our new President. "Don't you understand ... without a Gentile at our head, our whole survival is at stake – they'll tear the coat from my back –"' I subside once more. 'If my name was Oberhuber, none of it would be necessary. And Jung himself, of course, now speaks all kinds of nonsense. We can ignore the Oedipus complex – and the libido, he thinks it sounds "too repressive". One day he's calling for a new spirit of religion in the world; the next he's on his knees begging my forgiveness.'

Minna seems utterly remote.

'Yet somehow I still believe ... he's the best of them. Once he outgrows these tantrums. Don't you think?'

She turns to stare at me.

'He still recognizes my authority. And despite everything – despite himself – he wants to like me.'

'Yes ... that much I do know.'

'You've spoken to him?'

She nods. As though the subject were perfectly commonplace, between the two of them. Minna looks away, too quickly.

'He wants your trust. Or so he says.'

'Then he must earn it.'

Do they discuss me, then? What more, what else? No; I dismiss the thought. And yet, 'That much I do know'. Strange formula.

Lightly, 'Only last month I wrote to him, to arrange a meeting – he never answered. I went; he wasn't there, Now he accuses me of posting the letter too late ... when the truth is, he kept it three days without opening it! The problem in a nutshell.'

Silent Minna. I shall burst.

Finally, 'I didn't know you'd spoken of such things with Jung ...'

Still she says nothing.

'One must be careful. I don't imagine you discussed personal matters.'

Now she must speak. Instead she turns to look at me, making no attempt to hide the truth. Rejoicing in it.

She waited ... and she chose him.

I stop, and she halts a little way away. Turning once more to face me, defiant. 'Why not?' The futile words come tumbling, her rage breaking first. 'Sometimes you behave as if you had no idea ...'

'Of *what*? How hard it is for you?'

'Yes! For me. And for Martha.'

'But *you* needed an audience for your suffering –'

Full force, 'And you don't?'

I see. So now I must pay for her guilt. While she tells me how hard it is. Vicious now, 'D'you think I haven't seen you together, you and Martha, working side by side with the same tender martyred air – brimming over with love for one another. Yes: for the first time in your lives! How you hated each other ... and now, at last, you have something in common –'

Minna gazing at me in pure disgust. I must finish.

'Don't misunderstand me: more than a man – you have a grief in common. What more could a woman ask?'

The cakes sit untouched on the birthday tea-table. Gugelhupf, Linzertorte. I have my book.

Through the open door I can hear cheerful muttering as they help Minna back up the stairs, step by step.

After a while, Marty's footsteps, coming closer, entering the room. She stands in the doorway, waiting.

I have my book.

When I glance up, I see her picking Minna's shawl off a chair beside me. She walks to the door and out, without looking at me. I must finish my book.

SIX

The measured English voice on the radio repeats: war. War for the best of reasons. War against the enemy. War for freedom, for the family, for decency. War.

England has been at war with Germany for weeks, and all we get are reasons. The women listen like spent Furies; only Anna seems to realize that I have work to do. She stands, cleaning my metal palate, rinsing the pieces of my artificial jaw.

When I have pressed them home, furnished my mouth, I nod to her: enough. She goes and switches off the radio. In the silence, they watch me sifting papers on my desk, searching. No-one offers to help.

'Must they destroy everything again ...'

Marty's perpetual lament.

'What do you think ... should we put a call through? Is it still possible?'

'I have work to do.' Summoning Anna. 'The book by Hérault-Lachaise ...'

'Which book is that?'

Which book? Are they all warstruck? Must we hear out every bulletin? '*Essays in Egyptology*. Big blue book – I had it right here –'

She approaches. 'I don't think we brought it ...'

'I was reading it today.'

Trying to control my temper. Anna nods.

'I'll ask Paula.'

'Paula?'

'Paula. The housekeeper –'

'I know who Paula is! Don't treat me like an idiot! What does Paula know about my books?'

Of all ironies: the metal monster only stays in place when I shout.

More quietly, 'It was here ...'

I sit, gazing at the desk, the patient figurines. Anna comes to me, stands close.

'Papa. Some things had to be left behind.'

Her tender, smiling face betrays nothing. But I smell of death, I know. Even the dog won't come to me now.

I look down at my eighty-year-old hand, in hers.

The mass of pine trees make the day seem darker. Papa leads me up the muddy track, my hand clasped in his. His long coat flapping. Sunday clothes, a Sunday walk.

Fog. No, steam. Bubbles floating in the broad sluices. The bath-house walls sweat.

Watch ... Teresa's huge hands lathering the soap, working the soap. She smiles.

'Again ...'

My voice, pleading. Mamma brings her palms together, rubs her soft hands together, rotating them until a thin scraping of skin is born, ravelled up, dirty from rubbing. I brush it from her hand.

'Again.'

Laughing, 'That's enough.' Her hand in my hair, bringing out a wisp of straw. 'What's this?' I stare. 'Tomorrow ... I'm going to Neu Titschein, with Papa.'

I follow her gaze, across the room. Teresa sitting by the window, in the last light, sewing. Somewhere a needle, in the blubber of her hands.

Mamma's voice. 'It won't be for long.'

Teresa, whispering.

'That's why we say our prayers and go to confession, my little blackamoor ... because when we come to judgement, the ones who have never repented, the ones who have done evil in their lives –'

Whispering.

'– wake up in hell. And the devils tie them down and brand their bodies with hot irons, for a thousand years, and then another thousand, and another ...'

Rocking back and forth. The oil lamp vanishing and reappearing.

'And the pain never gets less, The pain, the smell of burning and the thirst. Unending, without sleep, a thousand years and then another thousand.'

Back and forth, by candlelight.

'Would you like to come with me, to church?'

My hand in hers.

'Come with me.'

Hand in hers.

'Because when you die, my little blackamoor –'

I look up, startled, from the foot of the stairs. Swift steps, fading, on the landing above.

'Paula?'

Silence. Distant traffic, London traffic. A door, opposite; I reach it, put my weight on the walking stick, and turn the handle. The door swings open.

Girls at the kitchen table. Papa glares at me; the others turn back to their plates.

'He might at least have the good manners to shut the door!'

He is staring at me, straight at me. Dark with rage.

'Sigi!'

No-one stirs, the girls sit like effigies. Mamma comes, bringing food.

'Let him eat later, if he wants.'

As she sits, I hear a door slam, down the corridor. I turn, too slow. The corridor is empty.

In the silence, the sound of a piano, finger exercises.

Over and over: the same scales. Clumsy fingers in the next room, clumsy notes. I clap my hands over my ears, lean back against the door.

No: use the sound, to erase thought, forget the voices in the kitchen. Papa's face.

I hurry to my satchel, bring out the books, sit at my desk. Find the page.

The piano. Up the scale and down the scale, maddening, mocking. 'He might at least have the good manners . . .'

Pages crammed with diagrams. Up and down. Please God . . . I raise my fist and pound the wall with all my might.

Any moment now . . .

We wait, tensely clustered by the door, eyeing the patients. Some in geometric postures, as if posing for a textbook.

A voice comes. 'Meynert . . .'

A flutter as we re-arrange ourselves. I gaze at the living sculptures in the ward; their trance is catching. On the verge of speaking, on the verge of moving, poised for flight. Someone touches me gently on the arm.

Whispers, 'Meynert's coming.'

I turn as Meynert strides in through the open door.

I hear the door open.

Papa stands there, in the doorway of my room. Raging.

'It's not enough that you don't speak to us any more? Let alone eat with us! And must your sisters give up the piano now?'

Spittle on his beard.

'You expect them to fetch and carry for you –'

Pushing my book away, I stand and force my way past him, out of the room.

The whores call their teasing, mechanical invitations. A bright, feathery boa flicks across my face, spilling cheap scent, as I pass too near a doorway. Laughter.

'Sigi.'

I stop, glancing round in alarm. Faces turn to me, renewing their invitations.

Marty's voice: 'Sigi.'

I turn from the kitchen doorway. Under my hand, the walking stick. Marty, approaching down the corridor. She looks at me, hesitant.

'I came to see if you were working. We're in the garden . . . it's so warm you'd think midsummer.'

Slowly, I come to myself. How can I explain to her? Is this how the mind dies, not in one place but in many?

'Where's Anna?'

It is out before I can prevent myself. I see the hurt in her face.

'Why are you so angry with us, these last few days?'

'I'm not ... angry.'

The 'g' sticks, humiliating. Angry. I can say it in my head.

'You know what Minna said? Now everyone's declaring war, he doesn't want to be left out ...' She waits for me to smile. 'Is the pain bad?'

At least the words come out better, angry: 'I need to do some alterations to the Moses book. I must have the Hérault-Lachaise, the man's spent his life studying Akhnaton and his court –'

Such stupid questions. Is the pain bad? I fend her off with ... with Moses ...

But for once, she does not retreat. She takes my arm.

'We'll look for it together.'

We walk slowly down the corridor.

The drawing room is cool and dark. We stand, arm in arm. It was her voice, in Paris. My Marty, my beloved girl.

'Lucky man, to be a harmless archaeologist.' I pause; too many hard sounds. 'If I had my life over again, I'd give up all this spadework, leave it to others ... and devote myself to a new science. To the world of psychic phenomena.'

She gazes at me, amazed. I smile.

Peering at her, 'What do you think?'

I don't know which startles her more, the proposition or the question. Or my tenderness. She answers timidly.

'*Is* it a science?'

Dear, stupid, telling questions.

Fliess, at the desk. No statuettes, no figurines; only a heap of manuscript. His eyes plead: I speak in love.

'... believe me, you risk provoking quite unnecessary opposition – by your very claims. I don't deny the value of the work. But the evidence on which it is based is personal testimony ... guesswork ...'

I turn from the window, correcting him: 'Clinical observation ...'

'Of course. But with a definite and limited field. You make of it a medical philosophy! A scientist doesn't take a handful of insights and weave them into a hairshirt for the whole of humanity . . .' Exasperated now, seeing me shake my head, 'You say it's your experience that confirms your work: that's not a scientist's attitude. On that principle this book might as well be a gigantic novel –'

'Perhaps I shall live to see the day when Newton is reproached for his theory of gravity – because the apple fell on *his* head, not on someone else's!'

'But the theory of gravity is a *fact*. What you've got here . . . is a mythology!'

I nod: congratulations.

'In the true sense, Wilhelm: a universal story.'

Abruptly, I am in the theatre. Empty and dark except for one light over the stage.

Charcot enters, bull-like beneath the light. Swiftly, as a man might enter his own drawing room, without looking round, removing hat and coat. Then he pauses, looking out at the rows of seats, looking up to make sure he is alone.

Briefly, drily, no bow, 'Mesdames, messieurs . . .'

Without waiting for the echo to settle, he exits. Returns without the hat and coat, but carrying a sheaf of notes, and a chair.

At the lectern, he settles the notes, and glances at the audience, a token glance. A glance at the first page, murmuring to himself in private lecture.

Charcot looks round as if to establish in his mind his props and fellow actors. Then moves quickly to the chair, raises it to change its stage position. Looking up as he lifts it. Stock still now, chair raised, gazing at me in the back row of the auditorium.

'An unusual place to take lunch . . .' He smiles, putting down the chair. 'Or are you still here from this morning?'

When no words come, he gestures impatiently.

'Come, come.'

I make my way towards the dais. Into the light. Charcot nods, recognizing me.

'I'm used to seeing you at the front. But not for several weeks

174

now. You have decided to make yourself less conspicuous?' And seeing me still speechless, 'We seem to have interrupted each other ... you should be in your laboratory. So should I.'

He turns, picking up the chair.

'Good day.'

I watch him, in the darkness of the doorway, putting on hat and coat.

'Maître ... the patient you hypnotized this morning – the case of hysterical abasia. What would happen if her memory of the traumatic event could be removed completely? Permanently. As if her lover had never left her – or not in that fashion.'

'Is that desirable, do you think?' He returns a little way, to study me. 'What would Professor Meynert say to such a course?'

'Preferable, surely, to remaining a cripple. As far as we can tell it is the memory alone ... that she suffers from. Are we to leave people deranged by reminiscences?'

He smiles. 'There speaks the Jew.'

The smile is not unkind; clinical, merely. Charcot comes closer.

'Men of the world, to look at them –' he eyes me, 'not in the height of fashion perhaps ... but men of reason. Practical reason. Bloodthirstily intellectual. And underneath this plausible disguise: dreamers, riven with guilt, fleeing from ... what? Why so eager to eradicate the past?' Smiling now, 'You want to make this girl a wandering Jewess? Yes, you can make her forget. But which is more important – to free her into a different illusion, or to try and learn from her how the brain manufactures such diseases?' A moment. 'What you saw today was theatre. To understand the mind, we must wait for the biologists to tell us. Back to your microscope!'

Then, seeing my expression, 'Is it so tedious?'

He turns, bringing his gloves out of a pocket, and walks slowly towards the door, putting them on. I stand, mute once more. At the last moment he stops and glances back, relenting.

'Would you *like* to learn, then ... how to hypnotize?'

Dusty light from the slatted blinds. Sweat trickling down our

175

faces. Breuer like a Rembrandt prophet, an Oriental wearing European grief. His anguished eyes upon me.

The body is as malleable as a dream, Sigi ...

Jacob gazing up from the pillow.

'Help me ...'

Mamma stands in the doorway, vengeful Teresa in her eyes.

The patient's arms are raised to the ceiling, stiff, grotesque, devotional. Her hair sticks out in knotted clumps, her face is greasy with sweat. She is blind to us.

A space among the figurines. My hand descends, coarse-veined and old, to place the missing effigy among them: erect, miniature arms extended, bearing an invisible gift in open hands. The hands reach out to reclaim me.

Now I am dwarfed – as I dwarfed the figurine – by a gigantic Babylonian figure. Sphinx-like, oracular. I gaze up at it.

In the neighbouring hall, several people are visible amid the Graeco-Roman statuary. Parisians, two men and a girl. Their laughter drawing my attention, till they pass from sight.

Fleischl, submerged. Beside the wooden bath, all his daily requirements: books, medicines, paper, bottles, a glass. And a metal syringe.

He lies with his face just below the water, eyes closed, hair streaming. Surfacing gently to meet my stare.

'Alserstrasse ... number fifty-one. Take my tip.'

He ducks his face, vigorously now, shaking it as he emerges, clearing his eyes with his hands.

Fliess' voice: 'Twenty-three and twenty-eight ... the two cycles combining? Do you find it recurring often, in your life?'

Fleischl reaches for the bottle, makes to pour.

'Learn how to handle women – that make sure! The doctor knows one little place to cure ...' Pouring; replacing the bottle. 'A bedside manner sets their heart at ease – and then: they're yours, for treatment as you please ...'

His hand descends towards the glass. Beside it the syringe.
Fleischl looks up, and holds my gaze.

'We're almost twins.'

It is the night of our first meeting; no, of our first talk. All
through the night, Fliess and I have patrolled the city, unburden-
ing our past, our plans.

'The same mentors, the same ambitions ... and you're the
only one, I think – who knows what it's like to be treated as a provincial, an upstart. As if science were a bourgeois prerogative.'

He smiles, 'And hypnotism not even a science.'

'You find the same?' We walk in silence. 'What an age we live
in – more afraid of the unknown than the most primitive era.'

'At least savages hold number in awe: you can imagine how
my researches are greeted. They might as well be necromancy.
Divination.'

I could hug him.

'If I was to choose my epitaph, I should like it to be the one
that Sophocles accorded Oedipus: "Who solved the riddle of the
Sphinx –"'

'" – and was a man most mighty."' He gazes at me; full of
love. 'I've made a mental note of your date of birth. Find out the
hour for me. I promise you – it's not astrology. The cycles of
the body and the psyche have no need of the stars, to rule our
lives –'

I am still gazing at him. 'Are your parents devout?'

Startled, 'Yes. Thoroughly devout.' A moment. 'They're old-
fashioned in every way. Progressive Berlin doesn't exist for them
– on Friday nights we could be back in Galicia ... village Jews,
oblivious to the world.'

'Do you miss it?'

Fliess smiles: no.

'I do. Every day. When we came to Vienna, I felt ... enclosed,
surrounded by a greedy, squabbling tribe of brothers and sisters,
one after the other. Offerings to the city gods; to conquer or
submit to them. I was expected to be their leader, an example to
them. When all I wanted ... was to go back to Freiberg.'

Amused, 'Where you were king.'

'No. Something else.'

The little upstairs room. My parents, and my stepbrothers; Emanuel seated, talking to Papa. Philipp standing, surveying the group.

'. . . It was like being a spy . . . in an adult world. A world of men.'

Philipp, walking along the path towards the bridge. He pauses, looking round. Thick, silent foliage hides me from sight.

'My father had been married before, I had adult stepbrothers. They seemed like gods.'

My mother, coming down the path. Philipp sensing someone there. Turning.

'I had the freedom of the woods . . .'

I am sixteen; walking watchfully through the same summery woods, by the Lubina. Heart pounding.

Fliess' voice. 'Why did you leave?'

I see my quarry, walking by the river, and hurry after her.

'Just like your father, mine dreamed of a coach and four.'

'And have you never been back, since then?'

The girl walks slowly, idling, unaccompanied.

'Once. To fall in love . . .'

Tumbling down a bank after her, I stop, staring. Two lovers sitting overlooking the river, with their backs to me. Philipp . . . and Mamma. They turn, revealing strangers' faces. Total strangers. Ashamed, I hurry on.

'. . . I went to stay with friends, one holiday. The girl was sixteen, the same age as I was.'

Gisela, sitting on a sofa, beside her mother. Both silent. Both embroidering.

'Gisela Fluess.'

Astonished, 'Fliess?'

'*Fluess.* I mooned around – hopelessly – imagining myself a Hamlet, a Werther . . . the silly girl was perfectly insensible to passion. Until in sheer frustration I fell in love with Frau Fluess. Superior to her daughter in every way.'

Frau Fluess glancing at me, turning encouragingly to her daughter.

Gisela looks up, and smiles.

'I've often wondered what Shakespeare would have made of Ophelia's mother . . .'

'Frankly . . .'

Fliess' tone has changed. I glance round. I can't see his face.

'Frankly, the hero of this book is a romantic.'

Wilhelm?

Fliess looks up at me, from my desk, over the heap of manuscript.

'He finds adulthood a tormenting dream . . . every page tells us so.'

Fliess stares at me, mocking, across the desk.

'Life disappoints him. Everyone betrays him. Everyone rejects him.'

Darkness. And a foul stench of beer and spirits.

'Professor Meynert?'

'Here, my boy. Over here.'

The gloom lifts as the corner of a curtain is pushed back. Meynert, on a couch beside the window.

What I can make out of the once elegant room is now a midden of discarded books, papers, clothes, food. I make my way towards Meynert. His dressing-gown is stained with blood. The man is drunk, and dying. Lifting himself up to greet me.

'Housekeeper's disappeared. I'll give you her address.' Meynert reaches for pen and paper. 'Think you could find her?'

'I'll try.'

He scribbles. The red beard has yellowed with age, the hand shakes; he tears off a strip of paper, holds it out.

'I knew you'd help.'

Lies back, coughing, and shuts his eyes.

I glance at the address, then back at Meynert. Silence. The interview seems to be over.

Abruptly, his hand comes up, raising his right arm from the elbow. One eye pops open.

'See this?' Squinting at me; shaking the arm as if it were fly-ridden. 'Can't feel a thing.'

He smiles, defying me to act the doctor. Lets the arm down to the couch once more.

'My father was a policeman. Did you know that?'

I nod.

'Police surgeon.'

He stares at the arm, as though contemplating cutting it off.

'He used to lock me in my room, as a boy.' Glancing at me, 'Without a pot to piss in.'

Meynert's gaze slides past me.

'Would you like to have my books, when I'm dead?'

Faltering, 'To – have them ...'

'Yes, have them. My library.'

'Surely there's no cause to –'

He interrupts. 'That's not why I sent for you.' A pause, then 'You shouldn't have gone to Charcot. What you get up to with your lady patients ... that's your business. I was married twenty years.'

His eyes range the room for a photograph. I remember: it used to be on his desk. Gone now. He is rambling again.

'You talk a lot of rot about hysteria – in the male. Charcot taught you that. Neurotic Frenchman. Male hysteria! I denounced you, didn't I, in front of everyone. Well, I've got something to tell you.' With a sudden, gleeful grin, 'I've been a hysteric all my life.'

He nods, triumphant. Lifts the right arm and lets it fall heavily back, at once, like a truncheon.

'Well? What do you say to that?'

'I knew ... you suffered from a palsy –'

'Don't play pussyfoot with me! What's the matter with you?' His leonine head bloated, dreadful. 'Haven't you got any emotions? Take a drink ... from the skull of the enemy. Take some books, damn you –'

A spasm beginning to rack him now.

'Enjoy it!'

Coughing. Blood coming from Meynert's lips.

Fiercely, '*I* became a criminal at twelve!'

Without criminality, no achievement. I search for a handkerchief, something to staunch the blood.

Meynert, hissing:

'In the desk –'

I turn, rising, and hurry to the desk. Open the drawer.

A voice, 'Quickly –'

Open the drawer. The great metallic barrel of a syringe, loaded and ready.

Quickly. I pick it up and hurry back across the curtained room. In the gaslit bathroom a naked figure sits shuddering in the wooden bath.

Fleischl, shaking, nodding, half in spasm, half in pleading.

I plunge the needle into his arm and as I do so he surges up out of the bath towards me, flinging his free arm around me in a lover's embrace.

I hear the choral shout of the mass.

You'd think midsummer. I am lying in the canopied swing, in the garden, walking-stick at my side. Beyond the garden table where Martha and Minna sit, the sun-drenched, ivy-covered London house. I lie, still haunted by the curtained room, by Fleischl's shout, reverberating in the bathroom.

Soft murmurs, subdued voices. The women think me asleep.

The house is bleached by light, windows and doors empty.

A figure, black-coated, bow-tie, emerges from the utter darkness of the French windows, into sudden light. Blinking at the heat. Coughing.

Minna cries out in welcome.

The sleeping compartment is lit by steady pulses of light as we enter the station, rocking slower and slower, the light less frequent and longer.

The train stops, jolting me awake; the connecting door flies open; through the doorway, Mamma with little Julius at her breast –

'"It was evening when I arrived, much fatigued by the journey I had often made so easily ..."'

Beside me, in a neat hospital bed, lies Ignaz. Coughing.

I am sitting beside him, reading. The book is his: he has marked the passage for me. His eyes on me.

'"... for eleven years, I had not seen Joe nor Biddy with my bodily eyes – though they had often been before my fancy in the East – when, upon an evening in December, an hour or two after dark, I laid my hand softly on the latch of the old kitchen door."'

Now he looks away. Face bloodless, a terminal consumptive pallor.

'"I touched it so softly that I was not heard. There, smoking his pipe by the kitchen firelight, as hale and strong as ever though a little grey, sat Joe; and there, fenced into the corner with Joe's leg, and sitting on my own stool looking into the fire, was – I again! 'We giv' him the name of Pip for your sake, dear old chap,' said Joe, delighted when I took another stool by the child's side (but I did *not* rumple his hair), 'and we hoped he might grow a little bit like you, and we think he do.'"'

Ignaz, no longer listening. I read on, keeping one eye on him.

'"I thought so too, and I took him out for a walk next morning, and we talked immensely, understanding one another to perfection. And I took him down to the churchyard, and set him on a certain tombstone there ... and he showed me from that elevation which stone was sacred to the memory of Philip Pirrip, late of this Parish ... and Also Georgiana, Wife of the Above ..."'

Ignaz has turned back to me. Anguished, intent.

'Tell her ... I release her. From all vows.'

I cannot speak. The lachrymose reading has robbed us both of sense. His eyes, pleading. Insisting.

... In order to understand ...

Fliess gazes up at me from the candlelit table, in the university square. His face a deathmask. Breuer turning to me, sorrowful.

... In order to rid yourself of the confused emotions ...

Fleischl screams, soundlessly, his body crawling with imaginary, invisible insects.

... Which haunt your adult life ...

Cousin John, running full pelt beside me. We descend like avengers, like a pair of wolves.

... You must go further back: back to a time ...

I open the connecting door, and look in.

... When your very presence threatened to destroy your parent's love ...

We descend like avengers on our quarry.

... and when your demands made a lover of one and an enemy of the other.

Philipp; and Mamma; their backs to me, undisturbed.

... This inexorable family drama returns ...

Some of the audience are on their feet, elders abusing me. I continue in perfect calm.

... Disguised, in adulthood: a landscape peopled for the grown-up boy by figures of threatening authority, and reincarnations of motherhood, rivals and lovers. As it is for the grown-up girl by jealous maternal counterparts, and likenesses of her father ...

Silence. Wind, sweeping the hillside. Subdued sobbing, Pauline with her head buried in Teresa's skirt. Teresa leans towards us with black bread, the bread of absolution.

Ignaz staring at me, intent, insisting.

... A landscape of ghosts.

Insisting: '*Tell* her.'

Minna turns back to gaze at the piazza, the houses in shadow, the evening passers-by. We sit, sipping our drinks.

'*Voi che sapete* ...' half humming, under my breath, '*che cosa è l'amor* –'

Minna's voice, more suitable and more melodious, joining mine.

'*Donne, vedete, s'io ho nel cor* ...'

'The past! That great excuse!'

Jung, the accuser. Gazing at me from his full height.

'No wonder your patients are grateful. They learn to attribute all their ailments to some long-lost experience ... only too glad to be distracted from who and what they are. From what they could be – if they weren't at the mercy of their childhood!'

I sit in silence at my desk, laden like an Etruscan tomb with funerary tribute.

'You don't want to cure them, you've said so yourself: it's not the cure that counts, but knowledge ... and submission. How could they hope to change? Imprisoned by the monstrous, unalterable past.'

Sadly, 'It's just the opposite. You understood that once ...'

I hear his mocking tones:

'The patient is free – when he knows he *cannot* change ...'

You think I should lie to them, to win their trust?

'Lie to them? Not when they prefer the bitter pill of truth! You call it adjusting to the facts: telling them the decisive events of their life are over, gone, it's all too late, what's left is civilized despair. The beast must be tamed! The human animal chained to his daily round, to smile and work and suffer for his sins. Unto the seventh generation. That's why you hate religion so – seven generations aren't enough for you, the very thought of joyous aspiration must be checked before it leads to chaos. Social anarchy. And pleasure: that must be taken secretly. Tip-toeing back into the garden of childhood desires to pluck the celandine. The well-tempered neurotic . . .'

Go on.

'In one respect, you're right: neurosis is not a thing to cure. It cures *us*. It is nature's attempt to heal. Through fantasy. But *you* think a happy person never fantasizes – only an unhappy one. There speaks the introvert. The narcissist. Dreams can be whole-some . . . joyous and creative. Poor man, how could you under-stand? You think everyone is a pampered child who needs to be woken to his fate. That's your vision – of your own life. It's not mine.'

Now: the coup de grâce.

'And what I find repellent is the way you glorify this lonely, tragic destiny – the sacrifice of instinct in a higher social cause . . . while seizing whatever guilty pleasures come your way. Ruth-lessly. The very essence of civilized behaviour: to be a conformist in public, a moralist in print, and in private – a cynic. An adulterer. Your ideas . . . I find merely pitiful. But your hypocrisy disgusts me!'

Silence.

'It seems to me –' I permit myself a smile '– that your father has much to answer for. And that this destiny you fear so much . . . has found us out. Hasn't it?'

Turning to him.

'Why do you hound me . . . with such a *venom* – when you know quite well that clandestine affairs are hardly my preroga-tive? You don't shout yours from the rooftops. Nor do I expect you to! But *I* . . . must I be your Christ – to the last?'

My own voice, distorted.

'If I'm wrong . . . enlighten me . . .'

The tears come, in a rush, at last.

'Why do you hate me so?'

Two voices, in unison.

'*Voi che sapete . . . che cosa è l'amor . . . donne, vedete, s'io ho nel cor –*'

Anna takes my arm, laughing at my counter-tenor. She continues, solo, as we walk. Faltering at last, under my gaze. I nod: go on.

'Good that someone in the family has a voice . . .'

She laughs; it's patently untrue. She squeezes my hand in hers, happy.

'Next summer you must come with me to Italy.' I glance at her. 'Will you come? I warn you – I exhaust my travelling companions. You'll come back with your mind full of cathedrals and railway stations . . . totally confused. The railway stations are the ones where you have time to admire the architecture. I shall introduce you to the wine which killed a member of the Fugger family – the first Jew to succumb to the pleasures of mediaeval Tuscany, but not the last. You'll go to bed drunk and dream significant dreams, and I shall explain them to you in the morning . . .'

'Oh I do hope not.'

I laugh with her, releasing her to walk beside me. The path is steep here, and I need my alpenstock. She takes small steps, watchful in case I fall.

Her face, still pensive. Italy . . . she need not fear: I *know* her dreams.

'Is it hard, to be an analyst's daughter?'

'To be *your* daughter.' Smiling, 'I've begun to realize how hard that is.'

'No. It's not hard. In time, you'll be an analyst; you'll probably marry an analyst. I could have told you that when you were twelve. Of all my children you're the only one who is gifted in that direction. Naturally gifted.'

'That makes it harder.'

'No. No – you'll see: it makes it easier. Or it will do, when I've analysed you.'

Now she looks startled, for the first time.

'Is that permitted?'

'Permitted? It's inevitable. And better taken by the horns. Don't you think every conversation that we have, you and I, every silence even, is a kind of analysis? Every encounter between father and child, between husband and wife ... however brutal, clumsy – it's always an adventure of self-revelation; or self-deception. And analysis is no more than a conversation, an honest one, between enlightened friends.' I study her. 'Don't you believe me?'

She walks on in silence.

'Are you afraid?'

A quick smile. 'Am I allowed a father complex?'

'If you didn't have one, I should be most offended. And you have one great advantage ...' I meet her glance, straight-faced. 'I don't take it personally ...'

I laugh at her puzzled expression; and pause, at the stile. Dear stile, old friend: these days I must use you to catch my breath.

Anna sits, beside me.

'Perhaps I shall exhaust *you*, in Italy.'

I nod. Taking her hand once more. After a while, her voice comes.

'Is it bad for a daughter to have so much of her father in her ... and not mind?'

'You're aware of the likeness, that's what matters. That's why I say, it isn't hard for you to be who you are. The hardship in life – the only hardship – lies in trying to be someone different.' I caress her hand. 'Yours is the easiest task of anyone I've ever met.'

I can see it in her eyes: she doesn't believe me for a moment. Then she rests her head against my shoulder, in silence. When she speaks it is in a different tone.

'I wish we could stay like this for ever.'

I bring my arms around her, against the loss that must come.

'Help me ...'

I cannot. I cannot move.

Jacob's eyes, pleading, full of horror.

'I don't want to die here –'

I wake in a sweat, fully clothed on the bed; the room a blur of brightness. Is my sight failing? I try to rise: I cannot move. One hand pressed stiffly to my cheek. The other hand – I reach out blindly, and my fingers mesh in soft material. The gauze of a mosquito net, covering the bed.

I lift the net to see the room bathed in afternoon light, no longer a glistening blur. As my senses return, the pain comes with it. I have been sleeping with a handkerchief pressed to the hole in my cheek. The flies get into it; creeping under the mosquito net.

Such pain. Why can't the brain answer: message received . . . enough!

I let the net down and lie back in my bright cocoon, giving the pain its head. A distant sound: the doorbell.

Little wonder if I dream of childhood, on this day bed. Swathed in gauze, as in a crib; the drawing room hidden by light. Perhaps I've found a useful therapeutic tool . . .

The doorbell comes again, insistent. If death calls, I shall meet him on my feet.

Clamp the handkerchief once more to my cheek. Force myself erect, straighten my tie, and wrestle with the netting.

A young man in a dark blue uniform, standing on the doorstep. Clutching a parcel. Postboy? He looks a raw recruit.

Staring at me: severe old gentleman holding his face.

We gaze at one another. Then he glances at the parcel.

Reading out, 'Professor . . . Sig.' He hesitates.

'It's short for *Sigmund*.'

Sig-mund. The metal sticks; I work it with my tongue. He looks up, at the strange sound, then back at my parcel.

'Are you . . .'

'Freud. Do I look like the butler?'

The boy eyes me, indifferent. 'There's a charge, that's all. Not enough stamps on it.'

A charge?

'You want money?'

'Just four shillings, if you please, sir.'

What to do? I turn. Without my stick, I have to pull myself in by the door frame. There must be money somewhere.

Turning back, 'Can you wait?'

Women's coats, in the vestibule. Empty pockets; no money. I lean back among the coats, exhausted. Let him wait.

187

Voices. I open my eyes, in relief. Voices, behind the little lobby door. I push my way towards it, brushing garments aside, so many of them ... and open the door.

In front of me, the Landtmann seethes with people. Café regulars, theatregoers, waiters. These days even to reach the toilet one must risk a duel; I push aside the bulging coats, push them back into the vestibule and shut the door behind me.

Koller waves, from a far table. Beside my empty chair a waiter is unloading drinks. Koenigstein, dealing cards. And Fleischl, one hand raised – insisting – bringing out a purse. As I approach through the mêlée, Koller signals once more, jabbing a reproachful finger at Fleischl, for my benefit, as if to say: *again* ...

Fleischl's purse disgorges two small coins, amid laughter, as I come to the table. Seeing me reach into my pocket, he turns to the waiter.

'I'll sign for it.'

And then, meeting my eyes, lightly: 'Princes never carry money.'

I sit and pick up my cards, ashamed at giving in once more to his largesse. Koller and Koenigstein study their cards.

Fleischl still gazing at me.

'Coming to Breuer's tonight?'

'Perhaps ... I don't want to stay out late.'

Rosannes, passing with his glass, perambulates behind us. Eyeing our hands in turn. We play. Slowly, pleasure returns, the gossip and the camaraderie envelop me once more.

'He's fallen in love with one of his patients. So I understand.'

'Again?'

Koller nods. 'Young enough to be his daughter ...'

Rosannes leans forward, sheltering from the surrounding noise.

'Breuer's fallen in love with his daughter?'

'*Pappenheim*'s daughter. Go *away* ...'

Rosannes does not move. I hear my own voice come.

'A dream ... is the expression of a wish.'

A dream? Faces staring at me. Koenigstein laughs. I turn to him.

'I'm going to Hamburg in the morning –'

But Breuer sits in Koenigstein's place.

'*Again?*' he answers, in patient despair.

Silence around us. I am playing cards at Breuer's.

'Must you reproach him?' Mathilde Breuer comes to my defence. She smiles, touches my hand. 'He wants to marry the girl.'

An irritable noise from Breuer, and he rises to fetch a decanter.

'But does she want to marry *him*?' Fleischl my partner now, opposite me. He sings, sweetly, '*La ci darem la mano ...*'

Breuer still glaring at his wife.

'I've begged you not to encourage this folly –'

Fleischl raises a hand.

'I think I speak as a neutral here ... being unmarried – and without any prospects of marriage –'

I am playing cards with Minna. Alone, the two of us, in the Berggasse.

She looks up at me, smiling.

I draw Marty towards me, kiss her. As I draw back, she studies me, unmoved. I smile.

'You're very pale.'

'I'm quite well, thank you.'

I take her by the shoulders, but she struggles.

'Don't – don't ... someone will see –'

Slipping from my grasp.

'Some women ... are afraid to go out, on their own. Shopping. Or just – walking. Even during the day.'

I gaze at the bookcase above their heads. Minna, sitting, reading a book. Marty beside her, waiting obstinately, as the evening passes.

'Do you know what that means?' I meet Marty's eyes. 'It means they are accusing their mothers of unfaithfulness.'

Minna laughs, derisive. Barely looking up.

'How can you be so absurdly dogmatic?'

'I am deliberately dogmatic, to provoke you.' She puts down her book, in answer. 'So. Let me explain. The strangers she meets – on the street –'

'The reason why women do not go out alone is that they are ashamed.'

We turn to look at Martha, startled by her tone.

'They are ashamed of the world.'

'Ashamed of the world?'

'I'm speaking about Jewish women. They are ashamed to live in a city where ...' faltering '... a man can get up in public and talk about putting Jews into ships and sending them out ... to be sunk at sea –'

I shake my head, disappointed. 'That's not why women won't go out alone ...'

'*I'll* tell you why.'

Minna shuts her book.

'Because every stranger in the street is more attractive than her husband.'

'Very good.'

'And that's why they come to *you*. Because they've married rich, unattractive men, and they can find nothing better to do than come out in hysterical symptoms.' Calmly, 'That's why your consulting room is full of women.'

I nod, weary. Will neither of them take the bull by the horns? Must I, then?

'There's another reason.'

I look at them, in turn.

'Recently, a woman patient told me that she'd dreamed about a visit to the butcher's, in the Margravplatz. Where they have the market – the "meat market", she called it. But it was shut. In her dream. Of course ... the phrase "the meat market is open" ... has a secondary meaning. Or implication.'

Minna, unable to stifle a smile; I do not meet her eyes.

'Naturally, I did not oblige her. My meat market remained shut.'

Martha, rising to her feet. I meet her stare of loathing.

'In other words: women come to me to retrieve the penis they found so distressingly missing ... in childhood.'

I hold her gaze until she turns and walks from the room, closing the door. A long silence, then Minna puts her books aside and stands up.

Quietly, 'Couldn't you have spared her that?'

Before she can leave, I move quickly to her. As she turns to fend me off, my hand brushes her shoulder, unbalancing her, and she falls back onto the sofa.

Minna glancing up at me, shocked. Then bursting into laughter at my clumsiness.

The sudden sharp noise of the door opening.

A gilded, rococo door, a door of Mozartian fancy, opening. A flunky steps in, and halts at once, embarrassed, murmuring.

'Forgive me, Baroness ...'

I am clasped to her bosom. The Baroness detaches one arm to wave the man away, and he withdraws.

I pull free, gazing angrily at her; but she retrieves my hand.

'I've never met a creature ... so afraid of his own heart.' Tenderly, 'How can you be a doctor, if you're not a man. Come ... you see ... how feminine you are ...'

She reaches up to stroke my face. I stand, formal, watching her smile fade.

'I'll attend you in the morning.'

She takes it like a slap, begins to moan, doubling up in pain.

I hesitate, lost.

And with a sudden cry she strikes a rigid, agonized, ecstatic pose.

I sit beside her, take her arms, massage them. At once she pulls me against her, calling at the top of her voice:

'Manfred! Manfred!' Laughing now, 'Rescue me ...'

Hurrying footsteps.

... Don't! Don't ... someone will see ...

I turn to the door. No-one there. Minna beside me, on the sofa. Studying me.

'You watch me all the time ... in the house. In the corridors. At mealtimes.' She smiles. 'I know your secret. You're a voyeur.'

The laboratory door opens, a man backs into the room, carrying a heavy bucket. Turns and heaves the contents into the sink. Under the water, a seething mass of eels, writhing as though in a last frantic copulation.

Charcot looks up from the lectern, smiles at the empty auditorium.

'Today ... we address the problem of seeing.'

Once more, the door opens.

Paula, in hat and coat, carrying shopping. She stands inside the front door, staring at me, with a parcel in one hand.

I can see it in her horrified eyes: I'm supposed to die in bed, not in the lobby.

I beckon to her, and she brings the parcel, puts it in my hand.

'I've paid.' And, taking my arm, 'Now ... *please* ...'

'Manuscript.'

From the feel of it. Another unsolicited offering. I peer at the writing on it.

'When I was nineteen ... here in England – I decided to call myself Sigmund.' Holding her gaze. 'Sigismund ... is a stupid name.'

She nods, not quite daring to push me towards the corridor. My fingers fumble on the string, the parcel falls. Paula gathers it quickly.

Soothing, 'I'll take it.'

Let her take it. More important things to do.

'I've lost a book.'

She nods.

'Fraulein Anna told me.' A moment. 'Have you ... looked in the library?'

I stop short, in the doorway. All around me, the bookshelves are empty.

'Where are they?'

The room is stripped, devastated. Bare shelves.

'Where are my books?'

'Papa –'

Anna, beside me.

'Don't you remember?' Warning me, with her eyes. 'You donated them to the Institute. In Zurich.'

Warning me. Of what? In the tone one uses to remind a thoughtless child of some forgotten stratagem.

'Fraulein Freud ...'

I turn. There is a stranger sitting at my desk, dark-suited, busy with papers. Glancing at Anna, I see it in her face: Gestapo. Ignoring me, he addresses my daughter.

'Your brother Martin has smuggled them into Switzerland. Illegally. There is no question of a donation: they must be returned, to their proper owners.'

'Their proper owners?' I force the man to look at me. 'These are my books!'

'Which you will not be taking with you. They are to return to your publishers. To the Verlag. To be destroyed.' A pause. 'I have the inventory here.'

'This is perfectly ridiculous! The Verlag know my wishes –'

'We own the Verlag, Herr Freud.'

He sifts through papers, in silence. Then, finding the one he wants, he pushes it towards me.

'I understand . . . you owe your publishers thirty-two thousand schillings. Sign here, please. Once you have paid, you may leave Austria.'

'I owe them nothing!'

Silence. What use is thundering now? To be treated as a debtor, a delinquent, it's a small price.

Anna's eyes on me, seeing me weaken, hating me for it. She turns to the desk.

'Are you aware that your men have ransacked this apartment, and broken into the safe? They have stolen our money. Six thousand schillings. Our entire savings.'

She has found the mark; I struggle with my rage, while the man slowly places a pen beside the Judas contract. Watching me.

'Sign the paper.'

I dare not look at Anna.

'And the exit visa?'

He does not answer. A small sound as Anna turns away. I step forward, take out my own pen, and sign.

He stands, filling his briefcase, and walks past me. A curt Heil Hitler from the doorway, a pause, and the front door shutting.

Neither of us moves.

'I think . . . it would be better to die.'

The voice of Jews. Her only bitterness reserved for me.

'Why? Because they want us to?' I come to her. 'D'you think I want to leave here? It's for *you* . . .'

I hold her, as the angry tears come.

'You know . . . I think we're witnessing a certain improvement, in human affairs. They burn my books. Once they would have burnt me.'

She looks up.

With revulsion now, 'So you forgive them.'

Forgive them? Look at me. Haven't we earned them?

I am back in the cocoon, under the bright, silky net.

Anna inside it, sitting on the bed, beside me. Holding a big blue book. She smiles.

'It was in the library ... I would have sworn on oath that we sold it.'

I am too weak to take it from her.

'Shall I read to you?'

The big, blue book. Burn it. Haven't we earned them, the barbarians?

'Would you rather sleep now?'

She sees my faint shake of the head, opens the book at the marker.

'Is this the place? "Akhnaton and the Court"?'

Akhnaton.

Reading, 'In changing his name to Akhnaton, "Beloved of the Sun-Disc", Amenhotep drew his subjects' attention not merely to religious innovations, but to a profound social and political transformation of the ruler's status . . .'

Jung's voice.

'No, surely the important thing about the man was not that he scratched out the inscriptions! He rescued Egypt from an impossibly cluttered theology – he was the first true monotheist ...'

Analysts trailing behind us, in the well-manicured gardens. Why must we gather in these empty palaces? To show we stand for civilization? Or to scratch out the old inscriptions?

'*Every* Pharaoh erased his father's name –' Jung testy now '– to re-invest the monuments with ritual significance. It was perfectly usual!'

'It was not usual!' I stop; must I shake the man out of his blind stupidity? 'How can you ignore the meaning?'

The shuffling analysts have stopped behind us, fascinated and alarmed. The great Freud shouting, apoplectic in the well-manicured gardens?

'All he erased, Herr Professor, was a title: Amon.' Jung gestures at the sky. 'The sun – as source of being! He was challenging a tradition, not a *man*. To break the power of solar worship! A ritual act –'

If he could hear himself! He points at the sun, but all his hatred is for me. Is this the way one challenges a tradition?

I roar, 'It was an act of parricide!'

'No, I say!'

My head throbs, as he turns away. I reach out. But nausea blinds me; I'm falling. Gravel scores my hands and cheek.

I hear Jung's mocking voice: 'Just like a woman ... contradict him and he faints!'

Arms cradle me. Bright sunlight in my eyes.

And Minna's fury. 'Yes ... why not? Am I to have no friends at all?'

You waited ... and you chose him.

'Herr Professor ...'

Arms cradle me. Faces before me, as my senses return. My own voice, murmuring.

'How sweet it must be to die ...' How sweet.

Be at peace: I chose him

Anna, watching me. She lets go of my hand.

When I turn, I see her through the netting. Standing watching me, with the book. I make to speak, but nothing comes.

'I'll leave this here.' She makes to put it on the bedside table.

Look at me. Take it. Take the book.

She does, and the words come, at last.

'Please ... call Doctor Schur.'

Look at me. It's all right.

Can she hear me? Smiling now, 'To be so old, and still afraid ...'

With one gesture, Fleischl sweeps the bottles to the floor, the brittle ones smashing.

'Did you know that Johannes Merck, the founder of this ... treasure-house ... was Goethe's model for Mephisto?' He gazes at me. 'I shan't be here when you return – you know it as well as I do. There have been days when I thought you would understand ... and not force me to suffer longer than was necessary. Perhaps – today as well as any other day –'

'Herr Professor?'

Schur, close beside me, inside the mosquito net, bending over me. Syringe in hand.

I nod.

I can see myself, standing by the desk amid the papers and the figurines, stirring a glass of cloudy liquid. Smiling. Be at peace.

I can tell that the injection is taking place, by Schur's expression, by the doctor's mask. Sated with pain, I feel nothing. He meets my gaze.

'Morphine. Two centigrams.'

Two? Is that all?

Yes, I can see it in his eyes. It's enough.

'Am I so close?'

He nods.

'Thank you. I knew you wouldn't fail me.'

He pushes blindly at the netting, hiding his face.

'Be so kind ...' Can he hear me? 'Remove the net. The flies can have their victim now.'

How easily it comes, the gallows humour.

'One moment ...' Schur deposits the syringe, returns to lift the net away, and fold it aside.

The room reborn before me, empty, sharply shadowed in the evening light. My hoard of honours, my Etruscan tomb. I glance at Schur.

'No need to stay.'

Nothing left; cleansed. Amortized.

Golden light.

My first view of the Forum, flooded with Italian evening light. Alexander smiles, seeing my joy.

Tenderly, 'Well then?' Humble brick and broken stonework. 'It seems a shabby sort of place, to me ...'

As it did to them, perhaps, who knows? But it's still here. The fountainhead.

Koller, and Koenigstein. Meynert. Black-coated students at my bedside, a strange crew.

Applause, as Otto Rank steps forward, handing me a small, slim case. Watching as I take out the medallion.

And read the inscription, barely able to believe my eyes.

... Who solved the riddle of the Sphinx, and was a man most mighty.

I bow, humbled.

Schur's voice.

'Should I ... fetch the Frau Professor?'

He can see the answer in my eyes.

'Tell Anna about our talk.'

He nods.

The morphine now, spreading, gentle reward. Schur bends to my moving lips.

'Frightened all my life. And now it's easy ...'

I can feel the warm, baleful breeze. Hear the blinds clattering in the dark.

... The body is as malleable as a dream, Sigi.

Papa's eyes in the drab light, gazing up at me, compassionate.

The slim hands turn to catch the lamplight. In one palm, a morsel of skin.

Mamma brushes it slowly from her hand.

... That's what we're made of. See? Nothing but earth.

She leans forward and lifts me up into her arms.

Everything is here.

WISE VIRGIN

A. N. Wilson

Giles Fox's inexplicable failure to win a Fellowship at Kings, the unfortunate loss of two wives and now the onset of blindness, have merely sharpened his resolve to astound the world with his interpretation of the Pottle manuscript, a little-known thirteenth-century tract on virginity.

But when Miss Agar, his academic helpmeet, impetuously proposes marriage, and when his daughter Tibba discovers the precocious and quite unmedieval charms of public schoolboy Piers Peverill, an intriguing new light is shed on Giles's investigations into the manuscript . . .

MONSIGNOR QUIXOTE

Graham Greene

A wonderfully picaresque and profoundly moving tale of innocence at large amidst the shrines and fleshpots of modern Spain, Graham Greene's novel, like Cervantes's seventeenth-century classic, is also a brilliant fable for our times.

'A deliciously funny novel and an affectionate offering to all that is noblest and least changing in the people and life of Spain' – Michael Ratcliffe in *The Times*

MORE ABOUT PENGUINS, PELICANS
AND PUFFINS

For further information about books available from Penguins please write to Dept EP, Penguin Books Ltd, Harmondsworth, Middlesex UB7 0DA.

In the U.S.A.: For a complete list of books available from Penguins in the United States write to Dept DG, Penguin Books, 299 Murray Hill Parkway, East Rutherford, New Jersey 07073.

In Canada: For a complete list of books available from Penguins in Canada write to Penguin Books Canada Ltd, 2801 John Street, Markham, Ontario L3R 1B4.

In Australia: For a complete list of books available from Penguins in Australia write to the Marketing Department, Penguin Books Australia Ltd, P.O. Box 257, Ringwood, Victoria 3134.

In New Zealand: For a complete list of books available from Penguins in New Zealand write to the Marketing Department, Penguin Books (N.Z.) Ltd, P.O. Box 4019, Auckland 10.

In India: For a complete list of books available from Penguins in India write to Penguin Overseas Ltd, 706 Eros Apartments, 56 Nehru Place, New Delhi 110019.